OCTOBER**BABY**

Center Point
Large Print

Also by Eric Wilson and available from
Center Point Large Print:

1 Step Away

OCTOBER**BABY**

EVERY LIFE IS
BEAUTIFUL

ERIC WILSON
and THERESA PRESTON

CENTER POINT LARGE PRINT
THORNDIKE, MAINE

ISBN: 978-1-61173-604-5

Library of Congress Cataloging-in-Publication Data

Wilson, Eric (Eric P.)
October baby / Eric Wilson and Theresa Preston. — Center Point
Large Print edition.
pages cm
ISBN 978-1-61173-604-5 (library binding : alk. paper)
1. Adoptees—Fiction. 2. Life change events—Fiction.
  3. Large type books. I. Preston, Theresa. II. Title.
PS3623.I583O28 2013
813'.6—dc23
                                                        2012038573

Dedicated to God's children,
the born and unborn,
all of whom He knits together
with purposes beyond our own understanding.

PART ONE

Chorion

"You watched me . . . as I was woven
together in the dark of the womb.
You saw me before I was born."
—PSALM 139:15–16 (NLT)

Chapter One

A Woman's Choice

Mobile, Alabama ~ October 1991

Try as she might, Nurse Rutledge knew she'd never forget the events of the past few days. Oh, heaven help her. How could she?

Last Friday, her own two feet had carried her to the clinic where she worked, a low-income affair squeezed between the buildings of downtown Mobile. She met with the patients, both walk-ins and appointments, and prepped them for their procedures. Mainly, though, she listened. In a place like this, it seemed like that went a whole lot further than running one's mouth with advice.

Most of the girls who came here, they trudged through the doors like they had nowhere else to turn. Maybe it was a boyfriend that brought them, or a relative. Maybe a taxi, or the city bus.

The *how* wasn't important to Nurse Mary Rutledge.

No, it was the *who* and the *why* that mattered most.

She welcomed the girls in, held their hands. Some unloaded their secrets and fears, while others spoke only through downturned eyes and shallow sighs. Some stiffened their jaws like it was no big thing to pay a visit to this place, and others, their lips quivered as they tried to convince themselves they were doing the right thing.

A woman's body was her own, sure enough, and she was free to do with it as she pleased. Yes, each of these girls had that choice.

Then again, that was sugarcoating the reality of the thing, wasn't it?

All of them, regardless, were scared as could be. They felt they'd run out of options, pressured by parents, or circumstances, or personal hopes and dreams. Some were white, some Hispanic, some with skin blacker than Mary's. Many were still children themselves, by no means ready to be raising babies of their own.

Midafternoon, between patients, the nurse popped the tab on a can of Diet Pepsi and leaned against the door frame of an empty operating room. She eased off a shoe and rubbed the sole of her foot against the top of the other.

"Where's our next appointment?" The doctor's voice startled her.

Turning, she swallowed her mouthful of soda. "Don't know, sir."

"Get to it. Go check with Josephine and see what's holding things up."

As the nurse nudged her toes back into her shoe, she spotted their last appointment slipping out the side exit at the end of the hall. The girl's head was down, brown hair draping her face. Porter? Yes, that was her last name. And barely eighteen years old. Behind her, the door locked automatically.

Mary told herself to check into it later and scurried to the reception area where she caught Josephine's eye. "Any word yet?"

"Quarter past three." The older woman shrugged. "And still not a peep."

"Doctor's getting fidgety."

"Well, don't let him sneak out just yet, dear. I've worked six years with the man, and I'm telling you, his mind's on the golf course before his body ever gets there."

Mary needed this job, and talk of this sort made her uneasy. Not only was it disrespectful, but it stirred unspoken concerns she had about the doctor's quality of work. He'd been known to overlook certain safety standards, and on the occasions when questions were asked, he shifted the blame to those who worked under him.

Josephine rose from her chair. "You don't mind, do you?"

"Sorry, uh . . . What was it you asked?"

"If you'd attend to the phone. I've waited a good hour to use the ladies' room."

"Oh, you should've said something. Go on now, Josephine. Go."

The receptionist hurried out of sight. On the wall, the clock's minute hand clicked forward.

3:18 p.m. Less than two hours till closing. Tonight when she got home, Mary'd massage some shea butter into these weary feet of hers.

The desk phone jangled.

She glanced down the hall. No sign of Josephine. Mary'd answered the clinic's phone before, but it was a task she avoided. Despite her college education and degree in nursing, she couldn't shake the insecurities of her cultural, conversational English.

Another jangle.

She closed her eyes and picked up. "Thank you for, uh, for calling Owens Clinic. Good afternoon. How may I—?"

"And what's so good about it? Huh? You tell me that."

Her eyes popped open. "Excuse me, sir?"

"I've been watching, and I know the kind of stuff that goes on in that place."

The man continued in a low, calculated tone, pouring words through the phone the way a torturer might dribble poison down a victim's throat. His rage, the vile curses, they churned in Nurse Rutledge's chest and belly. She was a good listener, sure enough. But this? This chilled her to her bones, and she hugged herself in the receptionist's chair.

Without a word, she hung up.

"Our three o'clock?" Josephine asked upon her return. "Was that her?"

"The police . . ."

"The police called?"

"No." Mary stood. "We need to call them, call 'em right away."

"Dear, just what is it you're trying to say?"

She hurried to the front window, where she closed the blinds and blocked out the autumn sun. "He told me he's gonna bomb us, bomb this place and everyone in it."

Mary knew such things'd been done before, and he sure didn't sound like he was making no joke.

"That last phone call?"

"He meant every word of it too." She shivered. "Said he's had his eye on us."

The doctor arrived midconversation. "A cancellation?" he ventured.

Josephine ignored his childish optimism and lifted the phone to her ear. She waved her free hand at Mary. "Lock that front door, would you?" Then, into the mouthpiece: "Police? Yes, ma'am, we'd like to report a bomb threat down here at Owens Clinic . . . That's right . . . Yes, that's the place."

At the door, Mary turned the dead bolt and cast a glance through the glass.

"Fantastic," the doctor said. "Another prank caller, huh?"

Josephine was still on the phone. "How long, you say? Well, we're inside with the shades drawn and both doors locked . . . No, ma'am, we're not going anywhere."

"Got that right," Mary muttered. "Nowhere, nohow."

Twenty minutes later, she was giving a statement to Officer Dodd.

Saturday morning the clinic doors reopened, and it was back to business as usual. The cops had placed suspects under surveillance and vowed to increase patrols in the area. In return, the doctor promised to report anything out of the ordinary to them.

For Nurse Rutledge, these were thin reassurances. She had a nice downtown apartment with a view, but she usually walked to work for the exercise and fresh air.

Not today. No, sir. Instead, she gave her older brother a call.

While she waited inside the building's front doors, she pulled back her hair into a tight bun and tried to block out the hateful words that'd echoed through her head since Friday. She turned her thoughts to thin-lipped Officer Dodd, the first to arrive at the clinic. He was a self-confessed rookie, newly married and new to the area, but he had kind eyes that went a long way toward making things seem all right.

There it was, the silky purr of her brother's Nissan 300ZX.

Mary slipped into white nurse's shoes and rushed down the steps to the car. Her brother stared at her from behind Oakley sunglasses stretched to their limit around his black, beautiful head. DeSean Rutledge was a hard-nosed defense attorney, a physically and intellectually intimidating man, and he delivered her to the clinic without incident.

"I'm off at five, DeSean. Come about ten after, and I'll be watching at the door."

"Sure thing." He lifted his chin. "Just call me at my office."

Although the morning hours crept by, she breathed easier after lunch knowing there'd been no additional threats or blistering phone calls. Looked to be a calm day, after all. Smooth as her grandma's molasses.

"We have a walk-in," Josephine called out.

Done with her prep routine for the woman in the operating room, Mary washed her hands and poked her head into the reception area. She found Josephine unlocking the door for a wide-eyed Ms. Porter, the girl who'd snuck out the side exit yesterday. She was one of those teens who from behind appeared normal as could be, and even straight-on, you'd never guess was twenty-four weeks along.

Was. Past tense.

Yesterday, this girl had gone through the procedure.

Why then, pray tell, was she gritting her teeth and cradling her belly, like she was holding together the split halves of a sun-ripened melon?

The sight of the girl's condition buckled Mary's knees, and she braced herself against the wall. Was never a good thing when a postabortive mother came back this soon, and the nurse knew in this moment that her own world was about to change. She didn't know how she knew. She just did. It was a womanly stirring. Something deep in her soul.

"How are you, dear? How can we help you?" Josephine asked.

"I'm fine," the girl said.

"You look a might pale."

"Please, I . . . Please tell him I'm here. I want . . . I need him to finish the procedure."

"Ms. Porter, is it? You're sounding out of breath."

"No, ma'am. I'm . . . I'm fine," the girl gasped.

Then collapsed upon the floor.

Mary stepped toward the girl now curled on the carpet, groaning, clasping her arms around her stomach. How could any nurse ignore what was plain in front of her? Mary might lose her job if she did what needed to be done, but at this point, well, she was more concerned with doing what was right. She, too, was a woman with choices, and far as she could tell, this young woman needed a ride to Mobile General Hospital. Needed it right quick.

Mary grabbed the phone from the desk and started dialing.

"What're you doing?" Josephine said.

"DeSean, that you? Hey, I know what I told you earlier, but I need you here now."

"Who's DeSean?"

"My ride out of here," Mary replied. "And Ms. Porter's too." She kneeled beside the fallen girl, then eased her onto her back, and propped up her feet with a cushion from the reception area's couch.

"Wherever do you think you're going to take her?" Josephine snapped.

"Just look at her. The poor thing, she's in labor."

"That doesn't answer my question, does it?"

"She's got to get to the hospital. Seems to me the only right choice."

By 1:45 p.m., a twenty-three-year-old nurse and an unwed teenage mother were being rushed toward Mobile General in a white Nissan 300ZX. Unexpected? It surely was. Wasn't just every day that Nurse Rutledge, an employee at an abortion clinic, helped one of her patients deliver a baby.

A living, breathing October baby.

Chapter Two

Wishes

Wilmington, North Carolina ~ October 2003

"There you go, Hannah." Grace Lawson finished lighting twelve candles on the chocolate cake with raspberry filling. "Make a wish."

Smiling at her mom, Hannah didn't even have to think about it.

She already knew.

Propped on the wooden bench in a pair of jean shorts, Hannah leaned over the park picnic table, and long chestnut hair slid over her shoulders. She'd shaved her legs for the first time this morning, sneaking her mother's razor into the shower. Now that she was practically an adult, she realized she had to start looking ahead. Her dad said you had to think about these things, you had to set goals if you wanted to reach your dreams. There were all these things to consider. What sort of career did she want? Where would she go to college? What guy would she marry?

And more immediate decisions, like what

movie they'd watch during tonight's slumber party. Mary-Kate and Ashley's *Holiday in the Sun*? Or *A Walk to Remember*?

Uh, that one was easy.

"Careful, honey." Her mom pulled Hannah's hair back.

"She's fine," Jacob Lawson said. "Let her blow them out."

"Dad, you didn't sneak in one of those trick candles, did you?"

"Tried to, but your mother said you're too old for that stuff now."

"That's not what I said." Her mom nudged him in the ribs. "It's her asthma. Hannah doesn't need to be blowing herself silly, trying to make one little wish come true."

"All that wish stuff, you do realize it's pretend, don't you?" her dad said.

Hannah and her mom exchanged an exasperated look. Sure, men knew all sorts of stuff about setting goals and making plans, but there were other things they didn't seem able to grasp. Sometimes a set of detailed blueprints was no more reliable than a simple heartfelt wish.

"C'mon now," he said. "That cake's calling my name."

"Okay, Dad. Okay."

As Hannah closed her eyes, the glow of the candles danced upon her eyelids. She smelled blossoms in the breeze, salt from the nearby

Atlantic, and a whiff of aftershave from her friend Jason on the other side of the table. He'd started wearing it since his own birthday six months earlier, like he was even old enough to shave. Of course, she didn't have to look over there to see his smooth face. She knew just what he looked like.

Jason Bradley, wide-eyed and wavy-haired. He was so . . .

"Honestly," Jason said to her, "if you won't blow 'em out, I'm gonna do it for you."

So annoying.

A grin spread across her lips, shiny and pink-glossed, thanks to her parents who told her she could now wear makeup—but *only* if she let them inspect it before she left the house. She blew out her candles. Acrid smoke rose into her nostrils, almost causing her to sneeze, and she leaned back and opened her eyes. Those around the table clapped.

Yes. She'd conquered all the candles with one breath. Didn't that mean the wish would come true? God heard the prayers of twelve-year-old girls, didn't He?

"Can we lick the candles?" Jason said, reaching for one.

Hannah adjusted a strap of her tank top. "We're not little kids anymore."

"So?"

"So, do you see the grown-ups doing that?"

Her dad plucked a candle from the frosting and sucked on the bottom of it.

"There," Jason said. "Your dad's not embarrassed. Are you, Dr. Lawson?"

"Never."

Hannah shrugged. "That's because boys have no manners."

"And girls," Jason said, "have no fun."

"Everyone has permission," Mom said, "to grab a candle before I start cutting." She tapped the air with a finger, counting those around the table. "There ought to be enough for everyone. I won't be having any, since I'm not a big fan of raspberry in my chocolate."

Hannah's grandpa, her aunt and uncle, her mom and dad, Jason, and her six girlfriends all indulged themselves, savoring rich chocolate frosting and wiping cake crumbs from their lips. The sun was an orange fireball on the western horizon, blazing through the branches of a wax myrtle, highlighting a chameleon as it scurried up the bark and puffed out scarlet pouches beneath his chin. Beside the cake, presents and gift bags waited to be opened.

"What'd you wish for?" Danielle asked. She was Hannah's newest friend from the church youth group, a tall, thin, African-American girl with shaped hair that set off high cheekbones and serious eyes.

"Sorry," Hannah said. "My lips're sealed."

"Let me guess. A million dollars?"

Hannah shook her head.

"For all A's this year?"

"Sounds like something my mom and dad would wish for."

"To be a model?" Danielle said. "You totally could be, you know?"

"Not with my legs."

"You have that girl-next-door look, and anyway you've got nice legs."

"That's not what I meant."

"It's her hips," Jason said. "When she was little she had surgeries and stuff, which is why she can't play sports. I mean, she can. Actually she runs pretty fast, for a girl."

"What're you talking about, Jason? You know I can still beat you."

"But if a joint pops out or anything, you'd have to get another operation."

"Is that true?" Danielle said.

Hannah shrugged. "You know how those models plant a foot and spin around on the runway? It could happen doing something simple as that. Too much twist. The wrong direction. There were some complications when I was born, so I guess I was kind of frail."

Her parents gave each other a furtive glance over the table.

"Not that's it a big deal," she went on. "I just have to be careful, that's all."

While Hannah shared her parents' love of sports and physical activity, she was the one in the family who had to be most mindful of frail limbs. She felt different enough as it was without drawing more attention to her inadequacies. She could run. She could play. She wasn't going to let those concerns slow her down.

"Let's get to opening these presents." Her dad spread his arms over the pile of gifts. His blond hair was a mop of curls. He had an infectious smile, and when he wasn't stressed out from work, he could make her laugh by simply pulling a funny face. "Or am I the only one dying to see what you got here?"

"Start with the cards," her mom said. "Let's not forget our manners."

"You tell 'em." Hannah's grandpa nodded. "Gotta raise these kids right."

"Can I start with yours, Papa?" Hannah asked him.

"Hmmph. I reckon so."

She stood at the head of the table, swatted away a mosquito, and presided over the cards and gifts with an air of adulthood. She thanked each person, never jumped or hollered or squealed, and acted every part the young woman. She received her own makeup kit with about thirty-two shades of eye shadow, a boxed set of *Anne of Green Gables* books, a twenty-dollar Kmart gift card, an artsy bird necklace made of gold, not to mention a certificate from her parents that allowed for acting classes with a professional local troupe.

This, above all else, made her want to jump up and down. That was one of her other wishes, to be an actor—that's what they called it now, even for women—and to bring people's stories to life on the stage. Maybe someday, possibly, even on TV or in the movies.

Goals. See, she was setting goals.

And hey, wasn't North Carolina a hotbed of artistic and acting talent? Weren't *Dawson's Creek* and *One Tree Hill* filmed around Wilmington? And what about all the recent films produced in this area? *A Walk to Remember*, for example. Nothing against the Olsen twins, but yes, Mandy Moore and Shane West's romance was soooo much more mature.

"Thank you, everyone. Seriously. I love the gifts."

As her parents enveloped her in a family hug, Hannah peeked out between their arms and rolled her eyes as though she were putting up with all this smothering for their benefit. The things kids did for their parents.

"These 'squitoes are getting thick," her grandpa said.

"About time to wrap things up," Hannah's dad agreed. "I guess all you girls're riding back with Grace and Hannah for the slumber party. I'll lock myself away in my room and try to get

24

some sleep since I have to be in my scrubs and at work by sunrise tomorrow."

"I'm sure they'll behave themselves wonderfully," Mom said.

"You really think they'll stay quiet?" Jason piped in. "I mean, they're girls."

"Wonderfully," she repeated, giving him a wink. "Like I said."

While everyone headed through lengthening shadows toward the parking lot, Jason bumped into Hannah's arm. She turned, still walking, and their eyes met.

"Hey," he said, "this is for you."

"What?"

"It's your, you know, your present."

Hannah looked down and saw a thin white bag appear in her hand. Jason's style was always simple and clean, and she suspected he had picked out the bag himself. Even in school, he laid out his supplies one by one on his desk, at sharp right angles, never crooked.

"I didn't wanna give it to you earlier, since it's nothing really. I mean, it's probably stupid. I just thought you might . . ." His voice trailed off. "Happy birthday."

"Should I open it now?"

"Up to you."

She peeked into the bag. "Stickers."

"Yeah."

"Butterflies."

"A buncha different kinds. Even glittery ones. I know how much you like 'em, and you're always telling me not to catch 'em 'cause it'll ruin their wings. Anyway, I just thought you might like some for your room or your books or whatever. It's dumb, huh?"

"I love them, Jason."

They walked side by side, and his hand brushed hers. For a moment she thought her wish might come true at this very moment. She imagined him cupping her face and kissing her. Did he know how she felt about him? Did he feel the same?

"So," he said, moving a step away, "what're you watching tonight? Your mom said I could stay for the movie, if I wanted."

"*A Walk to Remember.*"

"Ewww, a total girl movie. Think I'll pass."

"Uh, yeah, I'm a girl."

"Is that why you wouldn't run down to the lake with me yesterday? You think you're too old for that stuff now? You're all, 'Where's my lip gloss?' and 'I can't wear these socks, they don't even match.' I'm glad I never had a sister."

"I can still beat you to the lake."

Jason snorted. "Not even."

"Monday after school, soon as we get off the bus. First one into the water."

"That's two or three blocks."

"Look, Jason, if you don't think you're up for—"

"Soon as we get off the bus," he said.

"And no fancy running shoes or anything, just our regular old flip-flops."

"If you say so. I could beat you barefoot and running backward."

"Monday." She narrowed her eyes. "Guess we'll find out."

Chapter Three

Uninvited

The slumber party was a dismal, why-can't-we-all-just-get-along failure. As the DVD started, Danielle made one comment that set off one of the other girls. Soon the two were comparing the presents they'd given Hannah and which one they thought she liked better. It escalated to raised voices and harsh words, all so immature, but no matter what Hannah said, it only added fuel to their argument.

By ten o'clock the other girl's mother had arrived to "rescue" her daughter from this "toxic" environment. Grace Lawson came downstairs in her robe and house shoes to apologize, but there was no appeasing the woman.

"I'm sorry about that," Mom said, combing Hannah's hair back from her face. "Are you going to be okay?"

She hugged her mom and nodded.

Mom kissed her forehead. "Go on and watch your movie. Just try to keep the volume down somewhat, since your father has to get up early."

"We'll be good."

Mom headed back to her room.

Five minutes later, Hannah and the remaining girls huddled in their sleeping bags in the living room, and she heard them complain that everything was ruined.

"It's all my fault." Danielle paced in her yellow shorts and white T-shirt. "I know I should've kept my mouth shut, but that girl, oh, she just gets under my skin."

"She's that way with everyone," Hannah said, "but she's still my friend."

"I ruined your party. I'm so sorry. Why do I do that? Talking and talking even when it's time to drop it. If I'd just learn to—"

"It's okay, Danielle. Can we watch the movie now?"

Danielle plopped cross-legged onto the floor.

Hannah wrapped an arm around her friend's shoulder. "Honestly, having you all here is like the best present anyway. Thanks for staying."

A half hour later, though, Hannah's newfound maturity melted away and all she wanted was to

28

be by her mother. The other girls'd fallen asleep, sprawled across the floor in the glow of the TV, but Hannah was restless. She padded up the stairs to her parents' room and hopped up beside her mom in the large bed with the polished oak headboard.

"Honey? What's wrong?"

"Nothing," Hannah said. Then she cuddled closer and cried.

Smelling like peaches and vanilla lotion, her mom held her and let her vent.

At last Hannah spoke, her words barely a whisper. "I guess I just get my hopes up, you know? I imagined all of us laughing and having ice cream and getting into a pillow fight. Instead, one person's gone, another's upset, and the rest of the girls, they were practically snoring before we even got to the good part of the movie."

"You were left watching it all alone?"

Hannah nodded. "I hate that." She used her sleeve to wipe at her eyes.

"Maybe someday we'll get to see you in a movie, huh?"

"Doubt it. I can't even walk right."

"You can walk just fine."

"Why'd I have to be an only child? Did you ever think of having more kids?"

"Thought about it, sure." Mom stroked her hair. "But that wasn't the way things worked out now, was it?"

"You could still have a baby, couldn't you?"

"Oh, honey."

"I'd change diapers, if I had to. I'd even do dishes without you asking."

"Tempting." Her mom chuckled. "Very tempting."

On the other side of the bed, Dad snorted, rolled over, and continued snoring. They both stifled a laugh. They held each other in the moonlight that oozed through the curtains, and Hannah decided that even when she was a full-fledged grown-up, she wasn't ever going to stop hugging her mother.

"Mom?"

"Yes?"

"Does God hear our prayers even when we don't say them aloud?"

"The Bible says He knows our very hearts better than we do."

"You mean He knows what I wished for today?"

Mom embraced her a little tighter. "You're His daughter and He was smiling as you blew out your candles. You know how much your dad loves you? Well, God loves you that much more."

"Why didn't He give me a little brother or sister, then?"

Her mom blinked and her arms stiffened.

"I mean, it's okay," Hannah said. "But I just, I don't know . . . I just wonder what it would've been like."

Her mom's voice sounded thin. "Look at it this

way, Hannah. At least we have you all to ourselves. Now, how about you and I go watch that movie together? We'll have to keep it down, of course, for your father's sake. You cue it up while I get us some ice cream."

"Right now? For real?"

"For real. You're my birthday girl, aren't you?"

With the movie over, her mom kissed Hannah's forehead and trotted back up the stairs. Hannah squeezed one last bit of spray from her inhaler, felt her lungs respond to the bronchodilator, and wedged herself between the other slumbering girls in their sleeping bags. She folded her pillow under her head, pulled her legs toward her chest, and dozed off.

The nightmares came uninvited. As they had since early childhood.

She was warm at first, cocooned and protected, almost peaceful. Voices cut through the silence. Distant cries. And were those sirens? Her heart pounded and she shrank back from flashes of bright light.

Something was out there. It was coming for her. She tucked herself farther back in her small space. She couldn't move.

The sirens grew louder, and a sickly warm blast of air warned her of an approaching storm. She recoiled from it, and as she did so, she brushed against something in the darkness.

An elbow? A fingertip?

Someone else was hiding here too.

While she was relieved to know that she wasn't alone, she feared the presence of another person might draw attention to her location. She heard a door open. The light, she realized, came from arcs of lightning. The storm was just outside, brewing, swirling. She curled tighter, huddled in the dark.

Please don't see me. Please don't hurt me.

The tornado roared into view now, winds sucking at her, trying to pry her from her hiding spot. She cried, kicked. *No, please. No, don't . . .*

"Don't hurt me!" She bolted upright. "Stay *away!*"

The darkness subsided. Hallway light cast a pale glow over the family room.

"Hannah? Hey, it's me, Danielle. You okay?"

Hannah's forehead was wet with sweat. She looked around. She was in her home, in her sleeping bag. "It was coming for me. It was . . ."

"It was a dream, that's all. You're okay now. Just a bad dream."

Chapter Four

Something Wrong

Hannah sensed something was wrong. She'd sensed it before. Her dad barely looked at her mom as he drove, and Mom sagged in the front seat the way she did when she was worn out after an argument—except Hannah hadn't heard them say a cross word.

Sunday morning service was over, and as they arrived back home, Mom tromped up the stairs and said something about taking a nap, while her dad settled into the leather recliner in the living room and watched the game between the Carolina Panthers and the Indianapolis Colts.

Football. Ugh. Talk about boring.

Hannah stood out of sight, holding open the refrigerator door as though contemplating what she would have for lunch.

In reality she just wanted to know what was going on. At times it seemed that adults lived in a world where unspoken words were louder than those spoken, where a look could be loaded with meaning, and stony silence could be as ominous as the gunmetal-gray clouds that billowed over the surf in the hours before a hurricane. Sure, kids

33

had their secret messages and handshakes and glances, but adult secrecy felt layered and thick.

"You want a Coke, Dad?" she called over the noise of the TV.

"Any of that Code Red Mountain Dew left?"

"I thought that stuff was bad for you."

"So's just about everything except asparagus. And I really don't like asparagus."

"Even the way Mom cooks it? Roasted, with lots of butter?"

"Hey now, you keep that just between you and me, sweetheart. Far be it from me to ever complain about the food that's set before me."

"Are you and Mom fighting?"

Her father walked into view, rested a hand on the door frame. "What makes you say that? No, not at all. It's just, well, they're things that got stirred up today by the pastor's sermon, things that're hard to talk about, much less think about."

"Like what?"

"Are you gonna close that door? I can feel the chill all the way over here."

"Sorry." She pulled out the two-liter of soda and poured her dad a glass.

"Thanks, Hannah." He took a swig. "Ahhh."

"Code Red! Somebody call a doctor."

"Oh," he kidded back, "but wait, I am a doctor."

Hannah's shoulders slumped. "You're not going to tell me what's wrong, are you?"

"It's nothing, sweetie. It's . . . There's a time for

everything, and your mom thinks that time is now. As for me, I think we should wait. Simple as that."

"Why does it have to wait?"

"Because I don't think you're—"

"I'm what? You mean, this has to do with me?"

"It's complicated, Hannah. It has to do with all of us, and I for one don't think the timing is right. You've just turned twelve." He pulled her close, tousled her hair.

She groaned. "Dad."

"Sorry." He tried to smooth it down. "Look, you're a smart, talented young lady, and you have so much to look forward to. In a coupla years you'll be driving on your own, right? Well, when you drive you have to stay alert at all times, and that means keeping your eyes on the road ahead. Your mirrors're there to let you know what's behind you, but you can't drive a car by only looking through your mirrors, can you?"

She shook her head.

"Sweetheart, this is a metaphor I'm trying to share with you."

"I know what a metaphor is," she said. "I'm not a kid anymore."

"Your mom, she just thinks we need to be using our mirrors a little more and trying to make some sense of the past. Not me. I'm all about what's ahead."

"Setting goals," Hannah said. "And making plans."

"Attagirl."

She backed away before he could tousle her hair again. She combed her fingers through it. "I'm going up to write some goals in my journal. Mom says every goal starts with a wish and a dream, so it seems to me that we need windows *and* mirrors. You know what I mean, metaphorically speaking?"

As she climbed the stairs, she heard her dad mutter, "Twelve going on twenty."

She grinned. But still had no idea what was wrong.

Chapter Five

Not Just Any Girl

It was Monday, a beautiful sunny day, and Jason could think of one thing only.

The race to the lake.

Was Hannah here at school? Had she chickened out and stayed home sick? With him being in seventh grade and her in sixth, he usually only ran into her at lunch and sometimes in the hallways between classes. Up to last period, though, he still hadn't seen her.

"Hey, Truman," Jason called out, jostling in his shorts and striped shirt through the crowd toward the idling school buses. "Hey, wait up a sec."

"What?" Sporting carrot-orange hair, a skinny kid swiveled around.

"You seen Hannah?"

"Lawson? Sure, we had English together. A real snooze-fest, by the way."

"Was she all right? I mean, she didn't try cutting class or anything?"

"First off," Truman said, peering through black-rimmed glasses, "she never misses class, never shows up late, and never leaves early. Her parents? Real sticklers, from what I hear. Second, I'm into blondes, blondes all the way, so it's unfair of you to assume I'd know her whereabouts. She's a brunette, if you haven't noticed. Definitely not blonde."

"Duh. I know what she looks like, Mr. Wise Guy. Where is she?"

"Why does everyone assume I know these things?"

" 'Cause you know everything, Truman."

"Correction." The kid held up a hand. "I know many things."

"Fine. Just tell me where she went."

"See, you're doing it again, Jason. Assuming. And, uh, if you must know, her ETA's in about ten seconds."

"Her what?"

37

"Estimated time of arrival. Three, two, one . . . Hello, Hannah."

Jason felt a tap on the shoulder. He turned, eyebrows raised, and found wide brown eyes staring into his. Was that mascara Hannah was wearing? And were her fingernails painted? She wore an unbuttoned, light-blue shirt that flapped about her pink tank top, and she looked . . . Well, she looked really nice, not that he'd ever say that out loud. She looked older in a way that made him feel older too.

"You actually showed up," he said. "I'm surprised."

"Our bus leaves any second now."

"This is it, your last chance to surrender."

"Uh, over here." Truman waved a hand. "I did say hello."

"Hi, Truman."

"Last chance," Jason said again.

Hannah rattled her inhaler. It was decorated with his butterfly stickers. He wanted to smile at that, but he wasn't going to show any weakness today.

"Butterflies." Truman pointed. "Do you know much about their eggs?"

Jason scrunched his eyes. "What're you even talking about?"

"They grow into caterpillars," Hannah responded. "Into larvae."

"Yes. See, Jason? Hannah pays attention. It's a miracle that any egg survives, considering weather conditions and natural predators, and they'd never make it if weren't for this hard shell called the chorion. The chorion keeps the growing larva from drying out and dying. In fact, pregnant women also have a protective layer in the womb and—"

"Ewww," Jason said. "Honestly?"

Without another word, Hannah took one squirt from her inhaler, tossed her hair back, and marched toward the bus in her jean shorts and flip-flops.

Truman used his best Yoda voice. "Young and confident she is. No fear do I detect."

"Whatever, Truman." Jason pushed past him. "You sound like Kermit the Frog."

Ten minutes later, the bus circled through a northeastern suburb of Wilmington called Murraysville. It was a growing neighborhood, with its own set of lakes and docks, subdivisions and cul-de-sacs. Jason and Hannah lived about two blocks apart, sharing the same bus stop in the middle. A few blocks west, Smith Creek Park was a regular after-school hangout, and they'd been known to spend hours there, climbing trees, catching crickets.

Okay, so she was a girl, but what else was he supposed to do? His parents both worked full-time, hardly ever around, and he hadn't found any other guys his age in the near vicinity.

The bus careened around the corner, brakes screeched, and Jason felt the heat of the transmission and engine radiating through the floor. He stood, ready to rush past his competition two rows ahead.

"Stay seated," the driver barked, "until we come to a complete stop."

"Sorry."

Hannah threw him a smirk.

The bus jerked to a halt. "Now," the driver said, "you may exit the bus."

Hannah rose, nearly tripping over a kid's foot in the aisle. Jason skidded into her. They tumbled down the steps, out the door, onto the sidewalk, and sprinted toward the cutoff to the park. Behind them, kids cheered from their seats, and then the bus was rumbling away, and it was only the two of them huffing between fence posts into a field of knee-high grass and yellow flowers.

Pollen and dust hovered in the sunlight. Grass-hoppers bounced in various directions from their slapping flip-flops. Beyond golden stalks and tall thistles, the lake's sparkling waters beckoned from between hemlocks and oak trees.

Jason slipped at a turn in the path, scrambled, touched one hand to the ground, and jetted forward again. He was a few steps behind now.

A passion butterfly was perched on a stalk straight ahead.

Hannah's shirt and hair flowed about her, and her legs churned up dirt and grass. She was breathing hard but giggling too, and he grinned at the sound. He thought of the stickers in the white bag, paid for with his lunch money. Thought of the glittery decorations on Hannah's inhaler. Thought of summer days and inner tubes and playing Frisbee together.

On velvety, orange wings, the butterfly took flight.

Hannah reached the dock first, feet padding on the wooden planks. Jason accelerated and pulled even with her. They kicked off their flip-flops in unison, and he wondered now why it even mattered who won. No one was watching. No one else cared. As they raced side by side toward the water, their fingers touched and he took hold of her hand.

With their free hands, they plugged their noses.

Launched off the end of the dock.

Kaplooooosh!

Plunging. Paddling. Water swirling. Warm near the top, and cooler a few feet down. An explosion of bubbles. Spears of sunshine. Then cool refreshment and liquid blue.

Jason pulled himself up onto the dock, stomach brushing the wood. He rolled over, then reached back and offered Hannah his hand. She pretended to accept, then pushed wet hair back over her forehead and pulled herself up unassisted. They sat only inches apart, water spreading from soaked clothes onto smooth timbers.

"Guess it was a tie," he said.

"I let you catch up."

"Did not. You just couldn't deal with my last-second surge."

"Fine." She wrung out her hair like a towel in her hands. "Call it a tie."

He leaned back, propped on his elbows. His feet dangled in the water, and he thought for a moment about snapping turtles and alligators and water moccasins. Not that he'd ever seen any in this lake, but they could be found in the swamps along the nearby coast and even on the banks of the Cape Fear River. He loved all that sorta wildlife, as long as it wasn't nibbling at his toes. Of course, a lot of girls wouldn't even swim in this lake for fear of being gobbled up by some lurking creature.

Hannah was definitely not just any girl.

"You know what?" Jason said.

She tilted her head, wiggling a finger in her ear to clear the water. "What?"

"This is gonna sound stupid, so don't think anything of it, okay?"

She stopped. Moisture ran along her arms and curled down her neck.

He looked away. "I shouldn't even say it."

"Nope, you have to say it now."

"Forget it." He stood, slipped his feet into his flip-flops.

"Fine." She coughed. "If you don't want to tell me, it's not like I care."

"It's just, well, I guess I realized that you're . . ."

"What?" She gazed at the rocks and trees along the opposite shore. "I'm what?"

"You know, I always wanted a little sister, and now it's like I've got one."

She coughed again. Choked. Pounded her chest. Maybe she'd swallowed some of the lake water, maybe even a leaf or a twig. Then she rose to her feet, tears pooling in her eyes, probably needing help and too stubborn to admit it. Or maybe those weren't tears but just droplets from her hair. She grabbed her inhaler and flip-flops and took off running even faster than she'd run to get here.

"You okay?" he called out. "Hannah? Hey, what's wrong?"

She didn't respond, and he watched his "little sis" bolt toward home.

Chapter Six

Through and Through

Mobile, Alabama

Mary Rutledge loaded her grocery cart with what things she could, figuring as she didn't have a whole lot of money these days. Coupla rolls of toilet paper, some canned goods and supplies, bag of frozen chicken breasts, and a packet of spices. She'd be good. She'd be all right. Not like she was starving, nothing as bad as all that.

Did she miss those days back at the clinic?

"Lordy, no." She pushed the cart outside. "Ain't no going back."

A greeter at the doorway approached her. "Did we do something to upset you, Ms. Rutledge?"

"Not you. You done fine. I'll be by again next week."

Way things were, she'd be here even months and years after that. Which was okay, but she hoped someday to have a place where she could invite over DeSean and his family, a place that wouldn't run them off by sundown. DeSean's wife, she was one for fancy clothes and things and didn't take kindly to her children tramping 'round this part of town.

Mary drove home, parked her old Chevy Celebrity beneath the streetlamp. DeSean said that was the smart thing to do, and he knew that sorta stuff, being a defense attorney and all. She stumbled into her apartment, bags hanging off her wrists and elbows.

"I'm home," she announced to her fish. "Home with some fixin's."

In the bowl beneath the window, two goldfish swam in excited circles.

What she needed, Mary decided, was more hours waiting tables at the seaside burger joint. It was seasonal work, and when the going was good, she'd bring home a wad of cash that could cover the rent if she saved up. But when it was tough, say, a patch of bad weather or when the kids were back in school, well then, things stretched real thin.

She flipped on the TV, heard the newscasters talk about troops in Iraq, an Oregon anarchist group being watched by authorities, and the rising price of gasoline. Trouble all around. She tuned out their voices, focused instead on the photograph atop her bookshelf.

"Why, look at you. What're you now, baby— twelve, I figure? Pretty as could be, I bet, and I pray that you are loved. Loved, yes, through and through."

PART TWO

Caterpillar

"So let it grow, for when your endurance
is fully developed, you will be strong
in character and ready for anything."
—JAMES 1:4 (NLT)

Chapter Seven

Onstage

Wilmington, North Carolina ~ February 2011

She was nineteen, a freshman at UNC Wilmington —*"Go, Seahawks!"*—and part of the theater group.

Why, then, did she feel so alone?

Hannah Lawson hurried across campus toward her performing arts class, knowing she could never admit these feelings to anyone. No, they were best saved for her journal. Still, she wondered some days if she was the only student who felt awkward crossing the broad lawns, like her entire sense of dignity might be jeopardized at any moment by one wild gust of wind or a slick spot of grass.

Maybe it was the fact that she didn't reside on campus that made her feel out of place. Not that she'd ever voice such a complaint aloud.

Her mom had homeschooled her the last three years of high school, prepping her for the rigors of a higher education, and her dad footed her college bill from his earnings as a doctor at New Hanover Regional Medical Center. Staying at home with them in Murraysville was the economical choice. Pure and simple. It was a short drive to the university, cheaper than living in Belk Hall and paying for cafeteria privileges. It also allowed her dad to keep a watchful eye on her.

Was that why he paid for her schooling?

Afraid of letting his girl slip away?

Sometimes she felt more suffocated than loved, even though she felt horrible for thinking such a thing. Since her twelfth birthday, she'd asked her parents to treat her like a grown-up and give her room to make her own mistakes. After all, she wasn't a little kid anymore. She imagined living one day in a beach house, writing short stories for literary journals, and acting in films that had something meaningful to say about life.

Now that adulthood was here, stretched out before her, the thought of leaving home scared her a little. She wasn't so sure she was ready to take that leap.

Where did she fit in?

Did she have anything to offer?

How, without her parents, would she pay bills while pursuing dreams of her own?

Speaking of which, this daydreaming would make her late. She adjusted her worn leather bag over her shoulder and jogged from the lawn up the steps into the building.

"You barely made it, Hannah," Professor

Watson said, glancing at his watch as she entered the hall. "We can't be having that."

"I know. I'm sorry, Professor."

Eventually she'd be forced to choose between the Master of Fine Arts program and the Department of Film Studies, but for now she honed her talents under the professor's mentorship. He was head of the theater group, as well as an up-and-coming African-American playwright, with one of his own productions finding success off-Broadway. He'd been featured in a *New York Times* article, and *Essence* magazine listed him in their "Top 100 Most Eligible Bachelors." Some called him cocky, while others saw him as confident. Figuring she had a lot to learn from him, Hannah set aside personal judgments either way.

"I'm ready to jump in," she told him.

"No more stumbling over your lines, I hope?"

"I'm good." She set down her bag on a chair in the front row, hitched herself up between the floor-mounted lights, and stood center stage. "I promise."

"That's what I like to hear." Eyeing her through fashion glasses, he loosened his tie and leaned back in a seat a few rows deep. "You'll need to prove it to me, though, or I'll be forced to go with your understudy, come opening night of our production."

"Julia Armen? No, you can't—"

"She's been practicing hard."

"So have I, Professor. I want this. I *need* this."

"Love the desire. Now channel that into your performance. Today's our last rehearsal on campus, and tomorrow we have dress rehearsal at Thalian Hall. You do realize that Oscar Wilde and Buffalo Bill Cody performed there over a hundred years ago? With all the history of the place, you'll find it's an entirely different sort of stress. Thousands of seats, the lights, the balconies. You'll need to know in advance what that feels like, otherwise it can be a tad overwhelming."

"Don't have to worry. I'll be ready."

"I'm holding you to that."

She cleared her throat, squared her shoulders. Though she wasn't in her Victorian gown, she had no trouble slipping into character. "Is that you, Desmond?"

"Hello, Annabella," responded her costar, Lance Prescott.

"You can dispense with the pleasantries," she said. "A bit trifle, don't you think?"

"Nice." The professor sat up. "I like the haughty tone."

She curtsied with all the grace of a nineteenth-century lady.

Truth be told, she felt more comfortable onstage than she did walking across those campus lawns. Here, in the spotlight, she could become someone else, stepping into the role, letting the words and actions live through her. She didn't have to try to fit in or figure what was expected of her. She knew what the audience wanted, and she squeezed reactions from them with vocal nuances, subtle body language, and facial expressions.

Put her onstage, and she *was* her character.

But once she stepped back down, it was so much harder.

In her everyday life she wondered if she were being true to herself. She had no script. No costume. No stagehands or symphony. She sometimes felt as though she were outside herself, watching herself be herself, and she carried around the fear that she would be asked to step aside and let someone else take her place.

"We don't need you, Hannah."

"You're not cutting it, Hannah."

"You're not being real." Or: *"Now you're being too real."*

"Lance makes a good point," Professor Watson was saying. Hannah snapped to attention, and heard him add, "The haughtiness is good, but keep it subdued through Act One. We want it to build. The story needs to escalate, until we're cheering in the final act for Annabella to stand up to Desmond once and for all."

"Escalation. Got it."

"Professor," Lance said, "maybe we should hear how Julia does it."

"What?" Hannah swallowed. Was she being undermined by her own costar?

"No, not necessary. Hannah, I like your inflections and the use of the eyes. Come Wednesday at Thalian, I'm counting on you to be in top form. Don't let me down."

Hannah saw movement at the front of Java City Coffee Bar, located in the campus library. Truman entered, spotted her, and started in her direction. She lowered her head, letting her hair fall forward as she nibbled on a square of raspberry chocolate. Her phone was in her lap and she texted her dad, who was picking her up on his way back home from work.

"Hannah?" Truman said.

After her last-period algebra class, she was in no mood for conversation. Her head hurt and her stomach was growling.

"Hannah Banana."

She'd learned to tune out that old schoolyard nickname long ago. She continued texting one-handed: in café, come quick.

"Try all you want, but you can't ignore me forever," Truman said. "It's the orange hair, impossible for me to hide. And let's be honest, why would I want to?"

She looked up. "Truman. Hi."

He turned a chair around, straddled it, and folded his arms on its back. "You're my only hope."

She raised an eyebrow.

"*Star Wars*?" he said. " 'Only hope'? Never mind."

"What do you want?"

"Comp tickets to *Annabella*. For me and a special someone."

That brought a grin to Hannah's face. "Oh, really? So, like, you're dating one of the girls on campus?"

He shifted on the chair. "Uh, not exactly."

"Is it someone I know, someone from our old youth group? Wait, it's Megan, isn't it? She always had a thing for—"

"She's a fake blonde. You might find it hard to believe, but I have higher standards."

"So that's the only clue I get? You know, I was given four comp tickets, and my parents already have two of them. I planned to give the other two to a friend, but hey, I'm a complete sucker for a little romance. Tell me who the lucky lady is, and I might be persuaded to help out."

"She, uh . . . well, she doesn't know yet."

"Smart," she said. "You don't want to get her hopes up before having the tickets."

"No." Truman glanced over his shoulder and lowered his voice. "Thing is, Hannah, she doesn't know that we're dating."

"By definition, that means that you're, uh, probably not dating."

"She is dating. It's just that . . . It's someone else."

"Oh." A nod. "Ohhh."

"Yeah. A minor technical difficulty." Truman pounded a fist on the table, startling Hannah and drawing the eyes of a barista with dust-colored dreadlocks. "But I won't give up that easily. No! If there's one thing a woman can't resist, it's being desired."

"We all want that, I suppose. So, who is this desirable creature?"

"That, I'm afraid, must remain my secret."

"Does she even know?"

"Not yet. But this is my chance to change that, and it's all on you, Ms. Lawson. Don't be an enemy of love."

"Well, I was actually thinking of giving the tickets to Jason."

"Jason." Truman's shoulders sagged. "Figures."

"With him saving up for the spring-break trip, he says he can't afford a pair of tickets right now, even taking into account our student discount."

"A pair?"

"He and his mom. Since his parents divorced, she's been working 24/7."

"His mom?" Truman dropped his head, thudding it three times on the back of the chair. "And how am I supposed to compete with that?"

"What about taking your own mom?"

"Not even a possibility."

Knowing very little about his family life, Hannah was ready to fish for more info when her father appeared in the doorway. She froze. Why hadn't he texted that he was in the parking lot? Twice the age of anyone else in the room, he was still youthful and full of vitality, but that didn't overcome her rush of embarrassment. This campus was her real-life stage. How was she supposed to respond to being picked up from school by a parent?

"Sorry, Truman. Gotta go." She grabbed her stuff and patted his arm. "Hope you make it to the play on Wednesday. I'm sure you'll figure something out."

"Right. You betcha." Head still down, he added, "I'm glad we had this talk."

Chapter Eight

Minutes Away

Jason Bradley stood inside the theater doors with his girlfriend, Alanna, and marveled at the opulent interior of Thalian Hall. Curved balconies peered down upon the broad polished stage, where huge decorative panels rose floor to ceiling on either side. Drawn tight until the show began, red curtains matched the seats throughout the hall.

Soft lighting along the mezzanine and box seats revealed that hundreds were already in their places, awaiting the opening act of *Annabella*.

"Wow, I forgot how cool this place was." Although he had visited years ago on a school field trip, he'd never come to an actual performance here.

Alanna folded her arms, seeming less impressed. Long, blonde hair framed her stately neck and fine features. She wore a strand of pearls.

"I hope Hannah nails it," he said. "She's dreamed of this since she was a kid."

"Why do you care so much?" she said.

"She's my friend. We go way back."

"Well, I left my friends and family in Massachusetts to come to college here. I don't go calling them every day and attending all their events. You know, Jason, you have to let go sometime. All part of life and getting older."

"She's part of my life, always has been."

Alanna rolled her eyes.

"Listen, you don't have to worry, okay? It's just, she's like my sister, that's all. Look at you. You're getting jealous, aren't you?"

"Of her? Hardly."

He touched her arm. "You look great, by the way. I like your hair like that."

"Thanks. I didn't mean to get huffy."

"Don't worry about it. It's fine."

"Where're our seats?"

"Up one level." He handed her a ticket and pointed toward the balcony. "I'm, uh, I need to go to the bathroom before the show starts. I'll be back in a few minutes."

He watched her leave, then found his way to the restroom, where he stood before the mirror and adjusted his tie beneath a dark canvas jacket. He brushed fingers through his wavy hair, patted down one unruly spot, patted again, then gave up. What you saw was what you got. Take it or leave it.

He wondered how Hannah was dealing with tonight's pressure. Acting was one of her passions. Was she behind those curtains now, practicing her lines, trying not to hyperventilate? It took true talent to stand out in this community of the arts, and with the recent surge of locally shot movies, Wilmington had been dubbed "Wilmywood." While Hannah had plenty of talent to get noticed, it was confidence she seemed to lack.

I should go talk to her.

What were the odds of him sneaking backstage? Could a bit of bluffing and boldness get him past the suited attendants at the doorways and aisles?

Only one way to find out.

He straightened his jacket, lifted his chin, and headed back into the hallway.

In the shadows behind the curtain, Hannah thumbed through her script and went over yellow-highlighted lines once more. The wooden floor shuddered under her feet as stagehands rolled props into place. She shuddered too, grasping the collar of her gown to her throat. She lifted her chin and drew a long breath. Her lungs expanded, and she felt the flutter of butterflies in her stomach.

That was a good sign, right? She adored all things butterfly.

Stay calm . . . just stay calm.

Through lips in the shape of a kiss, she exhaled and read her next scene. She fidgeted in this pale pink gown with its frills of antique lace, thinking that women in the past must've grown tired of tight bodices. She had a sudden suspicion that Julia Armen might've altered the dress to cause her discomfort, but that only sounded paranoid.

Hannah coughed. Her left hand searched through her bag for her inhaler. Although she didn't need it as often these days, times of stress drove her to it both for medical and psychological comfort. Something to hold on to.

She dropped it and mouthed her next line. The floorboards quivered again. A shape moved toward her through the glow of colored lights, but she blocked out the movement and remained intent on her dialogue. The performance was only minutes away.

"There you are."

She looked up. "Jason? What're you doing?"

"Good thing they're not protecting the president

back here. I brushed right by the attendant, even gave him a little chest-bump, like I had stuff to do and he was slowing me down. Shoulda seen it. He practically apologized and stepped aside."

"You're bad."

"Nah. I only think I am." He sauntered toward her, his lean form draped in a tie and casual jacket, his sandy-brown hair partially tamed around his wide, bright eyes.

He was no longer a seventh grader. That was a fact. He was a college sophomore now, a certified hit with ye lads and lasses at UNC Wilmington. He had that thing, that casual I'm-not-trying-too-hard aura that made others feel comfortable in his presence.

Well, Hannah wasn't fooled by any of it. He was still the same guy to her, her longtime childhood friend.

More like a brother, really. Her goofy big bro.

At least that's what she told herself these days. It was better than facing the fact that her preteen wish hadn't come true.

"You know," he said, "if you haven't learned your lines by now, probably too late."

"Thanks. Real encouraging."

"Nice outfit, though."

"I can barely move. I feel like one of those Victorian dolls that old ladies keep locked up in glass cabinets."

"You look like one."

"An old lady?"

"A doll."

"Yeah, right." She dropped her eyes to her script and tried to hide her satisfaction. "Well, I'm not letting Julia take this role from me, but you can bet I'll be changing back into jeans the second the show's over."

Jason smiled and squatted down across from her. "So. You nervous?"

"Yes."

And it sure felt good to admit it.

Around Professor Watson and the rest of the cast, Hannah sensed the need to hold it together and show no fear. They didn't realize how important this was to her. Only those closest to her had any idea that it was everything she'd hoped for since childhood, her big break, a chance to show what she could do before a large audience.

"You're gonna kill it," Jason said. "You don't have to worry."

"Worry? Who me? I mean, it's not like half the cast hates me or anything."

"C'mon. That'd be impossible."

"I got the lead fair and square." She cleared her throat. "So what if I'm a freshman and Julia's a junior? It's not right of them to hold that against me, is it?"

"They don't."

Hannah nodded. "They do."

"Okay, I'll admit that Julia does. While making

my way through the props, I saw her prepping her poison dart."

"Very funny, Jason."

"Seriously," he said, "you were born for this. Ever since we were kids, you could flip this switch and step right into any role you were given. You don't think that's a gift? I mean, sure, you used it the wrong way a time or two during middle school, but every gift can get abused, right? You know, when I was walking here from my car tonight, I passed the street signs at the corner of Third and Princess. Just around the corner. Do you think that's just a coincidence? Way I see it, this is your night to be a princess, and I believe you were given this role for a reason."

"You really think so?"

"I really do. I'll be cheering for you all the way."

"Thanks," she said. "So, where're you sitting?"

"Front row, center balcony. With Alanna."

"Oh. I thought that . . . Wasn't your mother coming with you?"

"She called earlier, said she couldn't make it."

"Not again, Jason. If anyone deserves a night out, it's your mom. The poor thing."

"It'll happen. Hey, the good news is that I get a night out with Alanna."

"Yeah? I . . . I didn't know she was coming."

"You kidding? We wouldn't miss it."

"So it's official, huh? The two of you?"

He toggled his eyebrows. "Since a few days ago, yeah."

"Good for you." She kept her voice steady. He had aspirations of his own, career-wise and family-wise, and she had no right to begrudge him that. "Alanna's gorgeous. And you . . . well, you deserve to be happy. Thanks for telling me."

"So whaddya think? I was hoping to get your opinion."

"Me? I hardly know her." She stifled a cough. "Listen, I better—"

"Yeah, I know. Almost time for the show."

"Yeah."

"Break a leg, or whatever that is you're supposed to say."

"Thanks."

She watched him slip around a faux-marble pillar that'd been locked into position, and then he was gone. She imagined him and his girlfriend in the balcony, her parents in the seats just beyond the orchestra, and her college classmates scattered throughout the hall.

She could do this. She *would* do this. No need to worry.

"Hannah." A deep voice turned her back around, and she found Professor Watson bearing down on her. "Since you seem to perform best under pressure, I thought you'd like to know . . ."

"Know what?" Her forehead furrowed. "Is something wrong?"

"Quite the opposite. You, Hannah Lawson, will be performing tonight in front of some scouts from New York and L.A. With my recent successes off-Broadway and whatnot . . . well, let's just say that I have some pull, and there are agencies interested in you."

"In me?"

"Does that come as a surprise?"

"I, uh . . . thank you, Professor. Thank you."

He peered over his glasses. "Now, you make me proud, you understand? I've put my neck out for you because I see something special beating in that chest of yours. You have a passion that can't be taught. Let me see *that* tonight. Let the audience hear it in your voice and see it in your eyes."

"I'll definitely try."

"Give it your best, and they'll be lining up to sign you."

Hannah's mouth turned dry. Her tongue felt swollen. She nodded and pasted on what she hoped was a confident smile. "I won't let you down."

Chapter Nine

Without Further Ado

Oh, bother. Where was he? Why'd he always get kept late at the worst of times?

Dressed in a long blue gown and jeweled necklace, Grace Lawson paced the pavement outside Thalian Hall and checked her cell phone again. Still no texts, no calls. Her husband kept his phone silenced while working at nearby New Hanover Regional and often forgot to check it. The problem was that he had the comp tickets from their daughter in his pocket. Grace didn't want to miss one second of Hannah's performance, and yet she had no way of being admitted through the doors.

"Come on, Jacob." She pressed Redial. "Please answer."

Nothing.

Across the street, a police car monitored the evening's activity. Behind her, some college kid squawked, "Got your tickets? Got your programs? Programs, five dollars."

Five dollars? Give it another minute, and that's what she would do.

Grace touched her hair with a finger. She had it

pulled up but worried that it might come loose and tumble down around her shoulders if she kept pacing the street.

"Programs," the kid said again. "Fifteen dollars."

Fifteen? She shook her head. Talk about inflation.

A familiar figure appeared far down the sidewalk to her left. Jacob. He raced around other theatergoers, blond curls touched with gray and sweeping his eyes, hands fiddling with his tie. She thought of what she'd say to express her frustration with him, but her heart softened when she noticed his haggard expression.

"Grace, hey." He gave her a hug and a kiss. "Boy, you look stunning tonight. Like a . . . I don't know, like a young Jackie Kennedy."

At that, her heart melted.

"And you look overworked," she said.

"Sorry I'm late. I got your texts, but then my battery died. Had a total knee that didn't start till four. Should've been done in forty-five minutes, and instead it took three hours." He threw his hands up, surrendering his tie to her care. "Will you fix this for me? I can manage a surgery but can't even master a simple knot."

"I thought you only had two surgeries today."

"Dr. Andrews wanted to go home."

She finished the tie and patted his chest. "One more year, Dr. Lawson. They need to stop treating you like a resident."

"Most of the younger doctors figure I must be a

resident at my age. It's my own fault, I suppose, for getting a late start on my career."

"That wasn't your fault, and you know it."

"All the same," he said. "So you've got the tickets, right?"

"What? No, I put them in your coat pocket."

He checked. Nodded. "Got 'em."

They hurried up the theater steps. A large security guard stood with hands folded behind his back, blocking one doorway. They chose the other door, where a college attendant looked less imposing in his loose jacket and untucked white shirt. He had orange-red hair combed to the side, and his eyes were magnified by black-framed glasses. Grace exchanged a knowing glance with her husband. As fans of the TV show *LOST*, there was no missing the fact this guy was a comedic, young Ben Linus if there ever was one.

"Sir and madam," he greeted them, "may I see your tickets real quick?"

Jacob handed them over.

The kid whipped out a penlight. "Let's just check 'em out, make sure these babies are legit." He clicked his tongue. "Uh-oh. All right, I see that you guys're bronze package."

"Is that a problem?"

"Well, you could look at it that way. Problems are nothing more than challenges in need of a solution, and I do have a solution. I could bump you up to platinum package. Very simple. An extra fee of twenty-two dollars, and it'd radically enhance your enjoyment of this evening's show. Plus, some of the proceeds go to a, uh . . . to a charity."

"Is that right?"

Grace shook her head. "You're Truman, aren't you?"

"Am I German? No, I'm . . ." The kid poked his tongue against his cheek and looked both ways, avoiding her eyes. "You guys on the board or something?"

"Actually, our daughter's in the show and it starts right away." Jacob grabbed the tickets from his hand and opened the door for Grace.

She turned to confront the young man. "Hannah's told us all about you."

Dropping his chin, Truman chewed on a fingernail. "It's nice to meet you too. I'm just trying to earn my own way here, that's all." Then, with barely a moment to recover, he spotted his next victims coming up the stairs. He caught the eye of a fellow in a cowboy hat and hooked his thumb at Jacob and Grace. "They just got the platinum package, so what about you, mister? I'm sure you won't be disappointed."

Grace sighed and followed her husband inside. They followed an usher down the center aisle and caused a small commotion getting to their seats. Jacob started to turn back, saying he'd check on Hannah before the show started, but the lights dimmed across Thalian Hall. On the stage the leader of the theater group appeared tall and proud.

"It's too late." Grace tugged on her husband's sleeve until he lowered himself into his cushioned seat.

"Do you think she'll even see us out here?" he whispered.

"She'll see us," she said. "More importantly, we'll see *her*."

From the balcony, Jason watched Mr. and Mrs. Lawson settle into their seats far below. He slipped into his own spot next to Alanna. She had her legs crossed, skirt riding just above her knee. She sat primly, with her back straight, and studied her program.

"Hey." He leaned over to give her a light kiss on the cheek.

"Hey, how're you? You get a program?"

"I'll go off yours."

"That took a while."

"Yeah," he said. "I, uh . . . I went to see a friend."

"Mm-hmm." Alanna stared forward. "And how is she?"

Jason knew he was busted. He squared his jaw. "She's nervous."

"Well, I guess I would be too."

He took her hand, glad to hear a few words of empathy. He'd hoped to have his mom here

70

tonight, but she had been kept late at her job. It was nice to have Alanna on his arm, at least. She turned the heads of every guy within ten rows.

From the stage, Professor Watson surveyed those in attendance. He was sharply dressed, and his voice gave no hint of anxiety. "Thank you," he said, "for joining us this evening, and a special welcome to our alumni and guests. Good to have you. I would ask that you please put away your cell phones and cameras. You're here to enjoy a play, not to update your statuses and send tweets, and I'm sure the gossip can wait." He pressed his hands together, swiveled in a half circle so as to address the entire audience. "Tonight, we are proud to bring you our spring production, one of the enduring traditions from our university. This year, we are featuring some fresh new faces."

Hannah was behind those huge red curtains, probably standing at her mark. Jason imagined her peeking through a gap in the fabric, eyeing the crowd, adjusting to the fact that she'd soon be center stage before thousands of paying theatergoers.

She could do this. He had faith in her.

Still, his stomach churned, and he shifted in his seat. He felt Alanna's gaze cut his direction, but he stayed focused on the professor.

"You can read more about each of our young thespians," Professor Watson said, "in your programs. With my own rich theater experience,

71

I have every reason to believe that some of these new talents will go on to bigger and better things. Perhaps on Broadway or off-Broadway." He paused, seemingly for those who knew of his recent achievements there. "Perhaps here in Wilmywood." Another pause for appreciative chuckles from the locals. "Or even in Hollywood. Yes, I do truly believe that."

Although the man came across as a bit self-important, his speech did heighten Jason's own excitement for the show. Not to mention the nervousness he felt for his friend backstage in the pink frilly dress. He'd never seen Hannah so dolled up. She wasn't just the giggly girl down the street anyway, was she? She looked perfect for the part, no matter what Julia Armen and her circle of people thought.

"You got this," he muttered. "You can do it, Hannah."

Tight-lipped, Alanna slipped her hand out from under his.

"So join me now," the professor said, "in welcoming to the stage our cast, as they perform for you an original play written by yours truly." Applause swelled through the hall. "Thank you, thank you, thank you." He patted at the air in false humility, then directed all eyes toward the curtains that billowed deep red between gold-gilded frescoes. "Without further ado, I present to you . . . *Annabella*."

Chapter Ten

The Wolf

❧⚬❧

Hannah took a deep breath. With fingers crossed behind her back and feet planted on the white tape on the floor, she felt the heat and glare of the spotlight as the curtains fluttered open. Her mom and dad were out there, as well as Jason, Danielle, and others from school and church. Julia sat in the front row, no doubt studying Hannah's every move and searching for things to criticize.

And where were the talent scouts seated? Were they already passing judgment?

It was now or never, she decided.

Time to shine.

She nodded and glided forward, sensing the eyes of the audience follow her. Her dress flowed about her. The cheers grew louder. She heard Dad's voice, "Yeah, Hannah," and knew Mom was beside him, beaming with that smile that matched her name.

Hannah soaked it all in, waiting, letting the moment crest and subside. Her gaze floated over the sea of heads, and the spotlight flared blue in her vision. In the gap between dying applause and golden silence, she ran through her lines in her head. She didn't want to forget, and neither did she want to rush. All about the timing.

Wait. Wait.

She had them in her palm.

For a second, everything wobbled in front of her, but she steeled herself, let her hands hang loosely at her sides, and drew in another breath through parted lips.

"Annabella," a male voice called to her.

She glanced over at Lance, directing the crowd's focus to her approaching costar. He appeared onstage in a light gray suit. He had a rakish goatee and mustache. Despite an unimposing stature, he looked priggish and pompous, and as he nodded at those in the seats, the cheering went flat. He was trying too hard, and those watching knew it.

"Is that you, Desmond?"

"Hello, Annabella."

Poised in her chiffon dress, she waved her lace fan. "You can dispense with the pleasantries, Desmond. A bit trifle, don't you think?"

"I don't understand," he said.

"Oh, I know where you've been."

As Hannah looked away in a show of annoyance, the rows of balcony lights, the colored stage lights, the blinding spotlight all flashed across her vision and caused something within her to click into a different mode. One moment she was functioning and alert. The next, her five senses seemed to be crisscrossing signals.

She wheezed. Set a hand on her hip.

"If you'd just let me explain," Lance continued with his lines, "I'm confident we would agree. You need to know that my family has, well, certain standards for me."

She tried sorting out the mixed messages in her head. She latched on to the dialogue she'd practiced backstage. "Standards? Standards which I do not meet?" She suppressed a cough. "Admit it, Desmond. Please—"

The breath left her lungs. She shifted her eyes away from the spotlight, sought for something solid and dark. She gulped. Fought for air. She'd endured incidents such as this during childhood, but of late they'd been far and few between.

Why now? No. This couldn't be happening.

Lance's gaze turned her direction, mouthing her next line for her.

That's right. She was supposed to say something here, wasn't she? This was her time to speak, her time to shine. Instead, a band of steel was strapped around her waist, squeezing her insides, causing her vision to blur and blacken.

From off-stage, she heard the professor feeding her words: " 'I've realized . . .' "

She coughed. Blinked. "I've realized that I . . . I have certain standards that *you* do not meet." That didn't seem quite right, but she forged ahead. "It's time I set sail on my own. It's time I discover the life I've always dreamed of but thought impossible. It's—"

She gasped. Lifted a hand to her chest.

The audience was still out there, watching. She felt their concern, their fear, and their ridicule. She was losing it. The carpeted aisles seemed to expand and contract, matching the efforts of her lungs.

"Hannah, get it together," Lance hissed through clenched teeth.

As though she were doing this on purpose.

As though it were her intention to squander this opportunity.

The hours of practice, the rehearsed script—it all seemed wiped clean from her thoughts. She had to do something, had to at least try. Improv was a tool in every actor's bag of tricks, and if she fumbled on, clarity might return and the show could proceed.

"I'm . . . I'm leaving, Desmond," she said, moving past him.

"Leaving?" Lance shot a glance at the audience and improvised along with her. "Where to, Annabella?"

The darkness closed in, a wolf prowling at the edge of her tiny circle of light. She thought she heard snarls, and her facial muscles tightened in terror. Her neck constricted. She knew that even the murmurs of all those in the front rows wouldn't scare away her foe. The wolf stepped nearer, fangs bared, eyes unblinking.

Her dad stood to his feet a few rows back.

Wheezing, she reached for the closest person to her. "I'm . . ."

"What?" her costar demanded.

"I'm sorry."

She lunged forward, tried to catch herself. If only she could reach backstage. Instead, she felt the blood drain from her face, and she collided into Lance. Arms barely raised, he watched her crumble at his feet. Coughing, she fought for even a sliver of air. Her lungs heaved. Cast members moved toward her while Lance stood stiff and unmoving.

"Hannah?" Her father's voice. "Hannah!"

Although her brain was sending signals, none seemed to reach their destinations. She told her legs to stop quivering, her arms to stay still. Her dad was leaning over her. She told her eyes to stay focused on him, but they rolled back and let the darkness roar in. Whispers and cries of alarm rose around her. Panic overwhelmed her.

"Can you hear me?" Hands gripped her arms. "Hannah, this is your dad."

The wolf took one step back and continued to circle.

"Sweetheart, where's your inhaler?"

She started convulsing.

"Call 911," her dad shouted the order, probably to her mom. Then to Hannah: "I need you to relax. It's okay." His head turned. "Lance, go get her inhaler. It's in her brown bag. What's the *matter* with you? Go. *Go.*"

"We, uh, we need her bag," Lance said, trotting off.

"Hannah?"

"Dad," she wanted to reply, "I love you. Where's Mom? Don't let me go. It's dark and cold, and I can't breathe, and I'm so scared that the wolf'll come and catch me and that I won't be able to fight it off on my own."

But these signals never reached her tongue.

The convulsions shook her entire body now, rattling her heels and elbows against the stage. Her eyes widened. Her ears rang.

"Hannah, no. No!" He cupped her neck. "Listen to me, baby. *Hannah.*"

She caught a glimpse of her mom on a cell. Her father had his ear bent near to gauge her breathing. Her eyelids fluttered. She couldn't focus. Every muscle spasmed in one desperate moment —an overload of sensory input, an imbalance of electrical impulses that failed to find their grooves—and she seized there on the floor. Her entire body lunged, her back arched, and the blackness descended.

The wolf.

The howling tornado.

Her enemy was before her eyes, blocking out all else, and she knew she was going to die. She hoped her mom and dad knew how much she loved them. It was no fault of theirs that she'd always felt like a misfit. She was different, always had been. The operations. The paranoia. The waking nightmares. Her parents would probably be relieved to be done with all the drama. And could she blame them? Not one bit.

Then, of course, there was Jason.

She kicked. Kicked up from this pool of darkness toward swirls of distant light. She was rising from a cold midnight mist into the liquid blue of sun-splashed waters. She was back at Smith Creek Park, twelve years old, swimming in her shorts and shirt, warmed by the voice of a friend and by the touch of his hand.

"Hannah? It's me, sweetheart. Your dad. We're getting you some help."

She flopped onto the dock, reassured by the smooth planks beneath her. Or were the planks part of the stage? Where was she? Did it matter?

Then the quiet came and stole her away.

Chapter Eleven

Crawling

Hannah had envisioned taking a final bow, basking in the "bravos" and "encores" of the audience. Instead she'd ruined everything, letting the curtains close over her amid gasps and muted cries. When she came to, she was in a room at New Hanover Regional Medical Center. They'd checked her vitals, ran tests, and held her overnight for observation.

This morning, she was perched on the hospital rooftop in a hooded robe and pajama bottoms. She wasn't supposed to be up here, but her dad had brought her to this spot years ago, holding her hand as he showed off the view from atop his workplace.

It'd since become one of Hannah's favorite places to relax, write, and sketch.

To think and to pray.

"What's wrong with me, God?" she asked now. "Sure'd be nice to know."

A mile or two to the west, the Cape Fear River moseyed through the city and fed into the Atlantic, where peach and lavender clouds decorated the sunrise. She smelled the ocean air, as well as the tar on the roof. She heard faint sirens and the drone of machinery. She glanced down at a worn leather journal that matched her leather bag and remembered receiving them as gifts from her grandpa on her sixteenth birthday.

"Reckon they'll be a reminder," he'd told her.

"What, are you're kidding, Papa? I'll never forget you."

"Not me," he barked at her, but she knew not to be frightened by his gruff manner. "It's the good Lord who gave you life, and you best not forget that."

"I won't," she said.

"You write to Him when you think of it. That's what your Meema used to do. You put it all down in that there journal."

"I will, Papa."

"Well, all righty then." He smiled. " 'Xpect that's about all."

He died five weeks later, and she still missed that prickly personality that had hidden a heart full of kindness.

"Put it all down in that there journal . . ."

She opened the leather-bound book and chewed on the end of her pen. She didn't know where to start. At times her thoughts and feelings seemed bottlenecked, all fighting for the right to burst out first. Her high-school youth pastor used to prod her for a response: *"Come on, Hannah, I know you have stuff to say. I can see it in your eyes."*

He was right. She did.

But trying to squeeze the words from her only clogged them at the opening. The more of them she had to say, the harder they were to formulate into sentences.

She smoothed the page and told herself to write one word at a time.

Alone. Scared.

Then a sentence.

Actually, it's not being alone that scares me.

Once that first line was done, she was on her way.

It's being with other people that reminds me I don't fit in. I want to hide. All around, others laugh and go through life like they belong here. Do I belong? I don't know. I look normal, whatever that means, but I sure don't feel it. That's what I like about being onstage. I can play somebody else, fill their shoes and recite their lines. I don't have to wonder if I'm spouting off some random thoughts that make everyone just stop and stare.

She winced at that and set down her pen. That was enough for now.

She blew on the page to dry the ink, closed her book, and wandered from the roof back into the stairwell. She descended to her floor. Her room was empty. An orderly passed by with a laundry cart on squeaky wheels.

Hannah stepped to the nurses' station, where a man thumbed through charts on a clipboard. "Hi. My dad works here. Dr. Jacob Lawson. Do you know, is he in surgery?"

The nurse checked the schedule and shook his head.

She clutched her journal to her chest and meandered past a patient in a wheelchair. She hit the Down button on a staff elevator and exited on the floor that had her doctor's office. A few steps later she spotted her dad through the office door, deep in discussion with Dr. Stewart at his desk. Why weren't they talking to her? Shouldn't she be included in their conversation, or was there something they didn't want her to know?

Dad noticed her in the hallway, turned in his white jacket and scrubs, and came toward her. He pulled his hair back from his face. "Hi, sweetie. Long night, huh?"

"Uh-huh."

"You okay? Where were you?"

"Just needed some fresh air."

"Lemme guess. The roof?"

"You should've seen the sunrise, completely gorgeous. You know, I went looking for you and couldn't find you. What was that all about, with Dr. Stewart?"

"He gave me an update on how you're doing."

"Does he, uh . . . does he know what happened?"

"No," her dad said. "No, not yet. Full test results won't be in for another coupla days, but your PEF levels were fine, and he thinks it's good for us to go on home."

"Is that not what you think?"

"Uh, yeah. No." He nodded. "I mean, yeah, I agree with Dr. Stewart. He's a specialist, and we need to do what he says."

Hannah got the impression he was protecting her from the full truth. She wrapped her arms tighter, concealing her journal. "All right. Well, I'm going to go get changed, I guess."

"Sure. And why don't you give your mom a call."

"You haven't talked to her yet?"

"She's been worried sick, Hannah." Her dad rested a hand on her forearm. "She just needs to hear your voice."

A cool evening breeze rustled the curtains above Hannah's bed. Her Bible was beside her. Her mom's kiss was still warm on her cheek. She curled into a fetal position on top of the covers, legs pulled tight to her chest, her back to one edge of the bed so the expanse of blankets stretched before her in the other direction.

She felt so small. So fragile.

Her journal was open next to her, barely readable in the pale moonlight.

I am drowning. Seems like I can't breathe. I know it's just the asthma, but it feels like it's always here, even when I've used my inhaler, this sense that I can't get air. Why am I forever crawling? Just once I'd like to be able to fly.

Chapter Twelve

Wish Me Luck

She had barely stepped back on campus, and already the rumors swirled around her. Friends and strangers wanted to know: Had she been dropped from the lead role in *Annabella*? Was Julia Armen poised to get her part? She couldn't really blame the professor. What was he supposed to do when some freshman succumbed to a panic attack only minutes into the opening act?

Standing in torn jeans in the morning sun-shine of late February, Hannah hefted her leather bag and faced the steps leading toward the university's cultural arts center. A bell rang from the distant tower. Birds chirped in the trees.

And all she wanted to do was crawl back home.

Not like that would help anything. Time to face this.

She took a deep breath, adjusted the strap of her red and white striped tank top, and touched the gold bird necklace she'd received years ago at her twelfth birthday party. Still one of her favorite pieces. She climbed the wide steps, wondering what she'd say to Professor Watson. Surely, he'd heard of her medical condition. She had a valid excuse, after all.

Across the lawn, Jason was chatting with a group of friends. The moment he spotted her, he broke away. Had he been waiting for her?

"Hannah," he shouted.

She kept walking.

"Hey." He jogged toward her. "You okay?"

"Oh, so there's at least one person on this campus who'll talk to me."

"What?"

"Rumors are flying, and you'd think I had the walking plague."

"Aren't you being a little hard on yourself?"

"Oh, look," she mimicked. "Here comes that girl who ruined the spring play."

He chuckled. "Yep, there she goes."

She punched him. "You mock my pain."

" 'Life is pain, Highness.' "

The quote from *The Princess Bride* made her smile. That was one movie he'd actually watched with her when they were younger, overlooking the romantic bits for the sake of the Fire Swamp and the Rodents of Unusual Size.

As they reached the top step, Hannah saw Alanna approaching in a pair of form-fitting fashion jeans, teardrop earrings, and an emerald top. Truman followed in her wake the way seagulls trailed an inbound fishing boat, and Hannah realized that Alanna must be the object of his affection.

Well, get in line and take a number. And good luck fighting Jason off.

"Morning, Hannah," Alanna said.

"Morning, Hannah," Truman echoed.

Hannah lifted a hand in greeting.

"You doing okay?" Alanna said. "We were all worried last night, weren't we, babe?" Her face showed no expression as she hooked arms with Jason.

"I'm all right," Hannah answered.

Truman filled the empty spot on Alanna's left and asked her, "How can you call him 'babe' when you just caught the guy flirting with another woman?"

"Flirting?" Jason laughed. "With Hannah?"

Hannah diverted her eyes. She knew he meant nothing by it, and that only made it hurt that much more. They were friends and nothing more, so she had no right to expect anything different. Of course not. Sure would be nice, though, to know he even saw her as the type of woman worth flirting with.

Just get to class and get through this day.

"Yes, with Hannah," Truman shot back. "She's a grown woman now, you know?"

Alanna snapped her chin around. "You are so annoying, Truman. Leave us alone."

"I have as much legal right to be on this property as you. In fact, I'm not only enrolled here, but also an employee in the campus bookstore. Yes, it's true. They hired me yesterday. And considering my GPA, I'd guess that the administration views me as one of their more promising—"

"*Spare* me. Babe, please tell me he's not still going on spring break with us."

"Uh, he's the one hooking us up with the van."

Alanna shook her head. "I'm scared already."

"So where're you guys going?" Hannah said to Jason, hoping to deflect the negative attention from Truman. She knew how it felt to be the outsider, and she didn't like the way he got treated by the beautiful crowd. Didn't the Bible, in the book of James or something, talk about treating everyone as equals, not preferring those with stylish clothes over the beggar in rags? Or in this case, over the students who lacked the cool factor?

"We still haven't decided," Jason said.

"Seriously? It's, what, only a week away, right?"

"Yeah. Until we know how many people're coming, we don't know how much gas money we'll have. And until we know how much gas money we'll have, we don't know how far away we can drive. It's hard getting people to sign on when you don't have the place picked out."

"What's wrong with right here? Our beaches're some of the best around."

"Because," Alanna tipped her head at Truman, "we want to get away."

"Which," Truman noted, "is why they call it a getaway."

Alanna groaned. "Jason, please get *him* away."

"Ah, Truman's harmless."

"Then get *me* away."

Head down, Hannah waited for Jason's response. The reasons for his physical attraction to Alanna were obvious, but he seemed too softhearted for this woman made of stone. Was it her New England upbringing? Sure, those from the Northern states could be brusque, but she had met Southerners who covered backbiting and gossip with a veneer of politeness. It was too easy to make geographical assumptions. Were there other reasons for her demeanor?

"Hey, Truman," Jason said, "you don't mind giving us a little time to ourselves, do you? And about spring break, you and I can talk later and nail down a destination."

"Good. Let's say Friday, when I show you the van."

"Deal."

Alanna tugged on Jason's arm, and they hurried off.

Hannah waited till they were out of earshot. "So she's the one, huh, Truman? I don't get it. Why do guys ignore the nice girls and go for ones who'll break their hearts?"

"Hmm." He frowned. "I suppose in Cro-Magnon times, we needed our women tough, to guard the fire and fight off saber-toothed tigers while nursing our young."

"Okay. What about now?"

"She's hot, Hannah. What do you want me to say?"

"You think that's why Jason likes her?"

"Is this a trick question?"

"Forget it." She hefted her shoulder bag and stomped off.

"You know, you're not bad looking. You ever think of going blonde?"

She spun and glared. "I could ask you the same thing, couldn't I?"

"Fair enough, fair enough. You know, I really like your spunk, Hannah."

"Spunky and brunette." She fluffed her hair. "It's all the rage."

As she swiveled back around, her bag tipped and dumped books and papers onto the lawn.

Truman bent to help her. She scurried in a half circle, gathering the items before the wind made her look like an even bigger fool. Math syllabus. Science. A copy of *A Tree Grows in Brooklyn*. Pens.

Where was her journal?

She pawed the grass and rummaged through her bag. She must've left the journal at home or on the passenger floor of her family's gray-and-gold Acura Legend. Her heart and soul were in those pages, and the idea of anyone reading them was more than she could deal with at the moment. She told herself not to stress. It was probably lying on her bed. It would be fine.

"Missing something?" Truman handed over her inhaler.

"Oh, thanks."

"I appreciate you stepping in for me, Hannah. You're a good friend. I admit, I'm not exactly a hit with the ladies. But have you ever seen the yearbook photos of Brad Pitt or George Clooney? You know, some of us get better with age."

"How old are you?"

"Just shy of the big two-oh." He clicked his tongue. "That's right. A quarter of the way to my life expectancy. You always liked butterflies, didn't you? Well, you might say we're caterpillars right now, still crawling along and chomping on leaves. Just you wait, though. You'll see. One day, Alanna will be begging for another chance with me."

"You never know. Listen, I better run. Drama class."

Truman pulled a face. "The moment of truth, huh?"

"Yeah. Wish me luck."

Still worried about the journal, she jogged across the grass. The closer she got to the cultural arts center, the more she worried about her role in *Annabella*.

Chapter Thirteen

All I Have

Drama students and theater-group members stampeded past Hannah, up the stairs, and out onto the campus quad. When she tried to stop Lance Prescott and ask what was happening, he wouldn't look her in the eye. Not a good sign. He mumbled something about class being cancelled and continued on his way.

Pulling her shirt tighter around her tank top, Hannah slipped into the theater's wings. She heard voices. Professor Watson was reciting lines as Desmond.

"If you'd just let me explain," he said, "I'm

confident we would agree. You need to know that my family has, well, certain standards for me."

She felt compelled to step from the shadows and respond.

"Standards?" Julia Armen said. "Standards which I do not meet?"

Hannah peered around a stack of storage totes and saw her rival, center stage, script in hand. Julia was thin and pretty, her hair styled and highlighted. A few rows back in the theater, the professor read from an iPad. He looked relaxed in a vest and tie. His female assistant sat beside him, making notes on a clipboard.

Julia continued. "Admit it, Desmond. Please."

"Hey." Hannah walked onto the stage. "What's going on?"

Professor Watson dropped his chin, shook his head, and then looked up. "Hello, Hannah." He tapped his assistant's arm. Once she had smoothed her clothes and scooted off down the aisle, he turned back to his student onstage. "Julia, could you give us a second, please?"

"Sure," she said in a treacly tone. "Whatever I can do to help."

"Don't go too far."

Julia strutted past Hannah. Her elbow jarred the leather bag and knocked the corner of a book into Hannah's ribs. Sucking air, Hannah tried to hide her pain. She gathered herself and faced her instructor.

"There's no class today," he told her.

"Then why was Julia still here?"

"Yes, well, I'm going over individual parts, evaluating our options."

"I stopped by your office earlier, but you weren't there. I wanted to . . . wanted to talk to you about the play."

Professor Watson looked up from his iPad, his glasses reflecting its glow. "Yeah, about that. How are you feeling? Are you okay?"

"I feel fine." She took a seat on the edge of the stage. "The doctor says I had an acute asthma attack and a seizure, which were worsened by stress and anxiety."

"Stress and anxiety?"

"Yeah, but . . . No, it had nothing to do with the play."

He looked at her over his glasses, and she held her shoulders steady. She wanted to prove to him that she was up to the task of the continuing production. She couldn't let this slip from her grasp.

"Seriously," she said. "I really am fine."

"It's nothing to be ashamed of, Hannah. It was our opening night, and you felt all eyes upon you. Perhaps I share some of the blame, telling you about the talent scouts in the audience. You're not the first person to experience a case of stage fright and the jitters."

"Jitters?"

"Your health is what's most important right

now, and we cannot run the risk of something like this happening again. As a school, we could be held liable, and—"

"It won't happen again." She hated the quiver in her voice. She was supposed to hold it together here.

"How do you know?"

"I *know*."

He steepled his fingers under his chin. "I'm sorry."

"What're you saying?"

"I'm saying that I don't think you should be part of theater group. Not now."

"No." She stood and rubbed a hand hard across her forehead. "No, you don't understand."

"Maybe next year. When you're well."

"Professor Watson, you can't do this to me. You can't . . . This is crazy. Do you even understand how important this is to me? This is my life."

"Hannah."

She paced the floor, holding her head. "How can you take that away from me?"

"Hannah."

"And what about my scholarship? It's the only way of helping take some financial pressure off my dad. I mean, he's a doctor and all, so it shouldn't be an issue, right? But he's still paying off college debts of his own. He got a late start. What's he going to say when he hears that I've wasted all his hard work and—"

"Hannah, stop. Enough."

"Sorry," she whispered, folding her arms around herself. "I didn't mean to react like that." She closed her eyes, took a breath, then looked at him with all the sincerity she could convey. "It's just that when I'm performing, that's the only time I feel *alive*. I'm asking . . . no, I'm begging you. Please don't take that from me. This is all I have."

The professor didn't move.

She thought back to her first acting class at twelve years old. She'd been so excited, so thankful to her parents. Although she was one of the youngest in the group, her instructor treated her like one of the adults. She practiced elocution and inflection. She ran through scenes in a Southern drawl, in an English accent, and with no speaking at all. She learned to communicate emotion with the slightest of gestures and, in the process, gained confidence.

While onstage, Hannah could be who she wanted to be.

" 'I being poor have only my dreams,' " she now quoted to her professor. " 'I have spread my dreams under your feet . . .' "

" 'Tread softly because you tread on my dreams.' William Butler Yeats."

She nodded, biting her lower lip.

Professor Watson met her gaze and offered a smile. "Hannah, Hannah. You've always been a great student. When I invited those scouts, I was putting my own reputation on the line, and I did that because I have faith in your heart and your abilities."

"And I let you down, I know."

"It's not about that. It's really not. You do understand, don't you, that you can't live your life being someone you're not? That'll eat you alive. This is about you getting healthy and finding out who you are. Until then, you won't be ready for the demands of the stage."

A lump formed in her throat.

"We're going in a different direction," he said. "We're going with Julia. I'm sorry."

Hannah swallowed. She opened her lips to speak, but no words came out. How was it that a few days earlier she'd been on the verge of stardom, and now she was being tossed aside? She pivoted, looked back once, then left the theater behind.

Chapter Fourteen

Unspoken

Dr. Jacob Lawson stood in the doorway of Hannah's room, eyes on the unmade bed. He thought of her as a little girl, still in flip-flops and a Backstreet Boys concert T-shirt. He loved her beyond words and wished that one fatherly hug could make her pain melt away.

How had it even reached this point?

Should he tell Grace what he had done?

As parents, they had made sacrifices Hannah couldn't even imagine, all in an effort to cover infant operations and hospital bills. When Hannah was ten months old, they moved back to this area where Grace had grown up and leaned upon Grace's parents—Papa and Meema—to get back on their own feet. They raised Hannah here in Murraysville, and Jacob finally finished his schooling at age forty.

Since then, he'd served at New Hanover Regional, where they kept him on as an attending surgeon. Some of the newer residents weren't much older than his own daughter, able to run circles around him in the OR.

"But," Grace had always reminded him, "you make up for it in life experience and good, sound judgment."

Sound judgment? Today, he questioned that.

Yes, Hannah had grown into a beautiful young lady, able to manage her medical conditions with a variety of prescriptions, but her seizure at Thalian Hall had undone years of vigilance and prayer. She hadn't suffered one since she was five, and until two nights ago he'd believed life might actually be normal for her.

Normal? Jacob despised that word.

As an orthopedic surgeon, he treated many patients with deformities, and his daily encounters reminded him that *normal* had very little to do with the way one's bones were shaped. It had a lot more to do with the heart.

And Hannah had a big heart.

Which explained why she felt things so deeply, both the good and the bad.

"You're home early," Grace said from behind him.

He hadn't heard her come up the stairs, and he jumped at the sound of her voice. "Oh, hey. How ya doing, sweetie?"

"You nervous?"

"What? No."

"Why the guilty look?" Grace asked.

He moved out of the doorway and sidestepped her question. "You know, I'm really worried about Hannah. I spoke with Dr. Stewart the morning after the seizure, and he suggested we all sit down tomorrow and discuss what's going on."

"And what's going on?"

"You thirsty?" he said, heading down toward the kitchen. "I'm thirsty. I could use some Mountain Dew."

"What's going on, Jacob?"

"He thinks with the seizure and all, there may be other factors involved, stuff that could've altered the effects of her medication."

Grace filled a glass with ice water at the

refrigerator door and followed him into the dining area, where he sat with his soda. He pulled the *StarNews* across the counter, glancing over the front page.

"You already scheduled the meeting, didn't you?" she said.

"I did."

"Without talking to me first?"

"Grace, please." He shoved a hand through his mop of hair. "I don't wanna argue about this. I'm trying to look out for my daughter, that's all."

"*Our* daughter."

"Of course. That's a given, isn't it?"

She eased into the seat next to him and rested her hand on his arm. "Is there something you're not telling me, Jacob?"

"I think it's best if we, you know, just deal with this tomorrow."

"Right." She folded her arms. "At the appointment you made without consulting me."

He sighed. "Will you just trust my judgment on this one? There isn't time to go into it at the moment. Hannah's gonna be home soon."

Hannah slouched in the passenger seat, her bag cradled in her lap. The last thing she needed was more trouble, and she wasn't sure how Alanna would react if she spotted Hannah in Jason's red '81 Camaro Z28.

"You sure about this?" she said.

"About taking you home?" Jason gunned the engine, and the entire chassis shook.

"I mean, because of Alanna."

"What? She knows we're just friends."

Just friends. Of course. How silly of her.

"And," he added, "you live like two blocks from my house, so it's really no big deal. Plus, I've got a load of laundry to get done, and I hate fighting the crowds at the dorms. It's cheaper back at Mom's, and maybe I can beg some cafeteria money off her while I'm at it."

"Are you that low on cash?"

He jabbed his finger over his shoulder. "You see that stack of papers back there? Those are financial-aid forms. My student loans're killing me, so let's hope I qualify for something, or I'll be calling it quits at the end of this sophomore year."

"How much do you owe?"

"I don't have a clue."

"Is the interest rate high?"

"Maybe." He shrugged. "Probably."

"Why's college have to be so expensive anyway? I mean, I want to be winning Tony Awards on Broadway, or maybe an Oscar. Do I really need Comp Science 102?"

"I'm guessing 'no.' "

She looked at him. "What if you just went for an associate's degree?"

"Won't work. Not if I'm gonna be a city planner."

She covered her mouth and looked out at the buildings along S. College Road.

"What?" he said. "C'mon, I saw that smile."

"No, it's just that every time you mention being a city planner, I get these images of you as a kid, the way you'd build cities out of LEGOs and blocks. And remember that whole town you drew on a flattened refrigerator box? You'd push your little cars and trucks around, making all kinds of noises."

"Better than Sims. Guess I needed the hands-on experience."

"You'll be a good city planner. Just don't do the *vroom-vroom* sounds."

"Very funny." He downshifted and took a hard right. "What about you? Did the professor have anything to say about what happened during *Annabella*?"

"He told me they're going in a 'different direction.' " Hannah folded her arms, more angry than sad at the moment. " 'A different direction'? More like, 'I'm not Trump enough to tell you that you're fired.' "

"So Julia got the part, I take it?"

"She took it, all right. Guess this means I'll be sitting center balcony during the next performance, right there with you . . . and Alanna, of course."

"Oh, man. I'm sorry, Hannah."

"Just that fast, I'm out of the theater group.

Kicked out because of my health. I mean, isn't that some form of profiling? Aren't there rules against that?"

"Wish I could tell ya."

She slumped further in the seat. "Don't mind me. I'm just a little devastated, okay? A little? Ha. And I'm so tired of thumbing rides back and forth with my dad. You know how embarrassing that can be? I mean, I appreciate you helping me out today. Really. But what about my own car? Why'd I end up with the piece-of-junk car? Every time I get one thing fixed on it, something else breaks. It's spent more days in our garage than out of it. Well, that's what I get for buying a clunker, right? My dad's great at repairing bodies, sure. But cars? Not so much. You know, if I had Alanna's money, I'd be driving a shiny black BMW too. Is that why you like her? Is it all about the car and the—"

"Hannah."

She huffed. "What?"

"We're there." He pointed out the window as they circled the cul-de-sac of large brick homes separated by leafy trees and hydrangeas. He parked behind an Acura and cut the engine. "Looks like your dad's home early. Is that normal? Doesn't he usually work some crazy hours?"

She frowned. "I hope everything's okay."

Jason trailed her up the walkway and through

the front door. As soon as they entered, Hannah heard voices locked in discussion. She stepped into the kitchen. Her dad was seated on a stool at the island while her mom leaned back, hands braced against a countertop. They both turned toward her and dropped their conversation.

What was that all about? She'd heard her own name mentioned.

Jason broke the silence. "Hey, Dr. Lawson. Mrs. Lawson."

"Hi, Jason." Her mom gave a halfhearted smile.

"I hope you don't mind that I gave Hannah a ride. I was coming this way and—"

"It's fine," Dad told him. "Thank you."

"Okay. Well, it's good to see you guys." Jason flicked his hand in a half wave.

Still trying to decipher her parents' mood, Hannah realized too late that her friend was leaving. She waved back, but he was already gone and she hadn't even thanked him. Her previous frustrations melted into sadness, and she wanted nothing more than to hurry to her room and avoid a parental interrogation.

"How was school?" Dad asked, before she could slip past.

She decided to flip it around. "I heard you guys talking. What was that about?"

Hannah's mom lifted her chin, her mouth forming a thin, flat line. Was she mad at Dad? Or maybe there had been some bad news? All the signals in this house seemed mixed right now, with things that remained unspoken.

"Don't worry," Dad said. "We're fine. How 'bout you, Hannah? Are you okay?"

"Yes. Just a little tired."

"Having trouble sleeping? Or any other, uh . . . problems?"

"Seriously, Dad, I'm fine. Why?"

"No reason."

Hannah shook her head. "You guys're acting weird." She cut toward the hallway.

Dad glanced at Mom, then asked, "You sure there's nothing you wanna talk about?"

"I'm sure." Hannah started up the stairs. "I told you, I'm fine."

She closed her door, dropped her bag on her desk, and kicked off her shoes. Instead of thudding to the floor as she had hoped, the shoes landed on a pile of unwashed clothing. She wasn't the most organized person, despite her mother's best efforts otherwise. She flopped onto the bed, pulled a pillow under her head, and tugged at her blankets.

There was her journal, pages open, right where she left it.

And those words still fit:

I am drowning. Seems like I can't breathe . . .

Chapter Fifteen

Lies and Betrayal

Why were they here? No one had sought Hannah's opinion. Oh, well, she was nineteen, still under Dad and Mom's roof, and if they wanted her to skip Friday classes and take a ride directly to the doctor's office—*Do not pass Go*—what choice did she have?

So be it. Two against one.

She fidgeted in the seat beside them. Slivers of sunlight cut through the blinds, illuminating Dr. Alex Stewart's cherrywood desk, his padded leather chair, and the shelves of medical tomes and manuals. She'd been in here more times than she could count. Dr. Stewart had overseen her care for more than a decade, and she knew he was one of the foremost pediatric specialists in the nation.

But could he explain her dreams last night, with their recurring themes and imagery?

The tornado. The howling wind.

The stage that swallowed her whole with a mouth of gleaming teeth.

Hannah shifted in her chair and chewed on a fingernail, the sleeve of her gray sweater pulled up over her knuckles. She wasn't the only one battling nerves. Mom had been dead quiet in the car, and Dad now twirled his key fob and stared straight ahead.

"Predictions?" Hannah said.

Grace and Jacob gave her confused looks. Her dad tossed his keys onto the desk, where they clanked into a black organizer.

"Is there something you're not telling me, Dad?"

"I was thinking of asking you the same thing?"

"What?" She shrunk from his penetrating gaze. "I don't know what you're—"

"You heard me."

She scrunched her mouth and furrowed her brow. None of this made sense. Sure, she'd suffered an episode, but that could be addressed with a change in prescription. Unless there was stuff they weren't telling her, she should be able to walk out of here in ten minutes with a signed slip and a few pats on the back.

Dr. Stewart strolled in with a clipboard. A balding, middle-aged African American, he wore glasses and a white coat over a shirt and tie. He said their names and touched their shoulders as he slipped behind them on his way to his desk chair.

Hannah stared down and fiddled with her sleeves. She turned her gaze out the louvered blinds to the midday sun that outlined Wilmington's downtown buildings.

This city was her home. She'd gone to public school here through ninth grade, then home-schooled with her mother and earned her high school diploma. She'd learned to drive on these streets. Many of her college classmates were old friends from school and the church youth group. She'd walked the decks of the USS *North Carolina*, on display in the port, and shopped along the boardwalk. Both her Meema and Papa were buried here.

She had every reason to belong. Why, then, did she feel so out of place?

"It's good to see you all again." Dr. Stewart straightened his tie and rolled forward in his chair. "Although I wish it was under better circumstances."

Her parents flashed brave smiles.

The doctor flipped through the papers on his clipboard. "We have a lot of history here to consider," he said to Hannah. "Bronchopulmonary dysplasia, acute asthma, seizures, multiple hip surgeries—most when you were too young to remember." He folded his hands under his chin and gave her a sympathetic smile.

She looked away. "Oh, I remember some."

"I'm really sorry you've had to go through all this, Hannah. How have you felt this week? Any new symptoms or problems?"

"Nope. I feel fine."

"Well, I've looked at your EEG and MRI, and

it seems as though we need to reconsider our current management of your epilepsy. Stress, sleep deprivation, and alcohol can all increase your risk of seizures."

She watched cars move through an intersection below.

"And drugs," he added.

Her eyes shifted back and met his. Was he being serious?

He shrugged. "Since you haven't had a seizure since childhood, I have to ask."

"Whoa, whoa, whoa. I'm not some stupid party-girl."

"Answer the question," her dad said.

"No, all right. No. That's my answer. And no, Doctor, I don't drink. I don't smoke. I don't do drugs, unless you count all that stuff you tell me to take."

"I see." Dr. Stewart nodded, perused her records again, and glanced at her dad. They seemed to be trading signals, as though this entire meeting had been rehearsed. The doctor removed his glasses. "Hannah, I believe everything you've suffered from is related."

At this point, she didn't care what secrets they might be hiding. All she wanted was an explanation and a road map out of here. Out of this hospital. Out of this city. Even out of this state. Sometimes she wished her life had a Reset button, a way to start fresh.

She leaned forward. "Why am I sick?"

Dr. Stewart pressed his lips together, tossed another glance at her mom and dad.

"Hannah," Mom said. "We're not your birth parents."

She swung toward her mother. This *was* her mother, right? She couldn't even process what she'd just heard. If the words had been spoken in a different language, they would have been just as hard to comprehend.

With eyebrows knotted, Hannah gulped for air. "What?"

Mom's right arm was wrapped around Dad's, and her eyes were down. She hesitated, then looked up at Hannah. Her face showed not only love and concern, but a hint of dread. Hannah didn't understand what this woman had to be afraid of. She was the one who'd just dropped a bomb on her daughter's world.

"We're not your birth parents . . ."?

How could that be? None of this made sense.

Her mother appeared ready to cry.

"Hang on." Hannah's father turned in his seat. "That's not how I, uh, wanted to tell you. Sweetheart, listen, your mother and I love you. We love you very, very much."

Hannah stared at him. If he *was* her father, how could he play such a cruel joke? This wasn't funny. Did he hear her laughing? And if he *wasn't* her father, how could he have lied to her all these years? Right now, his expressions of love fell flat. Until she could wrap her head around this, such words were meaningless.

"You were born very prematurely," Dr. Stewart explained. "At twenty-four weeks."

What, at six months along? This must be another part of the joke.

"Jacob and Grace chose to adopt you after . . ." He sighed and switched direction. "Premature birth, or low birth weight and a traumatic delivery, can be associated with this condition."

"I was premature." Hannah locked on to the people who called themselves her parents. But not her birth parents. Her adoptive parents. Was that the right term? She wasn't sure whether to scream or to burst into tears. "And that's why I'm sick?"

Dad nodded.

Mom reached out a hand, wincing as though biting back pain.

In most circumstances, Hannah would have softened at that look on her mom's face and took the hand. She didn't know anyone more tender-hearted and patient than Grace Lawson. Hannah had always hoped she might receive some of that same DNA, but now everything was . . . Well, if what they said was true, that hope was a waste of time.

She didn't move.

"Hannah," her doctor said, "we're concerned

about you because of the physical, and yes, the emotional symptoms that you are having."

"And hiding things from me was supposed to help?"

"I'm sure that was never the intent."

"Mom? Dad? Why didn't you tell me that I was adopted?"

Her father pushed his hair from his eyes. "It's complicated, baby."

"So what's that mean, 'emotional symptoms'? What're you trying to say?"

The ensuing silence served notice that more trouble was on the way.

Dr. Stewart slipped a piece of paper from his desk drawer. "Your father e-mailed me this." He put on his glasses, looked over the sheet, and read aloud. " 'Just once I'd like to be able to fly . . . Instead, I feel dead inside. No, something worse than death.' "

Hannah jutted her chin. She huffed, realizing she'd been betrayed. She watched her mom pull her hand from her dad's grasp.

" 'I am still a child,' " the doctor went on. "A child trying to find a place in this world. I have so many unanswered questions, questions I feel but can't even begin to speak. Why? Because there are no words to express them.' "

Her lip quivered.

" 'Something is missing. Why, God, do I feel . . . do I feel unwanted? Why do I feel I have no right to exist? Why do I spend more time wanting to end my life than live it?' "

Hannah could barely move her mouth. "You read my journal?"

Her parents said nothing.

"Hannah, I've been your doctor for years, and I believe that what you're feeling is normal and even expected."

"What's this . . . what's this all about?"

"You were adopted, and—"

"Yeah, I got that part."

"And you were born prematurely because you were the survivor of a failed abortion."

What?

Her vision blurred and went momentarily black. It seemed that a switch had been thrown, that all the air had been sucked from the office. She blinked. She snapped her gaze to her doctor and tried to stay connected to reality.

He nodded. "Your physical and, I believe, emotional symptoms can be traced to this, as they have been in other cases."

"Cases?" Moisture filled her eyes.

"Yes. I can only speak to your physical symptoms, but I suggest that you begin treatment for your psychological symptoms immediately. I'm prescribing a new medication to help control your seizures, and you'll need to continue taking your current medication."

Tears spilled down her cheeks.

"Now, there are side effects. I'll need to see you every week." He handed her a prescription, then stuffed his notes back in his drawer. "I want you to try to get some sleep and to avoid further stress. Hannah, please, this is nothing to play with."

Her dad thanked him and grabbed his keys.

Hannah shook her head. "I . . . I can't believe you read my journal."

"Honey," her mom said, "we didn't mean to—"

Hannah lurched to her feet, her legs like wooden stumps beneath her. They felt detached, barely responding to her commands. "I have to go." She lumbered toward the door.

Her father stood. "I don't think that's a good idea." He reached for her arm.

She twisted away. "Don't. Touch. Me." She heard him call her name and heard her mother stifle a sob, but none of it stopped her.

Hannah had to get out of there.

Chapter Sixteen

The Unveiling

Where was Hannah? Why hadn't she been at school today or responded to any of his texts?

These questions plagued Jason as he edged his red Camaro down a dirt road on the rural outskirts of New Hanover County. He braked to a halt alongside a large metal barn. In the dusk, his headlights revealed blackberry bushes, sheets of warped plywood leaned against the siding, and an old transmission that weighed down a stack of tires.

The address matched. This had to be the place Truman described to him. Still, Jason wasn't killing the ignition or unlocking his doors until he saw his orange-haired friend.

While waiting, he speed-dialed Hannah.

Still no answer.

It was strange for her to skip school. Sure, she could be somewhat scatterbrained, and her room had been a disaster area ever since he'd known her. All part of her charm. She never missed school or church, though. Her father made sure of that.

If Dr. Jacob Lawson wasn't exactly a control

freak, he definitely liked things done his way and on his schedule. Especially when it came to his little girl.

Jason tilted his head. Well, she wasn't so little anymore.

Screeechhh!

He snapped around in the driver's seat, believing at first that he'd heard a bloodcurdling scream. Instead, he watched large rusted doors roll open, metal scraping against metal, and a pair of bats flit from the barn full of junk cars. Dangling fluorescent lights flickered on, and a gangly form appeared.

"Welcome," Truman yelled, "to the Batcave."

Jason turned off the car and stepped outside. "So that makes you the Riddler?"

"Either that or the Joker."

"Man, I was starting to think I had the wrong place. This your property?"

"The Batcave? No, my uncle and cousin live here."

"Where's this van your cousin's loaning us?"

"Loaning?" Truman straightened his light-pink shirt. "No, he's driving."

"You mean, he's coming with us on spring break?"

"They share a bond, Jason. My cuz won't let her out of his sight."

"Her?"

"The van."

"Right. Okay. Well, uh, is he helping with gas, at least?"

Truman frowned. "You must be the Joker. Well, riddle me this. Who's the one providing the wheels?"

"Your cousin."

"So then, who do you think's exempt from all fuel costs along the way?"

"Your cousin."

"My *cousin*. You are, indeed, correct."

Jason strolled through the doors. "Where is she? Let's get this over with."

Truman dragged his hand along the panel of an old GMC. "Listen, I need to apologize." He rubbed the dust off his fingers. "I'm just going to say it."

"Say what?"

"You know *The Odyssey*, that ancient text?"

Jason folded his arms and waited.

"Yes," his friend continued, "I'm sure you know all about it. The truth is, Alanna is my 'face that sunk a thousand ships.' She's my Helen of Troy, okay?" Truman's eyes glowed in the lighting.

"Uh, I'm not sure that quote's right."

"See what I mean, Jason? I can't help it. I'm completely out of control."

"You're talking about my Alanna?"

"Actually, there are no legalities or technicalities that make her—"

"Where's the van?" Jason brushed past him. "As for Alanna, you really need to give that up, man."

"I wouldn't be so sure. She friended me."

"She what?"

"We've been talking online."

"Uhh. I'm pretty sure she wouldn't do that."

"You are correct. But," Truman said, "my avatar's a sophomore quarterback at Duke. I have a perfect smile and washboard abs."

"Seems I've got some tough competition." Jason smirked to show that he didn't take the competition seriously.

"And I do feel guilty."

"So what've you two been talking about?"

"She, uh . . . she told me her favorite color. Which, I'll have you know, I have been wearing every day since."

Jason rolled his eyes. "It's not pink, buddy. It's orange."

Biting his lip, his friend dropped his gaze to his shirt. "I've been played."

Jason clapped him on the shoulder and wandered farther into the barn, where work lamps and cords hung from pegs on the walls. He asked again to see the vehicle for their trip. They still hadn't decided on a destination, but they had narrowed the choices to Six Flags in Atlanta, the beaches in Destin, Florida, or Mardi Gras in New Orleans.

"Here she is." Truman gestured at a cloth-covered shape. "Our chariot awaits."

"I thought this was the Batcave."

"Well, she's definitely not the Batmobile. Behold . . ." Truman yanked with both hands at the moth-eaten canvas tarp and unveiled a 1970s Volkswagen van—Dharma blue, stock hubcaps, with a yellow smiley face in place of the front VW logo.

"Wow." Jason stared. "What a piece of . . . junk."

"It's vintage classic."

"It's vintage junk. Look at it. It's . . . it's dead. You really think she'd even make it past the county line?"

"It's not dead," Truman promised.

"This is your cousin's, you said. And what does *he* look like?"

Truman shrugged. "Not nearly as good as the van."

Jason questioned the wisdom of this entire trip. Maybe Hannah was right about staying close and hitting the local beaches. At the thought of her, he pulled out his cell phone and tried her again.

Same results. Same sense of concern on his part.

"Hey," Truman said. "I bet you're going to Danielle's party tonight. Do you mind if I catch a ride with you there, and then back to the dorms later?"

"Why not? We know that my car, at least, will make it off this property."

Chapter Seventeen

Hard Truth

❦

The waters of Smith Creek Lake rippled in the breeze. The last glimmers of daylight seeped through trees and foliage and dabbed splashes of gold upon the lake's blue-black surface. Hannah sat on a narrow platform that jutted from the shore. She loved this place with all its memories. She'd always imagined it as her own wishing well. How many times since childhood had she tossed pebbles into the water while whispering secret hopes and prayers?

At the moment, the lake was her hiding place. She didn't want anyone to see her like this and didn't care if her parents wondered where she had gone. Let them worry. What right did they have to know? Why had they lied to her all these years?

"We're not your birth parents . . ."

Hannah's throat was tight. The muscles in her cheeks and forehead ached from crying, and she tasted the salt from her tears on her lips.

If not her parents, who were they, then?

Her adoptive parents, yes. Dad and Mom, ever since Hannah could remember.

And who was she?

"The survivor of a failed abortion . . ."

Her real mother had wanted to get rid of her. That's what that meant, wasn't it? Why sugarcoat it? She wasn't even supposed to be alive.

Okay, so Dad and Mom hadn't exactly lied to her, but they hadn't come clean with the truth either. Not until today. Until she was nineteen. Until she had lived her entire life believing she shared their genes and their history.

She had never questioned the fact that her eyes were darker than her parents, that her skin was more olive toned. Even biological relatives had different colors of eyes and hair. That wasn't so uncommon. What about her love of chocolate mixed with raspberries? Was that a personal preference or something from her birth parents? And what about her messiness? With both her adoptive parents being analytical, organized individuals, she'd assumed that she had inherited their leftover personality traits.

The dregs at the bottom of the cup.

And all along, she wasn't even from the same cup.

Hannah pulled her legs closer, rested her chin on her knee. She was barefoot, in jeans. Fish nibbled at the water below, attracted by the evening's gathering bugs. The wind rustled the tall grass in the field behind her, and she looked back to be sure she was alone.

She clutched her cell phone. She had a flurry

of unanswered messages from her parents, from Jason, and from Danielle. She brushed her hair back and dialed Jason.

"Hello?" he answered. "That you, Hannah?"

She smiled. "What took you so long to answer? I was about to hang up."

"Uh, say that again. It's really loud in here."

"You at Danielle's?"

"Yeah," he shouted over the background noise. "Where're you? I thought you'd be here. I looked for you at school, and they told me you never showed for class."

"Long story."

Through the phone Hannah heard another voice rise above the din. It was Truman, bragging about grilling a cheese sandwich on an iron. A clothes iron? She didn't even want to know what hijinks that boy was up to.

"Hannah?" Jason said. "You still there? Did I lose you?"

"I said it's a long story. I'll explain later."

Truman again: *"Oh no, it's on fire! Look, I set the iron on fire."*

"Uh, I better go," Jason said. "Can I call you back?"

"Tell Danielle I'm sorry I couldn't make it."

"You made her a blanket?"

"I can't make it."

"Wow, it's unbelievably loud in here. Sorry, Hannah. Later."

"Sure. Whatever." She disconnected. "Bye."

In the stillness of the sunset, clouds hovered over the treetops. She dragged her lip between her teeth and cradled her face in her hands. There was no way she was walking home. Not yet. She scooped up a small rock on the platform and hurled it at the water. She didn't attach any wish to this particular stone. Her wishes had a way of failing to come true, so what did it matter?

She watched the stone rip a hole in the surface and plummet toward the inky depths.

The large decorative clock on the wall said it was past seven o'clock. Jacob Lawson buzzed Hannah's cell again with no reply. He turned off the TV and dropped the remote onto the couch beside his wife. There was no use pretending that a rerun of *House* would settle his nerves. His daughter was gone.

Hannah Elizabeth Lawson.

They had loved her from the moment he set eyes on her. He had cradled her in his hands while that postnatal cap was still big for her small head, and he'd fed her warm formula from a bottle.

"I dunno, Grace. It's not like her to ignore our calls."

"It's been a traumatic day," she said. "For all of us."

"She can't just run off and disappear without telling us."

123

"Honey, she's nineteen."

"She's our daughter. She still lives in this house and plays by my rules."

"I'd say *we* broke a few of *her* rules." Grace lifted her soft, blue eyes. "When I found the journal open on her bed and read what was on the page, I felt bad enough just sharing it with you. I certainly never wanted it to go any further than the two of us. You should've talked to me before you sent that e-mail to Dr. Stewart."

"I just, you know . . . I wanted to protect her."

"Well, we've completely violated her trust now."

"What was I supposed to do? I find out my daughter's contemplating suicide, and I'm supposed to do nothing? I don't think so."

"You overreacted."

"C'mon, Grace." He thumped his hand against the dining-room door frame. "You read what she wrote, and you were concerned too. You really think that I went too far?"

She gave him a disapproving look.

"It's not like that," a voice said from the hallway.

Jacob and Grace both spun toward their daughter. Hannah must've entered undetected through the side door in the garage, and she stood before them with crossed arms, reddened eyes, and disheveled hair.

"You had no right, Dad."

"Hannah," he said, "we need to talk to you."

"You've had nineteen years to 'talk' to me."

He watched her head toward the stairway, her arms still folded. He cleared his throat. "I understand why you would feel that way, baby, but please, I'd like to talk to you now. Better late than never, right? If you'll just sit here with us and—"

"I don't want to sit. I don't want to talk about it."

Grace rubbed the back of her neck, her eyes pleading with Jacob.

He didn't know how to interpret the looks from either his daughter or his wife. Why all of these arched eyebrows and unspoken messages? Why couldn't the three of them gather around the table and speak directly? Okay, then, he'd put the ball in their court.

"What it is you want, Hannah? Tell me what it is you wanna do?"

"I want to see my birth certificate," she stated.

Hmm. Well, that was pretty direct.

Grace glanced back over the couch at Hannah. "Why, honey?"

"Because I want to know who I am."

"This." Jacob motioned around the room. "This is who you are."

Without explanation, his wife stood and left the living room. Was this all too much for her to handle at the moment? He stared at his daughter, waiting for her response.

"I want to know who my birth mother is. I want to know how I can find her."

"Sorry," he said. "I can't tell you that."

"Why?"

"Because I can't. I just . . ." His eyes locked with hers, and he softened a little. "All right, I can't do that because I have no idea *who* your birth mother is. I have no idea *where* she is. After she gave birth to you, she changed her name and left town. She abandoned you. That's the hard truth. We adopted you a month later. So now do you see why I think it's best that you just drop the whole thing?"

"Guess there's nothing left to talk about then."

Grace reentered the room, a large envelope in hand. She didn't even wait for Jacob's reaction. "Here." She extended it to their daughter. "It's your birth certificate."

Hannah took it. "Thank you."

"Wait," Jacob said. "Hannah, I won't let you—"

She was already marching up to her room, and Grace stood at the base of the stairs like a sentry at her post.

It was nearly eleven o'clock. Tomorrow was Saturday and the last day of the month, with Jacob expected at the hospital in the morning. Yet he couldn't sleep.

He eased from the king-sized bed.

"Whereyagoing?" Half asleep, Grace slurred her words.

"Bathroom."

She closed her eyes and faded off.

After a detour through the master bath, he slipped down the hall toward Hannah's room. Was that crying he heard? Though muffled, the sobs were unmistakable. He hesitated at her door. This girl whom he loved so much, she must hate him. All he could think of was that final flash of disgust in her eyes.

She coughed.

"Sweetheart?" he whispered, knocking twice. "You okay?"

"Go away."

"Did you forget your inhaler downstairs? I can get it for—"

"I'm fine."

"Can I come in?"

"No, I'm . . ." Her voice was shaking. "I said I'm fine."

From memory, he pulled up a picture of his little girl running toward him, lip quivering, knees scuffed from a tumble on her bike. Even her simple "owies" made him mad. He didn't want anything to cause her pain, and today he'd been the one to do so.

"You get some sleep, okay, sweetie?"

She didn't respond.

Jacob pressed his forehead against the door.

Despite his desire to open it and go to her, he had already overstepped enough boundaries for one week. For an entire year, probably. He wished he could block out the sounds of his daughter's anguish, but he was not going to leave her alone in this condition.

Hannah had been abandoned once already, hadn't she?

God help him, he'd make sure that never happened to her again.

Slumping to the floor, he uttered a silent prayer for wisdom and forgiveness. He curled up on the carpet, tucked his head into his arms, and tried to get comfortable.

Chapter Eighteen

World of Pretend

March 2011

Another Monday. The last week before spring break. Hannah meandered in ripped jeans down the library's broad stairway, her leather bag heavy against her hip. She couldn't wait to be done with her midterms in Geology 102 and English Lit.

Jason was seated on the bottom step. "Hannah," he called up to her.

She didn't know what to say to him.

"Hey." He gathered his books and jogged up to her.

He wore a faded blue shirt with jeans and a white belt. Much too cute for his own good. Was Alanna dressing him these days? Heaven forbid. Or did he pick this out on his own?

"Hannah." He stopped a step below her. "Sorry I didn't call you back."

She looked past his shoulder, then down at her bag. "How was the party?"

"We missed ya."

"We?"

"I gave your message to Danielle. She totally understood. You know, her parents' new place is big, swimming pool and all, and for a second there I was scared that Truman would burn it to the ground." Jason nudged closer, tried to meet her eyes. "Not even a chuckle? Are you all right?"

"Yeah, I'm . . . I don't want to be late for class."

"Ms. Perfect Attendance."

"Not last Friday."

"Yeah, about that . . . Where were you anyway?"

"Maybe later, Jason. I don't feel like talking about it."

She felt his eyes on her as she finished her descent. A part of her wanted to spill everything, and another part wanted to paste on a smile and pretend nothing in her world had changed. She was still Hannah Lawson. Born in Wilmington, North Carolina.

Of course, her birth certificate indicated otherwise.

Propped on the edge of the leather sofa, Hannah used her body language to let Dr. O'Connor know she didn't feel comfortable here and didn't plan to stay a minute past their allotted time. Her mom had ferried her to this counselor's office after school. She had errands to run but promised to be back at five sharp.

Count on Mom to be prompt.

"Mom"? Well, what else do I call her? She's all I've ever known.

"Thank you for coming," Dr. O'Connor said.

"I didn't exactly have a choice."

"All the more reason for me to thank you, Hannah."

He looked up from his notes. His eyes were kind, if not a little too intense for her liking. He sat in a chair to her left, dressed in a tan corduroy jacket, a clean dress shirt, and no tie. He chewed on the end of his glasses. "How long have you been keeping a journal?"

"A long time." She placed a hand on the journal next to her.

He gazed down again at his notes.

Nearby, the old ink-jet printer on the desk

squeezed out sheets of paper. An antique brass clock *tick-tock-tick-tocked* on a shelf. The sofa creaked. Every noise in the room seemed amplified, and her claustrophobia grew. Was that even a real Doctor of Philosophy certificate on the wall? Sure, Dr. Stewart had recommended this guy, but you never knew nowadays. Despite the cozy ambience provided by the table lamps, she just wanted out of here.

Dr. O'Connor fetched the papers from the printer, placed them in a binder, and returned to his seat. He pointed at her journal. "Would you like to read something to me?"

Hannah pulled it into her lap and stared at the floor.

"How long have you had feelings of isolation and guilt?"

She shot him a look.

"I'm trying to help here," he said. "Would you like to talk about it?"

She put her elbow on her knee and rested her chin in her palm. This entire meeting was a waste of time. Her privacy should've never been violated in the first place, and now it had led to this. Like she was some head case. Like she needed a shrink.

"You're not alone," the counselor said. "We often feel isolated and trapped in our problems. There are others, you know? Abortion survivors, like yourself. They have the same problems.

131

Some worse. Feelings of depression. Suicidal tendencies. Shame. Many of your physical issues can also be traced back to it." He put on his glasses and studied the first page in his binder. "Here's just one example, a five-year-old girl who recalls specific circumstances of her mother's failed abortion. The knowledge was suppressed in her subconscious, and every bit of it was corroborated by clinical reports from the day of the procedure. Fascinating research."

Hannah worked her tongue against her cheek, pretending that he hadn't piqued her interest. There were others? She'd never heard of such survivors until last week.

"I made copies of some other cases. I thought you might like to look through them yourself."

On the sofa Hannah pulled her knees to her chest. "Sorry, but I don't like being referred to as a 'case.' "

"Okay. Would you like to talk about that?"

"I don't want to talk about any of this."

"Hannah, I'm not judging you. I'm not labeling you. I just thought you might find some comfort in knowing the reality of your circumstances."

"Well, I don't. I find this very *un*comfortable. I don't want to be here, all right? I'm not just some . . . some case on a piece of paper."

"That's certainly not what I meant to—"

"I just want to feel normal."

" 'Normal.' " The doctor leaned back. "Would you prefer to talk about *that?*"

Talk, talk, talk. Was he serious?

She wanted to tilt her head back and scream.

A glance at that ridiculous brass clock told her it was five o'clock. All she wanted to do was race from the office into the arms of her adoptive mother. There was some irony in that, considering her reason for being here, but she didn't care. She knew beyond a shadow of doubt that Mom was parked outside, engine idling and ready to go.

"That's it." Hannah stood. "Looks like our time is up."

"Here, take this," the counselor said. "I compiled the binder for you."

She mumbled a farewell and grabbed it from him on her way out the door.

Chapter Nineteen

Stuck

Hannah sat cross-legged, skipping rocks across Smith Creek Lake. The moon spotlighted her on the dock, lending her a sense of security, but that sense evaporated the moment a car rumbled into the park's nearby lot. Who would be out here on a Wednesday night?

"Hey." Her voice cracked, and she licked her lips. "Who . . . who's there?"

A door slammed.

"Hello?"

Something rustled toward her, and she reached for her bag.

"It's me," Jason said, cresting the bank. "You can put down the pepper spray."

"How did you know I was here?"

"You kidding? You're way too predictable."

"I am not," she shot back.

He mimicked her exact words before she could even finish spitting them out, and she smiled. He was right. While her parents might not know this was her getaway, Jason had come here with her far too many times to be fooled.

He knocked on the air. "Can I come in?"

"No." She looked toward the opposite shore. "I'm mad at you."

He strolled across the planks, plopped down beside her, and peeled off his shoes.

"What're you doing?" she asked.

"I am taking off my shoes."

"And why're you taking off your shoes?"

His socks came off next. "Because I'm sorry. I don't like it when people are mad at me, especially you. I figure I should stay for a while." He rolled up his pant legs and dipped his feet into the water.

"Beware the snapping turtles," she said. "And water moccasins."

"They'll stay far away, if they're smart. I haven't showered in days."

"You're disgusting."

"Hannah." His wide, round eyes found hers. "Are you doing okay?"

She broke their gaze, shook her head. "No."

"You wanna talk about it?"

"Nope. Now you just sound like my shrink."

"Since when do you have a shrink?"

"Forget it."

Jason faced the water, catching the moon's reflected glow on his cheeks. He braced himself on his arms and kicked his feet. She tilted her head back, sneaking a peek at him from the corner of her eye. She imagined that twelve-year-old boy beside her, telling her that she was like a sister to him. He'd always been there for her, and that counted for a lot.

"You want to know what's going on?" She bit her lip, then tried to smile. "It seems my whole life is a lie."

"Why do you say that?"

She decided to take a roundabout approach. "You remember Oasis? I always loved that name, such a great name for a youth group. Oh, to be middle schoolers again, huh?"

"I'll pass."

"Really? Why? It was so carefree back then."

"Body odor. Hair under my arms. Girls. No, thank you."

"So what's changed?"

"Very funny." He splashed water at her.

"That was one of the first places," she said, "that I was given a chance to sing and do drama. It was at Oasis that I fell in love with performing. When I got up and did all those skits and stuff, I meant it. I felt it. Now, though, I wonder if I'm . . . I don't know. It's stupid, but a lot of nights I lie in bed and wonder if I'm being real. Does that make sense? I mean, who am I really? When I go through my day, am I even being myself?"

"Why's that sound stupid, Hannah? A fakey person wouldn't even care."

"It's just . . . I have all these questions, all these doubts. Have I got up onstage all these years to avoid facing the truth about myself? I guess all of it's part of being clinically depressed. That's what Dr. Stewart seems to think. He sent me to a counselor to work through my emotional issues, like it's any surprise that I'm upset right now."

Jason didn't push. He waited and listened.

"My parents," she said at last. "They're not my parents."

He turned toward her.

"So I guess that means there's a reason for all the doubts I've had. My hip surgeries, the bad dreams, asthma, the seizures . . . All of it's connected."

"Whaddya mean they're not your parents?"

"They adopted me because . . ." She winced, trying to hold back her emotion. "Because my birth mother tried to abort me. I guess I wasn't even supposed to survive." She sniffed. "And I barely did. Last Friday, that's where we were, in Dr. Stewart's office, and they dropped the bomb on me. I'm trying really hard, Jason, not to be mad at my birth mother. And at my parents. And at God, for things being the way they are."

"I think I'd be mad too."

"Yeah, well, I'm trying to hold it together. All I know—all they will let me know—is that I was born in a hospital in Mobile, Alabama. That's almost a twelve-hour drive, and I have no idea how I'd get there. Even if I did, what would I do? I mean, that was almost two decades ago. I just . . . I want answers. I want answers to all these questions. I want to be able to get on with my life, you know?"

He nodded.

"Because right now," she said, "I just feel . . . *stuck*. Like there's no way out. I'm stuck in this place that I hate, and I have no idea what to do." Her chin quivered, and the tears pooled in her eyes. When a droplet ran down her cheek, she caught his caring gaze and gave him a brave smile. "See, Jason? I told you I didn't want to talk about it."

"Wow." He scratched at his chin. "Hannah, I'm

sorry. I don't know what else to say. I imagine things must seem pretty terrible right now."

She dipped her head, felt more drops streak down her face.

"But they will get better," he said. "One day at a time, you know? One moment at a time. Sometimes all we can do is trust that hardship is a path to peace."

"That's, uh, really optimistic." She wiped her eyes. "And beautiful."

"Can't claim it for my own. I saw it somewhere online, I think."

"Well, it's beautiful."

"Hannah, things're gonna work out. I promise. You'll know what to do."

"What makes you so sure?"

"I know you."

Her gaze slid across the moonlit lake. "I don't even know me."

Admitting this made it easier to handle, and a tranquility she hadn't felt in weeks came over her. She caught a whiff of Jason's cologne over the scent of the damp pylons and budding flowers. She was reminded again of their childhood days, reassured by his nearness to her on the dock. It felt right.

And then his cell phone rang.

Glancing down at his cell, Jason caught the name on the caller ID. He scratched at his neck. This was really bad timing, and it was probably best if he just ignored the thing.

"Who is it?" Hannah asked.

"Uh, it's Alanna. I'll just call her back."

"No. Answer it."

"Right this second? Are you sure?"

"Please," she said. "Yeah, I mean, you should."

He pulled himself up, feet dripping water, and walked a few steps away to take the call. "Hello?"

"Hi, babe," Alanna said. "Where are you? Is something wrong?"

"Hey, uh . . . no, no, I'm just hanging out."

"I just spoke with Danielle, and she's interested in joining us for spring break. Will there be enough room for her, do you think?"

"Yeah, sure." He held up a finger to Hannah, indicating this would just take a minute. "She's gotta pitch in for gas, of course. Wait, does she know that Diego's gonna be coming along? Didn't they once have a thing or something?"

"As in, a romantic thing? They're adults, Jason. They'll be fine."

"Okay, well, I just don't want any drama."

Beside him on the dock, Hannah coughed. She took a hit from her inhaler.

"What was that?" Alanna said.

"Look, can I . . . actually, could I call you back? It won't be long, I promise."

Before she could press him for further details, Jason said good-bye and ended the call. He would explain more to her later, but he was needed by his good friend. He sat back down facing Hannah.

"I am officially the worst at planning road trips," he said. "Three days before we leave, and we have no idea where we're going. Awesome."

"One moment at a time. Isn't that what you told me?"

He grinned.

She lowered her head. "All I want to do is escape the moment I'm in."

"Am I that bad of company?"

"That's not what I meant."

"Hannah, I wish I had some magic wand I could wave, like that stick you used to wave at me when we were kids. You thought you'd turn me into a horse or a prince or whatever. Well, here I am. Still me." He shrugged. "There's no escaping your reality."

"Then what should I do?"

"Look, why dontcha let me take you home? That's the best I can offer. If I'm not mistaken, both of us have exams tomorrow."

She closed her eyes. "That's the last thing on my mind right now."

"I know, but we . . . or at least *I,* need to study." He stood and extended his hand. "C'mon. Just reluctantly agree, would ya?"

"Okay." She rolled her eyes.

"That's more like it."

She reached for his hand, then ignored it and stood on her own. "You stalker."

Chuckling, he watched her head toward the Camaro with bag and shoes in tow. Then his chuckling died out, and he found himself simply staring. Her hips swayed as she climbed the bank. Her hair tumbled over her shoulders in waves of chestnut brown.

An hour later, Hannah was curled on her quilted comforter, barefoot in gray sweats and her standard tank top. The nightstand lamp was on, and her Bible and journal were beside her. She chewed on her pen, tried to organize her thoughts, and wrote:

I've heard more secrets in the last week than I wanted to hear in a lifetime. So what's the deal? Why don't I feel some huge burden lifted?

The truth will make you free? I'm not so sure.

Chapter Twenty

Predator and Prey

Truman saw a light at the end of the proverbial tunnel, a pot of gold at the end of his rainbow. He hoped to win Alanna's heart, and that meant he needed to plan this spring break trip to perfection and drive a wedge between her and her current boyfriend.

Which brought him to Hannah.

She was a vital part of his twofold plan.

The plan went something like this: If he could get Hannah to come along on the trip, he might flirt with her and awaken some dormant jealousy in Alanna. When Alanna witnessed his suave ways in action, she'd be unable to resist. And in the event that Alanna *did* resist—unlikely as that was—Truman had a secondary strategy that involved matching up Jason and Hannah. While the odds of that working weren't as high, if it did work, Truman could catch Alanna on the rebound.

Hannah Lawson.

Everything revolved around her.

On this fine morning at the UNCW campus, Truman climbed the library stairs with all the stealth of a jungle cat. He was well aware that his prey was now studying for midterms at one of the tables on the second floor. Nose buried in her books, she would never see him coming.

He reached the top step. Turned. Scanned the rows of lamp-lit tables.

There, only ten feet away.

He slid into the chair across from Hannah and rested his chin on her stack of books. He was a crouching tiger. He stared at her through his black-rimmed glasses. She kept reading, her jungle senses evidently not as fine-tuned as his own.

He cleared his throat. "Hmm-hmmm."

As expected, this got her attention. She lowered her book and didn't say a word. Oh yes, she understood the danger now.

"Hannah, you . . ." He pointed. "You have a wild side."

"What?"

"I know you've got one deep down in there somewhere. I mean, don't you ever just want to . . ." He waved his hands and turned up the volume. "Go *crazy?*"

"Nope," she said. "I don't."

"But I *need* you to have a wild side, Hannah."

"What's this about?"

"From what I understand, every dejected girl-friend looks for an immediate rebound." He aimed a finger at himself. "I want to be that rebound."

"I have no idea what you're saying. I'm trying to study here."

Truman admired her bravery. Somehow she had managed to conceal the fear in her rich brown eyes. He noticed the pewter necklace around her fine neck and thought that she really was pretty good-looking, wasn't she? It was weird to admit that about a friend from his awkward middle-school years.

He leaned closer. "Subtext. I'd like to split up Alanna and Jason."

A flash of interest in her eyes.

You're mine now. You cannot deny the orange-haired tiger.

"That's mean," Hannah whispered.

"Be that as it may, I would like to . . ." He clapped his hands together, then spread them apart. "To cause a rift. Once Alanna leaves Jason, she'll . . ."

"She'll what?"

"Uh, here he comes. Jason's coming over here right now." Truman changed the subject and raised his voice once more. "Can I hear you say *Mardi Gras?*"

Shushes came from the neighboring tables.

Hannah shaded her face with a hand. "Shhh, Truman. And no, you can't. Are you even aware that you are in a library?"

Jason arrived and took a seat next to her. "So, did Truman tell you?"

"Tell me what?" Hannah asked.

This was supposed to be Truman's big opportunity, and now he felt his attack losing momentum. How was he to know that Jason would appear in this same corner of the jungle?

"About spring break," Jason answered. "We finally decided on New Orleans, and we want you to come, Hannah. You know, that is, if you can fork over the cash."

"Sounds fun, but I'd have to clear it with my dad. You know how he can be."

Truman jumped back in. "Come *on,* Hannah. New Orleans. *Mardi Gras!*"

She shot him an annoyed look.

"You know," Jason said, "Mardi Gras didn't actually start in New Orleans. No, it began in Mobile, Alabama." He shared a cryptic glance with Hannah. "Which is on our way. So I figured, you know, if we had time, we could swing by there and check it out."

What was going on here? Truman sensed a subtext different than his own.

"It's a pretty cool place," Jason added.

Some mysterious realization sparked in Hannah's eyes, and Truman knew it was time to reestablish his authority here. This was his territory. His prey.

He pulled his chair closer to the table. "Yeah, thanks for that history lesson, Jason, but we'll have *plenty* to do in New Orleans."

Another round of shushes.

"Of course. I'm just saying I don't want anyone to feel like they're . . ." Jason turned toward Hannah again. "Like they're *stuck* on this trip. I mean, if someone wants to go somewhere, I really think they should go."

"Listen." Truman directed a predatory glare at this rival cat. "I was doing just fine before you came over. I was in the middle of convincing her to go with us."

No one was even listening to him.

"Do you think I'm ready for a trip like that?" Hannah asked Jason.

"I think it's now or never."

"Hannah, Hannah," Truman said softly, trying to break apart their locked gazes. When the subtle approach failed, he turned to more desperate measures. "Hannah! It's . . . *now or never!*"

A guy stood a few tables back and threw his hands up. "Come *on*." Other students wore disapproving expressions. The guy at the table slammed his book shut and clomped toward the stairs.

"Sir," Truman called after him in a show of indignance. "Sir, this is a library."

Sliding down in her chair, Hannah pulled a notebook over her head.

Jason leaned over a course syllabus in his dorm room. All through Graham Hall, students were cramming for exams. Some met in study groups with bags of popcorn and cans of Red Bull, while others sat in isolation and pored over notes on their iPads. He preferred studying alone, otherwise his social side took over and his schoolwork fell by the wayside.

"Hey." A soft knock sounded on his open door. "Is it safe to enter?"

He turned at his desk. "Alanna. Yeah, let's just hope my head doesn't explode."

"I've been thinking about New Orleans. Are you sure it's a good idea?"

"You kidding? We'll have a great time."

She chewed on her cheek, ran a hand over a soccer trophy on his bookshelf.

"What's the real question?" he asked. "What's bugging you?"

"Why did you invite her?"

"Hannah, you mean? She's my friend. Why is that such a problem for you?"

"Are you blind, Jason? All last year I was your friend too. Who was there for you when your parents split up? I deserve to have my feelings considered in all this."

He pushed back in his chair and beckoned her to come closer.

She didn't budge. "Tell her she can't go."

"I can't do that."

"Why not?"

He sighed and shook his head.

"You know, *babe,* you have a funny way of showing me you care." Alanna tipped the trophy over, left if lying on its side. "These last few days, whenever Hannah walks by, you just roll over and do whatever she wants. Such a good little puppy."

"That's not true."

"Well, don't think that I'm that stupid." She swiveled toward the door, blonde hair cascading over her shoulder. She looked back at him, her blue eyes hard and cold. "Why don't you call me when you figure out what it is you really want."

"Alanna, wait just a sec."

She planted a hand on her hip. "What?"

He hesitated. While he didn't want to say too much, he needed to do something to salvage this relationship. "It's not all that you think. There's some stuff you need to know, stuff that Hannah's been dealing with."

Chapter Twenty-One

The Big Uneasy

Dr. Jacob Lawson sat at the head of the table, which he believed was the proper place for the head of a family. He wanted to lead by example, and he offered a prayer before supper.

"Amen," he concluded.

"Amen." Grace squeezed his hand twice before letting go.

He glanced at her. Was that extra squeeze a signal of some sort? She seemed to be aware of something he wasn't. Not as though that was unusual. Though Hannah hadn't spoken much since their encounter in the doctor's office, their daughter seemed more upbeat this evening. Either she was working through her conflicted emotions, or she was putting on her stage face for some other purpose.

Beside him, Hannah hopped up from her seat and poured iced tea for the three of them. She asked if anyone wanted butter for the baked potatoes. When he said he would love some, she dashed into the kitchen and returned with a yellow cube on a dish.

"What's going on?" Jacob said.

Hannah slid into her seat, spread her napkin on her lap, and salted her potato.

"Hello? Is there something my two ladies aren't telling me?"

Grace touched his arm. "Your daughter has a special request."

"Oh? Well, let's hear it."

"Dad, you know how Jason and some of his college buddies went to Myrtle Beach last year for spring break? He said it was great, and you know how responsible he is. I mean, you've known him since he was, what, nine or some-thing." She took a swig of her tea. "Yeah, so, this year they've settled on New Orleans. We're going to Mardi Gras."

"Who's 'we'?"

"That's why I'm bringing it up. Can you imagine, Dad? It'd be a fantastic cultural experi-ence for me. The city's full of so much rich history, and the Garden District alone is worth the trip. Have you ever seen the Garden District homes? The pictures. Truly stunning."

"I've seen some, yes. And I've also seen pictures of drunken college girls hanging over balconies."

Grace shot him a disapproving look. "Oh, is that so?"

"Definitely not the atmosphere I want my daughter in."

"Your daughter, that's right," Hannah said. "You've raised me to know better than that."

Jacob had to admit she made a strong point. He'd trained her up in the way she should go, and she knew not to put herself in compromising situations. Still, she was a teenager. Not even old enough to be able to buy a drink. The very thought of her wandering the streets of the Big Easy made him, well . . . uneasy.

Hannah wasn't finished. "I hear it's an amazing place. And did you know that Harry Connick Jr. is from there?"

Grace grinned.

Jacob sensed this getting away from him. "Thank you for that tidbit. I'll admit, Harry's not a bad singer, and I know your mother doesn't find him half bad-looking either."

"Oh, not nearly as handsome as you, honey."

" 'Course not."

"Does that mean I can go?" Hannah said.

"Sweetie." He leaned back in his chair. "Have you even heard of Bourbon Street?"

"Yes, Dad, I've heard of Bourbon Street. That's where the chickory coffee place is, Café Du Monde. They're the ones who sell those awesome beignets."

"That's actually on Decatur Street."

She shrugged and took another bite.

"There's a lot more to New Orleans than that," her dad continued. "A lotta stuff I don't approve of."

"Well, Jason's not into all that stuff, and neither am I. I hope, by now, you know that much about me. If I do go, I'll be focusing my energy on the positive."

"I'm positive, Hannah." He wiped his mouth with his napkin. "You're not going."

"What, seriously? Just like that? Dad, you don't understand."

He shook his head in disbelief. Did she think he would change his mind? He slid a glance at his wife, but Grace wasn't saying a word. She ate her food and observed their father-daughter exchange. Did she agree with him? Or think he was being too controlling?

"Hannah," he said, "I understand fine. You don't understand. You're nineteen years old, and you're not going to New Orleans. It's a dangerous city, and you have health issues to consider. Didn't you hear Dr. Stewart? Plenty of rest. Avoid stress. End of story."

She looked across the table for some backing from her mother.

Grace shrugged. "Your dad has your best interests in mind."

"And staying *here's* supposed to help me avoid stress? With all that's gone on the past week? This is the most stressed I've ever been. I need a change of scenery, need to get out and make some new friends instead of being the freshman who still lives at home and doesn't even have a car that works. Please, Dad."

"I'm sorry. I can't let you go alone."

"Without you, you mean. There's a group of like seven or eight people, so I definitely won't be alone. And Jason'll be with me. Okay, that sounds weird. But his mom trusts him to go, doesn't she? He'll be there to make sure we don't get into any trouble."

"Honey," Grace said, "I think you need to listen to us on this one."

"You guys're always saying how I need to be

more upbeat and be . . . Happy Hannah. Well, maybe this is what'll make me happy."

Jacob shook his head, glad to have his wife's backing. Pursing her lips, Grace looked back down at her plate.

"C'mon, Dad," Hannah said, injecting warmth into her voice. "At least think about it?" She wagged her fork at him and grinned, certainly playing up the role of cheerful, compliant daughter. "You know you want to let me go."

"You think so, huh? Okay, yes, I'll think about it."

"*Thank* you."

Grace shook her head, and Jacob could hear her telling him he'd been manipulated by the daddy's-girl voice and cutesy grin.

With a bounce in her step, their daughter took her dirty dishes to the kitchen. On her way back through the living room, she said, "I have a ton of homework, so I better get to it. You won't forget, though, will you? You'll think about it?"

He nodded.

Grace waited till Hannah was up the stairs. "I don't understand you, Jacob. One moment you're insisting on complete control, and the next you're letting her twist you around her finger. You'll think about it? Sounds to me as though you've already made a decision."

Jacob fished his cell phone from his pocket. Something was definitely up, and his daughter had played her role to perfection. He couldn't handle this on his own.

"Who're you calling?" Grace asked.

"Who do you think I'm calling?" He dialed. "It's time for some reinforcements. If I can't talk sense into her, maybe I can talk some into Jason."

Chapter Twenty-Two

She Can Hear You

Jason leaned against his Camaro and basked in the sunshine that spilled over the metal eaves of the Batcave. The area surrounding the barn was even more cluttered than it'd looked a few days ago at dusk. Did Truman's uncle and cousin clear cash from this as an auto-salvage site?

Or maybe it was just what it looked like. A yard of junk.

The '70s VW van was out of the barn, which was a good sign at least. The back hatch was up, the doors were open, and a large human form was sprawled in the dirt beneath the rear-mounted engine.

Truman walked over from the van.

"Is it okay?" Jason asked. "Does it even run?"

"*She.* Yes, she does indeed run. There's a minor issue with the speedometer, that's all. Since we'll be driving over 1,800 miles round-trip, it might be helpful to know how fast we're going."

"Or how slow. Judging by looks, I bet it won't . . . uh, *she* won't get over fifty."

"My cuz was clocked going seventy-nine last month."

"In *that?*"

"That is correct." Truman pushed his glasses up on his nose.

"And who clocked him?" Jason chuckled. "Did he get a ticket?"

"He got lucky. The officer, one of Wilmington's finest, was convinced it was an error. He said he'd best take in his speed gun for recalibration."

A Chevy truck approached on the dirt road, and Jason recognized it as Dr. Jacob Lawson's weekend vehicle. Oh, man. Hannah's father wasn't thrilled about her interest in this trip, and Jason wasn't thrilled about getting caught between the two of them. While Hannah may have been adopted, she'd still inherited a stubborn streak as deep as her dad's.

Truman blinked in the sunlight. "That looks like Dr. Lawson."

"Yeah," Jason said. "I'd stay outta this if I were you."

"Will do. I'll, uh, just stand here and keep these lips zipped tight."

The truck came to a stop. Jason tried to appear casual as Hannah's dad stepped down from the cab and marched in his direction. He was a broad-shouldered man, fit for his age, with wavy hair that fell across his eyes. Jason had always looked up to him and held him in even higher regard now that Jason's own father had bailed on his mom. The Lawsons were like his second family.

"Jason."

"Hey, Dr. Lawson. How are ya?"

"I'm fine. Thanks for getting back to me." He shifted his gaze to Truman. "Lemme guess. Truman, right? Otherwise known as the seller of platinum packages and the supporter of local charities?"

Truman itched at his neck and took a step back. "I am Truman, yes."

"And this?" Dr. Lawson nodded at the VW van. "This is the charity you were telling us about the night of the play? Well, I will admit that it looks like a worthy cause."

"I, uh . . . have no recollection of that event."

Although Jason didn't know the full context of their conversation, he was glad to be out of the spotlight for the time being.

Movement at the back of the van turned the heads of all three of them. A hulking form wiggled out from the shadows beneath the engine, a wrench in hand, and climbed to his feet. Even with the bushy beard, he didn't look much older than his cousin Truman. Grease-stained and sweaty, he wore a ratty T-shirt, knee-length khaki shorts, and black Vans shoes. His hair was his crowning achievement, a nest of dark brown fro-locks.

"Man, what is going on?" he yelled at his van. "I thought I fixed that."

Dr. Lawson frowned. "Tell me that van's not what I think it is."

"Yes," Truman said. "She is the classic upon which we'll be taking our voyage, our *Millennium Falcon*, if you will."

"Her name is Evelyn." Even from twenty feet away, it was now clear that the van's owner had his bushy facial hair gathered in a rubber band. "Hey." He peered at Dr. Lawson through glasses as thick as his cousin's. "Who's the old dude?"

"You remember Hannah?" Truman said.

"Yeah. The spaz?"

"Uh. Yes. Well, this is her dad."

"Ohhh. Hey, dude."

Jason pulled a face and wondered how much worse this could get. What a fiasco. Just being on this property made him guilty by association, and there was no way Hannah's dad would grant her permission to go on this poorly planned expedition.

"Who are you?" Dr. Lawson demanded of the bearded guy.

"I'm B-Mac, his cousin."

Truman raised his hand, owning up to the fact.

"B-Mac?"

"Yeah. And, you know, I'll be driving everyone to their . . . to their thing, 'cause this is my baby, you know?" He touched the van with an adoring hand.

"I'm sorry," Hannah's dad said. "What'd you say your name was again?"

"B-Mac."

"No, your name. Your real name. The one your momma gave you."

"Dude." B-Mac hitched up his shorts. "That is privileged information."

"Are you some sorta convict or something?"

"What? No. Look. Why does it matter what my real name is, man. Like, no one knows what Bono's real name is."

"Paul David Hewson," Dr. Lawson said.

"Okaaay." B-Mac brushed dirt from his elbows. "Duly noted. Look, I have tons of other nicknames, man. You can call me D-Mob, Grifter, Corney, Bulldog . . ."

Jason had seen that look on Dr. Lawson's face before and knew his patience had reached its limit. Jason wanted to laugh at this whole scenario, but the idea of Hannah missing out on their trip drained all the humor from the moment.

As B-Mac continued his roll call of nicknames, Dr. Lawson gripped Truman's arm. "I came here to talk to Jason. Do you mind if we have a little privacy, please?"

"Absolutely." Truman inched away. "You should do that."

"Chewy. Spaz. Warf . . ."

"Enough," Truman snapped at his cousin.

"Whatever, man. What's the old dude's problem?"

"It's your beard. You look like the Unabomber."

The pair of them moved around the corner of the van, and Jason shook his head. "Sorry about that, Dr. Lawson. What can I do for you?"

Hands on hips, the man loomed over Jason. "Hannah's sick. You and everyone else saw what happened to her on that stage. What gives you the right to invite her on this trip?"

"Uh, I dunno." Jason scratched his chin. "She's new at school, still trying to fit in, and I figured she might have fun. Honestly, I was just trying to help."

"Well, you're not helping, Jason. You're not helping at all. In fact, you've made my position very uncomfortable."

"I'm sorry."

"The truth is, Hannah's not listening to me right now. Her mother and I agree that a trip to New Orleans would not be in her best—"

"Dr. Lawson, I really can't get in the middle of this."

"Well, you're in the middle of this. Like it or

not, Jason, you are smack dab in the middle of this thing. You've been a friend to her for a long time, and she values what you say. I've got stuff going on in my house that you have no idea about, so I'd appreciate it if you would just take my side on this thing. Do you hear what I'm saying?"

"I hear you."

"Can you do that? Are we okay here?"

Jason wanted to voice his opinion about Hannah's age and her need to spread her wings. He pictured her butterfly stickers, the ones he'd given on her birthday years ago, and he wanted to say that confining her wouldn't necessarily make her stronger. It could, in fact, leave her unprepared for life's stronger winds. He'd never been a parent, though, and he had no place questioning a dad and mom who wanted only the best for their daughter.

Adopted daughter? Yes, but they had parented her since the day she was born. And if that didn't count for something, what did?

"Fine." He nodded. "Yeah, I can do that."

Dr. Lawson clapped him on the back and strode toward the Chevy truck.

Jason stared straight ahead, his jaw clenched.

Turning, Hannah's dad stabbed a finger at the VW van. "You know, I wouldn't go ten feet in that thing, if I were you."

On the far side of the vehicle, B-Mac's face appeared through the dusty windows. "She can hear you," he yelled. "That is not cool, man. Not cool."

The Chevy backed down the dirt road in a haze of dust.

"He's gone." Truman popped up beside B-Mac in a flash of orange. "I had no idea that sticks and stones could break your beard."

B-Mac slammed his wrench into the ground and walked away.

At the Camaro, Jason allowed himself a smile and his first full breath in minutes.

Hannah was waiting. Spring break started officially tomorrow, and students scurried in various directions across the campus. There. She spotted Jason as he passed beneath a large magnolia. Head down, he trudged toward her in a plaid buttoned shirt over torn jeans. What was wrong? Usually, he was the happy-go-lucky guy who took things a day at a time and tried to find the good in every circumstance.

Well, maybe her news would cheer him up.

She rushed his direction, bag over her shoulder. "Hey, look what I've got." She pushed back her thin, gold bracelet and reached into her jeans pocket. "A wad of cash."

He raised an eyebrow. "Yeah?"

"And I'll have more later. Here, take it. This afternoon I'm collecting from some of the students I tutor, so I should be good." She punched his arm. "Don't give me that look. I've been helping three high schoolers from the Christian academy."

"Nah, that's great. As long as it's not in math."

"Right. Not my best subject."

"So does this mean you're in?"

Hannah bounced on her heels. "It's now or never, right?"

"What about your parents?" He looked away, squinting. "And, you know, what if you're not medically ready for a trip like this?"

"Now you sound like my dad."

"Well, I think he's got a point."

She tilted her head to meet his gaze. "This is about Alanna, huh?"

"Don't even . . . Listen, Hannah, this is about you, all right? I care about you, and I don't think this is the right time to be adding more stress to your life." Jason closed her hand over the rolled twenty-dollar bills. "You keep that," he said. "I've gotta go."

Chapter Twenty-Three

Something Brewing

Hannah's luggage was open on her bed. Open and empty. She stared at her chest of drawers, where spring fashions begged for a trip out of town. She'd bought new sunglasses, tops, and jeans, using a Christmas gift card, and it seemed silly to squander this opportunity.

Of course, this wasn't really about the clothes, was it?

It was about Mobile.

Her birthplace.

According to Hannah's dad, her birth mother had changed her name and relocated, so it was pointless to search for her. The adoption was closed, which meant that even though the birth certificate showed the actual hospital where Hannah was born, it listed only the names of her adoptive parents. All details about the biological parents were unavailable.

Should she even waste her time packing?

Hannah touched the necklaces and bracelets in her jewelry box. She wanted to go. She did. Her dad had come to her room an hour ago and handed her that option. He admitted that he didn't think it was wise, didn't think the timing was right, but he trusted her as his daughter to make a responsible decision.

Fatherly guilt tactics.

As though he left her any real choice.

And then there was Jason, who had done a full 180 on this issue. He selected New Orleans as a destination, knowing they would pass through Mobile on the way. He hinted that she shouldn't be stuck. He was her personal sounding board and travel agent. Then earlier today, he refused her money and practically shoved it back at her.

So the two men she cared most about believed she should skip the trip.

Stay here. Stay healthy.

Stay happily Hannah.

She flopped back onto the bed and gazed at the ceiling. She had nothing to write in her journal. Like everything else, her own thoughts and emotions were a mystery to her.

Set on a timer, the coffeepot in the kitchen brewed an Italian roast. Jacob buttoned up his shirt in the bedroom mirror and inhaled the aroma that wafted up the stairs. He would grab a mug for his jaunt into downtown Wilmington.

The alarm clock sounded from the nightstand. He snapped around, but Grace had already pulled herself up in the bed and hit the button.

"I meant to turn that off," he said.

She shaded her eyes from the rays that cut through the blinds. "You're up already."

"Yeah." He turned back to the mirror and knotted his tie. "The sun's out, not a cloud in the sky. The world is a wonderful place." He grabbed his sports jacket. "I'm headed to work in a coupla minutes, but I wish I could go in scrubs. C'mon, it's a Saturday."

"Why so cheery? What's going on?"

"Well, I had a late-night chat with Hannah."

"About?"

"The trip. I told her I didn't think she should go, and I think she understood."

"Really," Grace said. "So she's not going?"

"I told her that we trusted her to make the right decision." He flashed a satisfied grin. "Yeah, I think we're good."

"Okay."

He ignored her doubtful tone. He didn't expect her to believe, since she hadn't heard his words of wisdom with Hannah last night. "I'm getting some coffee. You want me to bring you a cup?"

"Sure. That'd be nice," Grace said.

Jacob slipped into his jacket as he moseyed down the hallway. He knocked on Hannah's door, knocked again. She must be asleep. When he cracked open the door to say good-bye, he saw that she was gone. Did she have class this morning? No, spring break started today. Maybe she was up watching morning cartoons, cross-legged in her pajamas, crunching on a bowl of cereal, the way she did when she was a kid.

He entered the kitchen and grabbed mugs from the cupboard. Turning toward the coffeepot, a flash of white caught his eye. It was a handwritten note:

Decided to go . . . Be back soon.

Mobile, Alabama

Sergeant Dodd knew trouble was on the way. As a police officer for the past two decades, he had served the coastal community of Mobile and raised his family here. Every year, it was the same rigmarole with the spring-break crowd—the college revelers, the double-fisted drinkers, and the midlife-crisis folks who hoped to relive their glory days.

He did his best to stay calm and collected. When the glassy-eyed guys and their tipsy girlfriends hurled insults, he tried not to take it personally. He always reflected on that verse in Proverbs: "Answer a fool according to his folly."

And, yes, he would see his share of fools next week.

At seven forty-five, the sergeant met with his fellow officers before morning patrol, and they went through the usual spring-break routine of "getting Mobilized," as they liked to call it. A rookie raised his hand and asked how to handle any potential bomb threats.

"This ain't New York City," another officer said with a smirk.

"Ahh, he's a newbie," said another. "Leave the kid alone."

"No, he asks a good question." From the podium Sergeant Dodd gazed around the room at the men and women in uniform. "You think it can't happen here? My rookie year, a nurse at a local clinic received a bomb threat, and that was long before 9/11."

"Loooong before," one of the guys joked.

"Nothing ever came of it, but let's stay alert. Call it in if you see anything suspicious." Dodd closed his folder on the podium. "Be safe out there."

He was on his way back to his office when his wife rang. Pregnant, she had gone in for an appointment this morning. He closed the door on the dimly lit room and its cinderblock walls. Nothing fancy. But then he hadn't taken this job for a life of leisure, had he? He was here to protect the citizens of Mobile.

"Hey, Kelly. What's up?"

"Are you sittin' down, darling?" His wife's soft Southern accent hid a no-nonsense personality and a backbone of steel. She needed it for raising their three sons. "I just got back from my

OB-GYN, and she says we're gonna have ourselves a baby girl."

Sergeant Dodd dropped onto his hardwood chair. "Thank You, Lord."

Chapter Twenty-Four

Across State Lines

Savannah, Georgia

Truman thought his plan was ruined before the day even started.

No Hannah?

Not good.

By 6:00 a.m., all those going on the Mardi Gras trek had gathered outside Jason Bradley's house. Although exhausted from midterms, their excitement grew as they loaded B-Mac's van that idled in the driveway. Food, drinks, chips. Sleeping bags and pillows. Suitcases. Duffel bags. A red plastic gas can and a case of motor oil.

They were choosing seats when Hannah Lawson appeared on the sidewalk. She had dragged a piece of rolling luggage from her house a few blocks over, and she carried that big shoulder bag that went with her everywhere on campus.

"Hannah?" Jason stepped toward her.

"Don't even say a word," she told him. "This was my decision."

And just like that, Truman's plan was back on track.

They now drove south through Savannah on I-95, headed for Jacksonville, Florida. Though this route was longer, B-Mac promised lots of ocean views. B-Mac's beard was gone, and in its place, bits of blood-dotted tissue paper marked every wound from his battle with a razor. Truman was in the passenger seat. He hadn't said a word about the hack job for fear of being sent to the back, where the van's noise and vibration were the worst. The shave was a definite improvement, though. His cousin no longer looked like a person on the TSA no-fly list.

Truman turned, folded his arms over his seat, and stared through thick glasses at the other passengers. Tigerlike, he studied his prey. He knew more about them than they realized.

Alanna sat on one end of a bench-seat, nestled under Jason's arm. They were two good-looking people, but Truman knew things could never work between them. Jason was athletic, while his blonde girlfriend was too perfect to risk breaking a sweat. Jason had goals for city planning, while she was studying for a career in fashion.

On the other side of Jason, Danielle's slender figure was upright, and her dark-chocolate eyes kept drifting toward Diego. Diego, her ex-boyfriend, was reclined in another seat with earbuds poking from beneath his knitted cap. He was moody and quiet, a star soccer player for the UNCW Seahawks. The school paper reported that he came from Venezuela, from a family with nine kids, and that he hoped to one day bring them to America by playing in the pros. No one doubted he could do it.

And then there was Hannah. She had her bag on her lap, her legs outstretched, and her ankles crossed. The wind through the windows blew strands of dark hair across her face, and one stuck to her lips.

Truman shifted in his seat the way a cat wriggled down in the grass before launching an attack. Time to turn on the charm and stir Alanna's envy.

"Hey," he called to Hannah. "What do you think of this?"

She blinked, turned, and noticed him flicking the plastic-flower lei that dangled from the rearview mirror. "What about it?" she said.

"The lei is yours, free and clear, if I can't guess your favorite color."

"How many guesses do you get?"

"As many as it takes," he said, toggling his orange eyebrows.

Hannah seemed transfixed, and Alanna glanced his way from two feet behind her.

That's right, ladies. Try resisting my bold plumage. I dare you.

"You get one guess," Hannah countered. "That's it."

"You drive a hard bargain, milady. Very well." He stared into her eyes and searched for the answer. He thought of their years as schoolmates and friends. He pictured her various outfits, hoping for a dominant color to present itself.

She sat motionless, no doubt terrified by his feral ferocity.

"Uh, let's go with red," he said.

"Pretty close, actually. But there are dozens of shades of red, you know, and this one is very specific."

"Raspberry," he blurted, in a moment of inspiration.

"Really?" Her eyebrows arched. "How could you . . . how'd you know?"

He faced forward, rested an arm out the window, and left the ladies speechless. A bit of mystique went a long way. Best not to force the plan, but let it fall into place.

Jacksonville, Florida

With Savannah behind them, they zipped through the flat landscape of Jacksonville and turned west on I-10. Who knew the van would get this far this fast? She was a workhorse. Jason remembered his first glimpse of her, that anti-climactic unveiling in the Batcave. Factoring in food, gas, and potty stops, they could still hit the Gulf by sunset.

A romantic stroll on the beach with Alanna?

Sounded awesome.

Alanna was pressed against him now, hand resting on his leg. She smelled good, as always. An arm's length away, Hannah seemed lost in thought.

Jason knew it had taken some courage on her part to walk out the door of her father's house. He'd wanted to stand up to Dr. Lawson himself, for Hannah's sake, but he respected the man too much to do so. Hannah was still under her parents' roof, still their little girl. Until she completed this journey of self-discovery, she would be stuck—as she'd said to him on the dock—in a past full of questions and doubt. She needed to do this so she could move on.

He just prayed that her expectations were realistic. After all, what were the odds of her finding her birth mother or any additional details of her survival story? Hannah was delicate right now, and he would hate to see her heart crushed.

A debate raging at the front of the van broke through his thoughts.

"Fat Man's," Truman said.

"C'mon," B-Mac said. "Are you kidding me?"

"Fat Man's Burgers. Not even open for discussion."

"You are wrong, cuz."

"Their one-pounder?" Truman said. "Best by a country mile. You get your name on the wall if you finish it."

"No, no, no." B-Mac's fro-locks whipped back and forth. "You clearly don't know your burgers. I've got the top three spots on that wall, dude, and it does *not* compare."

Jason couldn't help himself. "To what?"

"Homer's on Fifth Street. Ahh, man. It is legend-*dary*."

Truman held up a hand. "Sorry to inform you that Homer's is disgusting."

"I'm not much of a burger person," Jason said, "but the City Deli is pretty good."

B-Mac looked at him through the rearview. "Those are sandwiches, man. If you call those burgers, you need help."

Diego surprised everyone by tugging on his earbuds and chipping in. "You know, the problem with people who say they love burgers is that after a while, they ditch the burger for some other kind of food. Right, Danielle?"

Jason cringed. Oh, boy. There was no mistaking Diego's real meaning.

"You talking to me?" Danielle shot back. "You are *not* talking to me. Yeah, I'm a . . . I'm a vegan

173

now, that's right. And you'd better believe, I am much, much happier."

"Why? Because burgers are cheap to you, is that it?"

"You know what, Diego, this isn't about cows versus carrots, okay? This is about you. And me. And the unfinished business we—"

Closing his eyes, he popped his buds in again and leaned back.

"Oh no, you *didn't* just put those in. Listen, you want to talk, Diego? Let's talk." She waited. "Mm-hmm, just as I thought. Attention, van. Diego doesn't want to talk about our problems."

"We *all* wish we had headphones at this point," B-Mac said.

Danielle flipped her hand, dismissing the apathy in this van, and Jason looked around to gauge the reactions. Hannah fought off a smile. Alanna rolled her eyes. Truman put his head out the passenger window and fiddled with the broken side-view mirror.

B-Mac gripped the steering wheel and brought the discussion back around. "There's a place out west where you can get specialty burgers that aren't even on the menu. Can you imagine? Dude, it's supposed to be killer. The Upside-Downer, the Double-Double, the Triple-Double, and the . . ." He paused, choked with emotion. "The Meat-Lovers.' "

Jason wanted to laugh out loud. He watched

the lines on the interstate that stretched ahead of them and figured they were due for another stop soon. He couldn't believe the path this conver-sation had taken—from burgers to breakups to breakdowns.

"Hey, uh, Hannah," B-Mac said. "What's your favorite burger?"

"What?"

"Burger. Favorite burger."

Jason saw her sit up and knew this was a subject she could expound upon.

"You know," Hannah answered, "I watched this documentary once, and it really freaked me out. Did you know that 35 percent of the meat in most burgers is meat fillers from little yellow pellets that come in a cardboard box? Yeah, and the rest of it's from cows that graze in their own manure."

"No." B-Mac shook his head. "That is not provable."

"And they're pumped full of steroids and antibiotics and hormones."

"Who says?"

"And they just grow and grow and grow. So where do all those chemicals and stuff go, huh? That can't be good for you."

At Jason's side, Alanna huffed and turned her gaze out the window.

"Like, seriously," B-Mac said, "when you cook a burger, all that bad stuff drains down into the grill."

"They bathe the meat in ammonia," Hannah went on. "And that's what—"

B-Mac cranked the radio and yelled, "Ignorance is bliss. Ignorance is bliss."

"That's what gets into your arteries."

"I'm not listening to you, Hannah. You're making me really angry."

"All of that junk, it's inside you. And—"

"Hannah!" Alanna shook her head. "Is this how you'll act the whole time? If so, it's going to be a long trip there and back."

All seven people fell silent.

Jason felt horrible for Hannah. Yeah, she could get to rambling on a subject and stumbling over her own words, but that proved she had passion and a desire to think for herself. He liked that about her. The only time Alanna got that passionate about an issue was when it benefitted her to do so.

Regardless, it was best to keep quiet and let the girls work through their own issues. Trying to pull two cats apart was just asking to get clawed.

By both of them, probably.

Jason tucked his Seahawks hoodie between his neck and the seat. Before he closed his eyes for a short rest, he saw Truman lean toward his cousin in the driver's seat. Jason was no lip-reader, but it looked like Truman whispered, "It's working."

What was working? What was that supposed to mean?

Tallahassee, Florida

Hannah stood beside the Dharma-blue van and gazed around this gas station on the west end of Tallahassee. It was getting dark. The others were lined up at the indoor restrooms or at the glassed-in counter, their arms full of Doritos and gummy bears and soft drinks.

This was the first time since her adoption that she had been back near the Gulf of Mexico. She'd been born on the Gulf's shores. Was she supposed to feel some connection?

B-Mac and Diego returned to the vehicle first, sucking on fountain drinks.

"Your real name . . ." Diego was saying. "Is it Alexander?"

"Are you kidding? If I had a name that cool, I would totally use it."

"Okay, hmm. Is it a name that could go either way, like Lesley?"

"Dude. How'd you know?"

"You mean, I actually guessed it?"

"No, man." B-Mac climbed behind the wheel. "Not even close."

Jason appeared from the store and extended a peace offering to Hannah. "Want my other Reese's cup? C'mon, you know you want it. All yours."

"No, thanks."

"You okay?"

"Just great," she said.

Inside the store's front window, Alanna stood watching them.

"Don't let her get to you," Jason said. "It's me she's mad at. I know she seems that way a lot, but underneath it all, she's not as bad as you think."

Although a number of responses flitted through Hannah's head, she kept them to herself. Jason was almost twenty. She would trust him to figure out his own relationships. She ducked back into the van, and he followed.

"You know," he said, "I'm proud of you for doing this."

"When my dad gave me the option, I don't think he expected me to take it."

"Your parents love you, Hannah. They mean well."

"That's not what this is about, Jason. I'm doing this for me."

"Exactly. I mean, you need to. It's important."

She settled into her seat. "I need to find my birth mother. I'm not going home till I do."

Chapter Twenty-Five

Killing Time

Mobile, Alabama

Something woke the thirty-seven-year-old woman from a nap on the couch. She blinked. Rested a hand on her stomach. Listened. She would swear that someone had called for her, and it wasn't the first time she had thought such a thing.

Always a young girl's voice.

But never this close.

Rattled, she walked to the kitchen for a glass of water. She saw herself in the window over the sink, and the reflection erased any signs of her age. For a moment, she was a young woman again herself. Barely seventeen.

In that lifetime, she was known as Alyssa Porter. She lived with her parents in Huntsville, where she graduated a year early from high school and scored high on her SATs. She accepted a scholarship to Auburn, planning to get a master's in civil law. People said she had the perfect life. She got all the breaks. Born with both beauty and brains.

The breaks ran out on July 2, 1990.

At 8:44 p.m., on her seventeenth birthday, she got the call. A drunk driver had crossed a median and plowed head-on into her parents. He suffered a few scratches and a broken ankle, while Mr. and Mrs. Porter died minutes apart at the scene.

Alyssa was sent to live with her aunt and uncle in Mobile, where her grief took over. One night she ran off with a friend and hit the local bar scene. She met an older guy who made her forget, for a little while anyway, her pain. They shared a night on the town. The next morning he was gone, but her pregnancy didn't come as any real surprise.

What happened later at Owens Clinic did.

And once again she ran.

Mary Rutledge tossed and turned on her sagging twin mattress. What with all the sirens, she couldn't get a wink of sleep. She rose and went to the window, not that there was much to see from a first-floor apartment in this lower-income section of town. Mobile had its nice parts, sure enough, and DeSean, he did all right for his family. Yessir, he did. But this building was old, and some days she had seen drug deals going down in broad daylight. The streets 'round here were rough. That was the plain truth.

More sirens. Off in the distance.

Must be the first of them spring-break kids coming and causing trouble, living it up in these warm coastal towns. Just kids being kids. Oh, they would learn.

And, well, who was she to talk? Even at her age she learned something new every day. Way she figured, the day you stopped learning was the day you stopped living.

Mary pulled on some clothes and drove her rusted Celebrity toward one of 'em nicer sections of town. She passed this way three days a week while going to work at the hospice center. Though she'd let her nursing credentials lapse, she couldn't help but care for people. Loving was all part of learning, wasn't it? Sure, the pay weren't great, but it was steadier than her days serving tables.

The bright lights of a Publix caught her eye. She parked and went in. Store was nice and clean. She wandered the aisles and thumbed through the magazines, just killing time.

And that's when she saw her, the woman from almost twenty years ago. She was reading the nearby greeting cards, also looking but not really buying. Just killing time, same as Mary. She had to be in her thirties, still pretty as could be with all that hair and them soulful eyes. A face like that, you didn't forget. Not after what they'd gone through.

Their eyes locked. Maybe five seconds, maybe ten.

"Ms. Porter?" Mary said.

"Excuse me? No, you must be mistaken."

"It's me. Nurse Rutledge. You remember me, dontcha? Surely you do."

"No, ma'am. My name's Hastings, not Porter."

Mary knew that some people, they liked their secrets kept buried. But Mary, she wanted to talk. She figured, as it was, she'd been holding onto things long enough.

She tried again. "I worked at that old clinic down on—"

"Please," the woman interrupted. "My apologies, but I have to go."

Chapter Twenty-Six

Beached

Destin, Florida

Hannah loved the ocean. These beaches felt a lot like those back home, except that in the Carolinas, the Atlantic tides displayed both northern and southern moods.

Tonight the moon was low over the Gulf of Mexico, and the cobalt surf wore caps of frothy white. She pulled a top over her T-shirt and strolled in jean shorts through the sand toward the bonfire. It felt good to stretch her legs and get some fresh air. Honestly, a van full of guys should carry mandatory air-quality alerts.

She ruffled Diego's hair and took a seat on a log of driftwood. Still attached to his iPod, he grinned at her. A few feet away, Danielle crinkled her mouth in disgust and turned her attention back to B-Mac, who was performing an original song on his guitar while Truman gazed into the flames.

Where was Jason?

Hannah spotted him down the beach. He crept up behind Alanna and grabbed her around the waist. His playfulness was met by a cry of anger and a shove. What did he see in her anyway? With the thick eyeliner and perma-scowl, she didn't look half as pretty as all the guys seemed to think.

"That's the meaning of life," B-Mac sang out. "That's the meaning of love . . ."

Beside him, Truman mouthed along.

"That's the meaning of everything, and that's all you need to know . . . about everything." B-Mac gave a final strum and let the music fade.

Hannah dropped her chin and smiled. While she was all for creativity, that last line needed some work.

"Wow," Danielle said. "You're really good, B-Mac."

Diego looked at Hannah, shook his head, and smirked, as though convinced that Danielle was trying to make him jealous. Maybe she was.

"Thanks," B-Mac said. "That was supposed to be a jingle for a barbecue company. You know, I meant every word, but they thought it was too deep."

"You should try out for one of those reality shows."

"I don't think so, Danielle. I'm pretty sure those things're rigged. You know, sometimes I write songs based on dreams that I imagine other people have."

"What about your own dreams?"

"I don't dream."

"Not ever?" Danielle shot a sideways glance at Diego.

"Well, I . . . I do dream of starting a burger joint someday."

"Big Mac," Diego said. "I bet that's what the B-Mac stands for."

"That, uh, may have something to do with it. But if you think I'm telling you my real name, you can—" B-Mac hopped to his sandaled feet and swung his guitar around by the neck. "Lights. Tow truck. Dude, it's about time."

Parked behind the VW van, the car with the rotating lights didn't look like any tow truck Hannah had ever seen. It looked like trouble. B-Mac seemed oblivious, though, as he lumbered past clumps of dune grass. Hannah wiped sand from her shorts and followed along with the others. They gathered at the back of the van, where the tires were up to the axle in sand.

"It's a cop car," Truman said.

"Good," his cousin said. "That's good. They sent in the big guns to help."

The police officer climbed from his cruiser. His face was stern as he shone his flashlight on B-Mac. "Step away from the vehicle, sir."

"Dude, tell me the tow truck's right behind you."

The light flashed up into B-Mac's eyes. "Have you been drinking?"

Hannah couldn't blame the officer for asking. A gust of wind was whipping B-Mac's fro-locks about his head, and he looked like a wild man, his face ashen, his eyes as round as the van's hubcaps. He was harmless enough. She knew that now. But the officer wasn't taking any chances.

"Sir. Answer the question."

"No, of course not," B-Mac said. "Why's everyone always think I've been drinking?"

The cop aimed his flashlight at the van. "Explain this to me."

"Ohhh, this? What? You know, nobody ever tells you that you can't drive on the beach. They do it all the time on TV. It looks fun, right? It's all a lie, man. All a lie. Also, running on the beach is not as easy as it looks. Have you ever tried—?"

"Mr. Curly-Top." The cop edged closer. "Do you see any hotels on this beach?"

"Yes. No. Uhhh . . ."

"Any restaurants? Bars?"

Hannah and everyone else shook their heads. This officer seemed upset about something. It was late, and clearly he didn't trust their intentions.

"Bars? No," B-Mac said. "Is that a trick question?"

"You don't see any of those things," the cop said, "because this is a land preserve."

"A land . . . Really? For what?'

"Set aside for endangered turtle eggs."

"Tur . . . turtle eggs?" B-Mac laughed. "Dude, seriously? Am I being punk'd?"

The flashlight beam cut toward a sign that stood crooked in the sand.

Land preserve.
$5000 fine.
Trespassers will be prosecuted.

B-Mac's jaw dropped. "No. No, that's not . . . No."

The cop's dark eyes were hard and unblinking.

"Five thousand dollars?" B-Mac gasped.

Truman jabbed a finger toward his cousin. "He's the owner and the driver."

"C'mon. Truman, you're the one who told me to drive here."

"I don't even know your real name."

"What is wrong with you?"

"Listen," the officer said. "I don't have time for this. Now, I need to impound this vehicle. I'm going to ask all of you to please pick up your belongings and make your way down to the curb. I'll also need your names."

"Our . . . our real names?" B-Mac asked.

"Excuse me?" The cop's light blinded him again. "Sir, if you're going to be belligerent, I will cuff you and take you downtown, where you can—"

"Officer?"

The man in uniform shot Hannah an exasperated look.

She responded with an expression of innocent desperation. While she had practiced such things in the mirror for her acting, there was nothing fake about it at the moment. She *was* desperate. She couldn't let a fine and a ticket—because of turtle eggs, of all things—end her quest.

"I'm sorry," she continued, "but can I please say something? This is my first trip like this, okay? I've never done anything like this before. I know you don't care about my sob story, but the only reason I came is because I have to get to Mobile, and I have a really good motive. Motive . . . You care about that sort of thing, right?"

"Ma'am, I don't have time for this. I want all of you to go ahead and—"

"No, listen." She lowered her voice. "Please, I promise I have a good excuse."

The officer turned off his flashlight and looked around at the others.

"See, I'm trying to get to Mobile because . . ." She moistened her lips. "Because I just found out that I'm adopted. Like, just last week. And this is my only chance to find out who I really am. To find my mother, I mean. It's like I've been caught in the sand the same as our van here, and I need to get out. You know what I'm saying? Or I'll be beached forever. And, well, I think she still lives in town. At least I hope so." She swallowed. "It's been . . . been nineteen years, so of course she could be long gone by now."

Hannah realized that she had just made her reasons for this trip public, reasons she hadn't meant for anyone except Jason to know. Would they all think she was pathetic? Just milking this situation for sympathy? Whatever. It felt good to get it out.

"So, look," she pleaded with the cop. "I understand you probably have to do this, and it's your job and everything, and we probably deserve everything you're trying to say, and we definitely didn't mean to harm any turtles or turtle eggs or anything like that." She dug rolled bills from her shorts. "If this'll help, I've got like ninety-three dollars and change. Here's a quarter, and this, this is a dime and some pennies."

"No, ma'am." He sighed. "Please."

"Just take it. It's honestly all I have."

"I believe you. Now if you'll put that back in your pocket, I'm not going to take your money." He tapped his flashlight against his leg. "What I am going to do is call a towing company, and I'm sure *they'll* be glad to collect every penny."

"Well, it's better than five-thousand dollars," B-Mac said.

"You. Curly-Top. Not a word."

Hannah stepped back in. "Thank you, Officer. I really . . . we really appreciate this." She glanced back at the crew, and they gave hearty nods of agreement. Only Alanna seemed unmoved as her eyes bored into Hannah.

Chapter Twenty-Seven

A Deep Wound

Truman stood with the others at the back of the van. In seconds they would push as the tow truck pulled. Soon they would be out of this sand trap and back on the road. In less than two hours they would reach their beachside resort on the fringes of Pensacola.

"You think you can take care of this?" the

police officer asked the driver of the flatbed tow truck, a gruff guy in a ball cap.

"Yeah, I got it."

"Push, y'all," B-Mac cried, as the tow chain tightened and the van inched forward. Packed sand spilled from her tire treads. She was moving, actually moving. "C'mon, Evelyn, you can do it. I know it's painful."

Everyone groaned with effort. Well, yes, almost everyone. Truman had only one hand on the rear corner.

"You're not doing anything," Diego snapped at him. "Push."

"Truman, we're not going to do this all on our own," Hannah agreed.

"I'm . . . I'm hurt," he said. "I hurt in my legs right now."

The van lurched from the sand's grasp, and the group of seven guided her up the flatbed ramp.

"You did it, girl." B-Mac patted the Dharma-blue siding. "You did it."

Alanna wiped off her hands and scrunched her nose. Such a fine specimen, she was not used to these menial tasks. And neither was Truman. They belonged together. He'd tried to make that clear by stepping back from the grunt work at the back of the van.

He had to give it to Hannah, though, who'd spared them all some grief by talking to that cop. Truman folded his arms and faced her now. "I had no idea you had that in you. I knew you were an actor, but that was amazing. Seriously, I . . ."

The police officer was approaching on his way back to the cruiser.

"Hey, thanks," Truman said to him. "For letting us off the hook."

"Don't talk to me."

"I . . ." Truman stepped out of the man's way. "Good. All right then."

"Smooth," Hannah said.

"Speaking of smooth, you need to go pro when we get back. I've tried improv, and I'm okay, but *you?* What a story, and it was so elaborate. Yes, I know you were acting and all, but I completely bought it as the truth."

Hannah stared at him. Jason came alongside her and stared as well.

What? Truman took a step back. Had he laid on the compliments too thick? While the plan to wow Alanna was not proceeding as hoped, here Hannah and Jason stood together. Maybe this was the better part of his plan, getting them interested in each other.

"The truth?" Jason patted Truman on the shoulder. "Yeah, well, uh, what Hannah said *was* the truth."

"You mean . . ."

"It's okay, Truman." Hannah patted him too, then walked off with Jason.

"So you're saying you are adopted?"

"Yeah."

"You don't look adopted."

Jason shook his head. "Go figure."

Truman realized his mistake. Just because *he* was adopted, just because he had orange hair that made him stand out at all his family gatherings, didn't mean all adoptees looked so distinct. He was a Bengal tiger dropped into a household of grizzly bears. He knew some of what Hannah must be feeling, though, in this search for her biological roots.

The flatbed had delivered the VW to solid pavement by the main road. Everyone was climbing in. Truman jogged that direction, glad to see Jason seated between Hannah and Alanna. The plan was coming together. If Alanna's scowl was an indication, she would soon be Truman's for the taking.

Later, he would come clean to Hannah about his own adoption story. He, too, had gone in search of his birth mother. With mixed results.

Wilmington, North Carolina

Grace Lawson couldn't get her mind off Hannah. She sat on the couch and peered through reading glasses at memorabilia from her daughter's childhood. Old school projects. Cards written in crayon. Report cards and certificates of achievement. Grace and Jacob had never let their girl travel so far away, and Grace worried they would never see her again.

Oh, sure, Grace had the usual concerns about auto accidents and medical emergencies, but there was something even more troublesome this time.

What if Hannah found her birth mother?

What if that bond was so strong that it undid everything?

Grace pressed her lips to Hannah's third-grade school portrait and blinked back tears. She loved this little girl with everything in her. *She* was her real mother, in all the ways that counted.

And yet, she couldn't stand in the way, could she? To do so would be to deny her daughter that deep need to understand her origins and purpose. Yes, letting go of her was a necessary step, but it felt as though Grace's heart was being torn from her chest.

Tears streaked down her face, and she wiped them away.

Oh, bother. Would you hold it together, Grace Lawson?

She heard her husband's Acura pull into the driveway. Late, as was often the case. They had the house to themselves, she'd prepared for a romantic evening together, but that mood was now gone and his dinner was stored in the fridge.

"Hello," he said, entering from the garage. "I'm home."

"You're in scrubs. You got your wish."

"Yeah." He dropped onto the couch cushions beside her, tipped his head back, and closed his eyes. "You talk to Hannah today?"

"I tried her cell a number of times."

"Maybe she left it behind. Or lost it again."

"That's five in the last year. She loses them faster than we can replace them."

"Right there." He tapped the school portrait still in Grace's grasp. "You know, that's how she'll always be in my mind. I don't think I want her to grow up."

"Well, we can't stop that from happening, I'm afraid."

"I should've never given her that choice last night, Grace. I should've put my foot down. I thought she was smarter than that, and now she's off in some other state in an old beater of a van. Mardi Gras? She'll see things I never wanted her to see."

"She's not interested in Mardi Gras, honey."

He turned on the couch, pushed his hair back from his eyes.

"She wants to find her birth mother," Grace said. "Don't you see that?"

"They're driving through Mobile. Of course."

She nodded and removed her glasses, unable to say another word.

"Oh, sweetheart." Jacob pulled her close, holding her to his broad chest. He cupped her face in his hand, kissed her forehead. "She'll always be our girl. I'll never forget the first time the doctor put her in my arms, and my wondering how some-thing so tiny, so small, could possibly have that much power over me. We've been there since day one, and this is *our* family. *Our* memories. No one can take that from us."

"I sure hope not."

"And no matter what anyone thinks," Jacob added, "I did see him smile."

She nodded. "When Hannah gets back, I think we should tell her."

"Tell her what?"

"Everything."

"No." He stood. "She can't handle it. Trust me."

"I think she can. I think we need to trust our daughter."

"The daughter who can't be trusted with a basic cell phone? That one?"

"And," Grace said, "we need to trust God."

"Right." He managed a thin smile. "I'm going to go and get us a snack."

Grace watched him through the doorway as he pulled items from the kitchen cupboard, rejected each one, then threw his hands up and headed for the stairs. So much for the late snack. He liked things to fit within his plans, always manageable and under control.

And she knew why. She understood, she really did.

Though Jacob rarely brought it up, she knew he still carried a deep wound.

Fort Walton Beach, Florida

Even if a bit behind schedule, they were on the road again. Hannah brushed her hair back from her face. She felt the stickiness of ocean humidity on her neck and face. She licked her lips. They tasted salty. She couldn't wait to get to their lodgings for the night and take a shower before bed.

Pensacola wasn't far away now. They would spend the night there and drive the last few hours to New Orleans in the morning.

Where was her birth mother right now?

Was she in any of these seaside towns they were passing through?

A Chris Sligh song played over the radio, and it started raining. Motel lights flashed by. The others nodded off while the van carried them along the wet roadways, but B-Mac remained alert at the helm.

"Hey, Hannah."

She looked up and caught the driver's eye in the rearview mirror. "Yeah?"

"Listen, I think that . . . I just wanted to tell you that I think it's really brave what you're doing. The whole thing with your mom. And I just hope that you find, you know, whatever it is you're looking for."

"Like that old U2 song," she said.

"Yeah. Okay, I know they're, like, old and everything, and these days I'm more into the Black Keys, but I do consider myself a fan."

"You too?"

He missed her attempt at humor, and she had said it only to alleviate the heaviness of their subject. "It's important," he said. "Don't let anything, or anyone, stop you from doing what you got to do."

She pressed her lips into a faint smile. Beside her, Jason opened his eyes and looked at her. Alanna dozed on his shoulder, and Hannah fixed her gaze straight ahead again.

"So," B-Mac asked her, "I really shouldn't eat burgers, man?"

"If you only knew."

"I guess it's just so hard for me to think of eating healthy food. I mean, it just weirds me *out*. So what should I eat? Fish burgers? And like tofu. What is that stuff? Who came up with the idea to take a bean and turn it into a sandwich that tastes like a hamburger? Remotely. I mean, vegans try to tell you that tofu tastes like real beef. That is untrue."

Hannah chuckled. "Don't let Danielle hear you."

"And a salad? I mean, me eating a salad. Are you kidding me? Dude, maybe if I could get like twenty buffalo wild wings on top of it."

"They're not made from buffalo, you know?"

"Ignorance is bliss." He whipped up a hairy pale hand. "Not another word."

Chapter Twenty-Eight

The Prescription

Pensacola, Florida

Truman should have suspected something was wrong the day he booked the rooms online. Pensacola was a beautiful place, so there was really no excuse. It was all on him.

Dark and foreboding against the distant city lights, the motel rose from the sand and gravel in one solid block. Not an ounce of style. No sign of a pool. Peeling paint and rotted railings. This was beachfront property? Yes, if you counted a half-mile barrier of dunes and grass as part of that beach. A sign with green neon letters said:

Windy Shores Motor Resort
~~No~~ Vacancy

"Is there ever a time they're actually full?" Diego said. "I doubt it."

"It's a quarter past midnight. I suggest we stick with the plan."

"The plan, Truman?" B-Mac leaned forward for a good look at the sagging outdoor walkway that skirted the second floor. "This is literally the worst hotel I've ever seen."

"It's a motor resort."

"What's that mean? Is there even such a thing?"

The others stirred in their seats, coming alive with disappointed groans.

"I will admit," Truman said, "that it did look better on the Internet."

"It couldn't have looked much worse," Alanna commented from the back.

"Where'd you search?" B-Mac asked. "At Norman-Bates-Hotel dot com?"

Truman figured he may as well fess up. "Uh, Hotel-Monkey dot biz."

"Dude, I'm sleeping in the van. She might need my protection."

Truman trotted to the office before the entire crew turned against him. A potbellied man in a stretched white shirt signed him in and delivered instructions. Truman returned to the van, swinging the room keys and hoping things looked better inside the place.

"They had our reservations. We are official. A side note regarding the showers."

"There'd better be showers," Alanna said.

"There are, milady. Even complimentary bars of soap. He was quite clear about that, even proud of the fact. Thing to remember is that you turn both knobs all the way to the left and give it a good two or three minutes."

"For the water to heat up, you mean?"

"Uh, no. Two or three before the hot water runs out."

"You *can't* be serious."

Gathered at the back of the van, each person fetched their belongings and Truman divvied out room assignments. He spoke in a loud voice, so as to avoid confusion, but nobody seemed thrilled with him this late, after this many miles.

"Diego," he said, "you'll be bunking with Jason."

"This place is a dump."

"Don't insult the man with the keys. I'd like to see you find a room for $14.99 a night. Has your lacrosse coach even told you about this thing called the Internet?"

"It's soccer, actually."

Knowing Diego's aspirations, Truman had made the mistake intentionally to annoy him. "Well," he said with a shrug, "you all look the same to me."

Diego was more than annoyed. "That's really racist."

"What?" This time the mistake was unintentional. "No, I meant athletes in general."

Shoving past him, Diego grabbed the key from his hand.

"Moving on," Truman said. "Hannah, you'll be rooming with Alanna."

Hannah's shoulders slumped while Alanna pulled hers back and shot an annoyed look over the mound of luggage and supplies. She asked if there wasn't another option, and Truman insisted there wasn't since Danielle had paid double for a room of her own.

B-Mac tried to get comfortable in the driver's seat. "She can have my room."

"No," Truman said. "That won't work because you were staying with me. And, uh, neither Hannah nor Alanna would want to share my room." Then, realizing the opportunity before him, he fixed Alanna in his catlike gaze. "Would you?"

She snatched her key from his hand. "Get away from me, Truman."

"I wore pink all month for you."

"Don't even start. Are you a quarterback at Duke? No, didn't think so."

"You do make a valid point." He grabbed his stuff and slammed the hatch.

"We're trying to sleep here," B-Mac shouted. "Respect, Evelyn."

Hannah propped herself against pillows. Her weight rattled the headboard, and the light flickered on the nightstand between the two single beds. She laid out four bottles of prescription medicine beside her journal and a glass of water.

"That's a lot of pills," Alanna said from the other bed.

"Yeah. I know it's ridiculous, isn't it?"

"What're they all for?"

"Well." Hannah pointed. "There're cortico-steroids for my asthma. This is an antiepileptic. And this one's for arthritis."

Alanna sneered. "Arthritis? You look fine to me."

"I don't feel fine. I was born with hip issues and low bone density. They, uh, the doctors say that arthritis is one of the side effects. Oh, goody. More pills for me."

"And what's that other one for?"

"It's, uh . . ." Hannah sucked on her lower lip. "It's new. It's for anxiety."

She waited for a reaction. She had no specific reason to like or dislike Alanna, yet they seemed to be rivals. Was it because of Jason? Was Alanna jealous of their long-standing friendship? If so, that was comical. Sure, Jason and Hannah shared a lot of memories and all, but that didn't mean there would ever be anything between them. Crazy to even think such a thing. He was brotherly, protective, and teasing. Nothing more.

"Well, look at you," Alanna said, her sharp tone turning Hannah's head. "Perfect. Just perfect, Hannah."

"What?"

Alanna glared at her. "You know what I think? I think you like to use this stuff so that people have to be nice to you. You know? Poor little Hannah. So wounded. So needy. Well, you're not the only one with problems."

"I'm sorry. I didn't mean to—"

"You never *mean* to do anything. That's the point, though. You still do."

"What've I done to you?"

"Ask yourself this," Alanna said. "Why'd you really come on this trip?"

"New Orleans. Café Du Monde. Just, you know, the whole thing."

"And to find this supposed birth mother of yours?"

Hannah recoiled from that. "She's not some figment of my imagination."

"Let's hope you find her, then. That'll make things just that much more perfect, and you won't have to wedge your way in anymore."

"You know," Hannah said, "Jason invited me on this trip."

Alanna's expression turned smug and full of pity. "He didn't want you to come. He's just too nice to say it." She turned out the light and rolled onto her side.

Stunned, Hannah stared at her back. That stuff about Jason? Could it be true? No, he was the one in the library who hinted at a stopover in Mobile. And his reticence at school yesterday had to have come from his respect for her dad. Ever since Jason's own father left his mother for a female coworker, Jason had leaned upon Jacob Lawson's wisdom and approval.

"Alanna, do you, uh . . ." She tried to steady her

voice. "I, uh, usually get up early, but I can set the alarm if you want. Whatever time you think would be—"

"What is *wrong* with you, Hannah? Just *go* to sleep."

The headboard squeaked as Hannah leaned back. Moonbeams poked through one of the missing slats in the blinds, washing her arms and face in a ghostly glow. She lifted her chin, tried to hold back a sniffle. The last thing she wanted was to let Alanna realize how much the words stung.

Lord, I can't deal with this.

She took her meds. Sipped at the water. Took slow, deep breaths. One one-thousand. Two one-thousand. Three . . . She imagined the whole next week stuck with this girl, not to mention the long drive back. And how was Hannah supposed to find her mom while others objected to any detours or special requests she made?

This time, she came up with her own prescription.

You've got to get out of here. Now.

Hannah slipped from beneath the covers, pulled on sweats, and collected her stuff in her shoulder bag. She snuck out the door without a word to Alanna, who was curled beneath her blankets with eyes closed. Asleep so quick? After throwing such sharp barbs?

Whatever.

Down at the van, Hannah eased open the hatch and searched for her rolling luggage.

"What? Who's . . . ?" B-Mac mumbled. "Agghh!"

He banged his head into the steering wheel as he snapped upright, and she told him it was just her.

He was disoriented. "Don't hurt Evelyn. Take me instead."

"It's all right, B-Mac. She's fine. Go back to sleep."

Hannah dragged her luggage from behind the case of oil, extended the handle, and set it on the ground. She closed the hatch and started toward the main road. It was past one in the morning. She was miles from downtown Mobile. There was no way, though, she was spending the rest of the night at the Windy Shores Motor Resort.

"Hannah? Hannah, what's going on?"

She swung her gaze toward the second-floor walkway. Jason stood there with a bed-head and sleepy eyes, his hands braced on the wooden railing.

"I'm leaving," she said. "Why do you care?"

"Look, it's the middle of the night. Can we talk about this in the—"

"Nope. I don't want to talk about it, Jason. I'm leaving, and you're staying here with your . . . your girlfriend. I realize that my being here is a problem and that I should've never come, so you can just . . . just *go* to New Orleans with Alanna and with your . . . your whole *posse,* and have fun. Have a blast. Whatever. I don't even care anymore."

"You're not making sense. What is wrong?"

She flung out her arms. "Apparently, *I'm* what's wrong."

"Hannah, c'mon."

Before Jason's words could calm Hannah, Alanna arrived on the walkway beside him. If that wasn't a gloating expression on her face, what was it? But the moment Jason turned toward his girlfriend, her sneering lips were replaced with a look of concern.

"Oooh!" Hannah grabbed at her hair and wanted to scream. "Look, I'm leaving. Do not follow me."

Jason stayed at the railing and watched her march off. Behind her, she heard B-Mac stumble out of the van. If he even got near her, she would deck him.

"Dude, not good," he said. "Her dad is gonna kill you, Jason. He's scary."

"She's a big girl," Alanna said. "She can take care of herself."

Hannah yanked the luggage along, her heartbeat racing and her forehead hot. She kicked aside an empty can of Pabst Blue Ribbon and cut toward the highway.

Chapter Twenty-Nine

Isolated

Truman woke to the pounding on his hotel-room door. Yesterday's journey had sapped his strength, and he marveled that sitting for mile upon mile could have such an effect on him. He scratched his head, put on his glasses, and checked the clock.

11:18 a.m. Sunday. How was that possible? He must still be at—what was this place called? —the Windy Shores Motor Resort.

Knock, knock, knockkk . . .

"Cuz, get up. We're starving, man. And if I have to break down this door, I am not going to be the one who pays for it. Right now, my stomach is very unhappy."

Truman shuffled across the threadbare carpet. He opened the door and shaded his eyes against the glare. "Whoa. That is some serious wattage."

"That thing," B-Mac said, "is called the sun. And this is the beach, sort of."

"Where is everyone?"

"We're all waiting down at the van. It's spring break, dude, and we've still got a few hours to New Orleans. Grab your stuff and let's hit it."

Truman hurried to the bathroom mirror, where

he wet his hair, combed it with his fingers, and patted it down. While thirty seconds was only half the time he usually spent, today's results could not be denied. The jungle cat was on the prowl. He sprayed his underarms with deodorant, waved it about his body as a form of cheap cologne, and sauntered with his baggage down the stairs toward the—

Whoops.

Missed a step.

He caught himself, straightened his shirt, and continued to the idling VW van. B-Mac peeled from the lot, and the vehicle's tires spit gravel.

"Didn't know she had it in her," Diego said with a grin.

Riding shotgun again, Truman turned and counted heads. "Stop. Go back. We're missing, uh . . . We are two short. We forgot Hannah and Jason."

"Seriously, you didn't hear the commotion last night?"

"No, B-Mac. I did not hear the commotion. It so happens that I sleep very soundly."

"You were spared. We almost had another visit from the cops, man."

Truman saw an opportunity. He pivoted toward Alanna, rested his chin on his elbow, and cocked a bright orange eyebrow—*use the plumage, work it.* "Is this true?"

She stared into his eyes.

Woooork it.

No doubt fearful of her own growing desire, she tore her gaze away. She pulled her long blonde ponytail over her shoulder. "Hannah was so annoying, the way she went on about how she needs all this medication and no one understands. Well, she got her wish, didn't she? She took off last night, and this morning Jason went after her."

"After Hannah?"

"Yes, Truman. He rented his own car. I say, let the two of them have their own little adventure. They can catch up with us later. Or not. I don't care."

The tiger couldn't believe he had done it.

He had isolated his prey.

There she was. Thank God.

Even from afar, Jason Bradley knew that signature strut of his childhood friend—admittedly, a little curvier now. With her multiple surgeries and daily medication, Hannah had fewer physical problems now than she did as a preteen, but she still had to use common sense when it came to exercise and activity. He could tell by her hunched shoulders that she was tired after the long over-nighter, yet her legs still churned forward. Stubborn as ever.

He approached her from behind in a rented Toyota. The sun beat down on the waters of the Gulf of Mexico, a fireball in the haze over distant oil rigs and cargo ships. Seagulls swooped along the sand dunes, and the grass waved in the ocean breeze. It wasn't a bad place to spend a night outside, but she must have been cold and scared and lonely. Or maybe she was mad enough to stay warm all by herself.

Yep. Probably the case.

Cars passed both ways along the coastal stretch of highway. As one roared by Hannah, she turned her head and wiped her brow.

Did she recognize him through her sunglasses? She couldn't know he was in this rental. She should realize, though, that he wouldn't leave her out here on her own. Not forever. Only long enough to let her mellow out a bit first.

He slowed and pulled alongside her, lowering the passenger window. "Hey."

She turned, scowled, and kept walking.

"Sorry it took so long." He kept pace. "The only rental place that was open was by the airport, and then I had to find you. Which, you know, wasn't on my itinerary."

"That's me. A big inconvenience."

"Not to me. C'mon. Get in."

She rolled her eyes and faced him through the window. It was such a cliché, but she really was pretty when she was mad. "I don't need your charity, Jason."

"Uh, yeah, you do."

"I can do this on my own."

He checked the odometer, pretended to make calculations. "Another fifty miles? Sure. You'll get there in, oh, I dunno, fifteen hours or so. I doubt you'll even think of being hungry or thirsty."

"What? So we leave the rest of the crew and just drive to Mobile together?"

"Beats walking."

"What would Alanna think?"

"Doesn't matter what she thinks. This was my decision, and she knows that." He nodded at the empty seat beside him. "Now get in. I don't have time for this."

"Why do you care?"

"I care about you, all right?"

Hannah removed her sunglasses. She leaned through the window, necklace dangling, hair blowing around her face. Her light brown eyes stared into his, and she gave him a flirty pout. "You know, I'm not the kind of girl who just gets in the car with anybody."

"Right. But you will hitchhike by yourself."

"I wasn't hitchhiking. I was walking."

"Yeah, well, that's equally smart."

She tossed her stuff into the backseat. "I would have been fine."

He cleared his throat, hit the power locks, and followed signs toward the city. She rolled her hand through the air. People were flying kites over the dunes. When he veered to avoid a bicyclist, she kidded him about his poor driving skills and grabbed at the wheel. Laughing, she honked the horn. He slapped her hand away and told her he needed to keep his eyes on the road. What had gotten into her? This dangerous behavior wasn't normal, coming from the Hannah he knew.

"Who is Hannah Lawson?" she said. "That's what I came to find out."

Ahead, a burger joint claimed: PATTY'S BEEF—"Best Beef Patties between Here and Biloxi."

"You hungry?" he asked. He didn't even need to wait for her reply.

Hannah was famished after a night walking the beach highway. Patty's Beef was one of those hole-in-the-wall places with a tourist vibe all its own. The servers wore old-fashioned outfits, spoke in Southern accents, and took pictures with out-of-town customers to be displayed on a stretch of corkboard.

When plastic platters with large charbroiled hamburgers arrived, Hannah thought she would cry. She took a bite. "This is amazing. So, so good."

"You know, it's probably got meat fillers in it, those little pellets that—"

"Ignorance is bliss, Jason."

Her phone rang on the table, and she stiffened at the sight of her dad's number.

"You're gonna have to answer it eventually," Jason said.

She picked it up. "Hey, Dad. Here's Jason."

Jason nearly fumbled the cell that hit him in the chest. He shot her a look, then spoke into the mouthpiece. "Dr. Lawson, how are you?" He tried to ignore Hannah, who acted as though she were hiding under the table. "We're fine. Things're going great . . . Yep, definitely . . . Uh-huh . . . I'd say, if anything, Hannah's been a good influence on all of us. Here, she's begging to talk to you."

Hannah punched his arm before accepting the phone. "Hi again."

Across the table, Jason mouthed that he was going to go outside to call Alanna.

"Baby, we've missed you," her dad said. "I know it's only been one night, but we care about ya. I know you're having fun, so I don't wanna take up too much of your time. Just be sure to take your pills and stay away from stressful situations, okay?"

"Dad, I have to go. I'll be back soon, don't worry. Tell Mom hi."

She ended the call. Through the glass, she saw Jason frown and end his as well.

Chapter Thirty

Awkward

Gulf Shores, Alabama

Back on the road, Hannah fed Jason directions from the dashboard GPS. They were looking for Mobile General Hospital, and she realized that it wasn't on the downtown grid but shoved instead toward the city's outskirts. Still fifty-two miles away.

Good thing she'd set aside her pride and accepted the ride.

She leaned against the window, chewing on her fingernail. She thought about her parents treating her like a little girl who still needed to be checked up on. And about Jason arguing on the phone with Alanna. Had it involved Hannah at all?

Not that she had any right to pry.

"It's okay, Hannah," Jason said.

She glanced at her nail, pulled up her sleeve, and turned. "What?"

"I saw you spying on me while I was talking to Alanna. You don't have to feel bad."

"Oh, now you're a mind reader?"

He shrugged. "I just know you. Listen, whaddya

say we take the beach roads and keep the trip scenic? I hear Gulf Shores is worth seeing, and they have an old pier by the ocean that's not far from here. That still gives us lotsa time to get to Mobile. It's your call, though. I mean, I know how important all this is."

Hannah returned his shrug. She wanted nothing more than to find her birth mother, but the thought of not finding her was horrifying. What if the trail went cold? What if it was a total dead end? That might undo her completely.

"I can put it off a little bit longer," she said.

"Is that a yes?"

She nodded.

Rather than take the route back to I-10, they drove the coastal highway alongside sports cars and SUVs pulling fishing boats. They followed signs to the pier, where they parked in a sand-sprinkled lot and jogged in jeans and tennis shoes onto the beach. The sun was warm. Birds circled. She stepped onto a large rock and did a balancing act, arms extended and toes pointed. Jason looked away when she caught him watching.

He led the way beneath the pier's towering structure, and they took off their shoes to wriggle their toes in the sand. Hannah sat against a pylon, and Jason sat facing her. While people fished and strolled along the pier overhead, it seemed like a world of solitude down here in its shadows.

"Do you remember the first time we met?"

Hannah asked. "Don't answer that. It was on our field trip to Airlie Gardens. You were in third grade, and I was in second. You'd just moved to Murraysville, the newest heartthrob of all us giggly girls."

"*Us,* huh?"

"Don't go getting a big head. Schoolgirl crushes never last."

"Well, I do remember Airlie Gardens. Have you been there since they put in that new butterfly pavilion? Figured you'd like that. I mean, it looks pretty cool."

"My dad was going to take me, but New Hanover Regional keeps him locked down most of the time. Maybe when I get back."

"One day at a time, right?" Jason scooped sand onto her foot. "That's part of the Serenity Prayer: 'Living one day at a time, enjoying one moment at a time, accepting hardships as the pathway to peace. Taking, as Jesus did, this sinful world as it is, not as I would have it . . .' And it goes on."

"Where'd you learn that?"

"Al-Anon. I go to meetings on Thursday nights, sometimes on the weekends."

"Really? Isn't that for children of alcoholics? A support group or something?"

"Yeah," he said.

"But your dad, he wasn't a big drinker, was he? I mean, I know he took off and—"

"It's Alanna. Her dad is an alcoholic. The

group's helped her come a long way, and she understood a lot of the emotions I was dealing with last year. She was there for me. Don't judge her too quickly, Hannah. She's had her own share of troubles. When she left Massachusetts, she did it because she needed a place to start fresh."

"She doesn't make it easy, you know?"

"I know."

Hannah gazed along the pier's structure, where the beams formed crisscrossing shapes. "What if I don't find my mother?"

"You will. I know you, and you don't give up easily."

"What if I don't? I'm afraid of going to Mobile and coming up empty."

"Taking risks is part of the deal," Jason said. "What, you wanna go home instead?"

"Why can't life just be . . . simpler?"

"The risks make the rewards that much better."

"Look, I know I can be hardheaded. But a risk taker? Not so much."

"I'll be there with you, Hannah." He scooped more sand over her toes. "We go, we dig around, and we see what happens. That's the only way you'll ever know, right?"

She nodded. She closed her eyes for a moment and let the breeze cool her skin.

"You awake over there?" He shook the sand

from his hands, scratched at his arm, and squinted into the sun. "You remember when we were maybe nine, I think?"

"Well, when you were nine, I was eight and a half."

"Thank you," he said, smirking, "for that unnecessary correction. Yes, I was nine. You were eight and a half, and we would go with the Thomson kids to—"

"They were weird."

"Weird. Yes. So, we would go with the weird Thomson kids to the quarry and—"

"Race to the water?"

"Exactly." He waved his hand. "This all just reminded me of that."

Their eyes met and they exchanged a mischievous look. They sat frozen, waiting like two Old West gunslingers for the other to flinch. Hannah moved first, vaulting to her feet and darting toward the surf. Jason hopped up right behind her, and the race was on.

She drew in the ocean air. She heard his laughter as he gained on her. She cut down the slope toward the foam-flecked tide, and he came alongside. His hand brushed hers, and the electricity of their touch tingled along her skin and spiked her pulse. They were twelve all over again in that footrace to Smith Creek Lake. They joined hands and plunged into the waves.

They splashed each other. He picked her up and

dunked her. She spluttered back to the surface. She swung the wet hair from her face, giggling like that schoolgirl with the second-grade crush. Along the pier, spectators pointed and stared.

"See, Jason," Hannah said. "I can be a risk taker."

"We all start somewhere, I guess."

In soaked clothes, they collapsed onto the sand. They rolled onto their backs and basked side by side in the springtime sun.

The hotel's automatic glass doors slid open. Hannah and Jason strolled barefoot through the lobby. Water pooled behind them on the floor. Clumps of sand fell from their jeans. Chuckling, they stepped up to the long marble counter, where the desk clerk waited and eyed the tennis shoes Hannah held in her hand.

"Good evening?" he said. More a question than greeting.

"Hi." She offered her best smile.

None of this was planned. When Hannah had marched off with her luggage last night in Pensacola, she didn't know Jason would leave all else and come after her. Or that he would insist on joining this quest of hers. And she certainly didn't know they would talk and roughhouse on the beach until the sun slipped and the horizon turned a deep copper. Tomorrow they would head into Mobile, but tonight it was best if they nailed down a place to stay before all the area's rooms were filled.

A solid plan.

Except this was their third hotel in the past forty-five minutes, and so far there was nothing available that fit their budget.

"How may I help you?" the clerk inquired.

Beside Hannah, Jason was a mess, his hair curly and wet, his gray T-shirt damp and clinging to his chest. He shoved his hands into his pockets. "Do you have any rooms?"

"We do, sir."

"Whew. That's good news. We were about to sleep in the car."

The clerk was a large black man with a double chin. He studied them through small eyes, as though deciding whether they were desperate spring-breakers ready to empty their parents' bank accounts, or just some lowlifes out to cause trouble.

"Here." Hannah dug soggy bills from her pocket. "I have $90 and change, or something like that." She laughed and added her cell phone to the wet pile. "I also have this phone that doesn't work because, uh, the ocean broke it."

"Oh?" Jason said to her. "The *ocean* broke it?"

"Yeah."

The clerk stared at the objects on his marble counter. "The cheapest we have is $110, unless you are Triple-A."

"Yeah, uh, we are." Hannah nodded. "We have them all, all three A's."

"All three," Jason said. "And we'll need separate rooms, by the way."

"That's right," she agreed. "Because we're not together . . . like that."

Jason shook his head. "No."

"Well, with Triple-A it's going to be $99. Only one room available at that rate, so you'll have to share. The other room I have is, uh . . ." The clerk sported a wide grin and slipped Hannah a wink. "The luxury suite. Only $299."

"Sounds great." Jason held up a hand. "But, uh, we just need the regular room."

"The very regular room," she said.

The clerk's face dropped, along with his chins.

"Standard," Jason reiterated. "You know, maybe next time, though."

As the clerk turned to grab keys and paperwork, Hannah looked to Jason, who lifted both shoulders and mouthed that he was sorry and it was going to be okay. Okay? The two of them in one room? Well, they would have to deal with it.

"Do you have a towel?" Hannah said to the clerk's back.

"Two," Jason said. "Two would be great."

The clerk came back with guest towels, programmed key cards, and a form to fill out since they were paying in cash. If they did damage to the room, the hotel would need to be able to track them down. And were their driver's licenses current? In other words, were they carrying false IDs? Again, the spring-break crowd.

"Enjoy your stay with us," he ended.

They thanked him and waddled in their salt-stiffened attire to the elevators. They were still chuckling when they nudged through the hotel-room door into a lamp-lit room. Hannah had figured there would be two beds, similar to the layout at last night's lodgings.

There was one. King-sized.

With mounds of pillows.

"Uh, this is awkward."

"Very awkward," Jason said. "Definitely only one bed in here."

"We go from the motor resort to a last resort."

"You think you're funny, dontcha?"

"So." She edged farther into the room. "What're we gonna do?"

Chapter Thirty-One

In the Dark

Hannah was stretched beneath the covers in the glow of the nightstand lamp. The hotel curtains were parted far enough to allow in some starlight. She heard Jason come back through the room door. She zipped her sweatshirt a little tighter and sat up.

"I did our laundry." He dropped folded clothes onto the corner of the mattress. "So. You are welcome."

"Thanks."

He uttered a weary groan and lowered himself to his blankets on the floor at the foot of the bed. He stretched out, fully dressed, arms crossed beneath his head.

She lay back and rolled onto her side. She tossed, adjusted her pillows. She pulled the covers to her neck. "Are you asleep?"

"Uh, I literally just laid down."

"Yeah, okay. Sorry."

She squeezed her eyes shut and felt like kicking herself. She wasn't sure how to act in this situation. She had never been stuck with a guy overnight, and the truth was that this day together had stirred some old feelings she tried to ignore. Since that day on the dock at twelve years old, she had put aside any romantic notions. Otherwise, she was only setting herself up to get hurt, right?

"Are you, uh . . ." She chewed on her lip. "You okay down there?"

"Well, you know, I usually prefer the king-sized floor. But this is all they had."

"That's funny. You're funny." She stared at the ceiling. "Do you think I'm being weird about all this? I'm not trying to be. It's just, you know, if my dad knew where I was right now, he would not be happy."

"Why are we whispering?"

She grinned. "Guess I don't want him to hear."

"We both have our clothes on, Hannah, and I'm stretched out on this scratchy carpet like a two-by-four. Are we doing something wrong here?"

"I don't want to give the appearance of evil. My parents're always telling me to avoid that. And you remember at Oasis how our youth pastor said to keep out of compromising situations? Not that this is compromising. I mean, you have a girlfriend and everything, and it's not that way between us."

"So what's the problem? Can we get some sleep?"

She flung her hands back on the pillow. "I don't know. I mean, you're like the popular college guy. Girls, they . . ."

"Uh-huh?"

"They find you attractive. And enjoy your company."

"Girls?"

"In general, yeah." She had enough risks to take on this trip without also presenting her feelings to be trampled. "Would you think it was weird if I said that I've . . . never *been* with anybody before?" She cringed. She couldn't believe these words had spilled off her tongue. "Physically speaking."

Stop, Hannah. You're only digging the hole deeper.

Jason didn't say a word. Probably thought she was an idiot.

She slapped her hand over her eyes. "Of course," she blurted, "that was purely a hypothetical statement."

"Uhhh . . ."

"Sorry." She giggled. "I, uh, didn't mean to get into all that."

When he remained silent, she reached over and turned off the light. What was he thinking down there? She'd just disclosed one of her secrets, not one you exactly bragged about at college, and she hoped for some response from him. Something. Anything.

"Good night," she said at last.

"Good night."

She heard him shift on his bedding. She

imagined him smirking at her. She pressed her lips together as her mind raced and her heart thumped.

Enough. This is ridiculous.

She bolted upright. "I can feel you down there judging me, Jason."

"What?"

"Like you think this is totally ridiculous. Like I'm some sort of Christian homeschooling freak."

"Nobody thinks that, Hannah. You get straight A's. Plus, I'm a Chri—"

"Don't deny it. You know you thought it."

"You wanna know what I think? I think you scored higher SATs than most of the—"

"Here's the thing." She flopped down on the bed, then bounced back up again. "What's so wrong with not having a wild side? I mean, I'm glad I haven't done all these things with other . . ." She picked at her nails. "And I do have a wild side. Have you seen me play Scrabble? You ever seen the words I come up with? That's just for starters. I also go up on the roof at my dad's work, yeah, way up top, and sit there and write in my journal. The roof's off-limits, you know? No trespassing. But does that stop me? Ha. No, because I'm *wild*. And who defines what wild is anyway?"

Hannah heard Jason shift again. Was he uncomfortable down there? She wanted to turn on the light and ask what was going through his mind, but it was best to keep this conversation in the dark. She had already said far more than she ever planned, and she didn't need him seeing her flushed cheeks.

Why wasn't he saying anything? Why wouldn't guys just express their feelings?

Fine. I'll make this easy for him.

"What're you thinking?" she whispered.

"I'm, uh . . . I dunno . . . I think . . ."

"You know what?" She threw aside her covers, whipped her legs from beneath the sheets. "I can't do this." She balled a blanket in her arms. "This is just . . . it's wrong. It's all wrong, no matter what the circumstances are. And I can't . . ."

She trudged past him on the floor, dragging her pillow and blanket. He moved aside, and his knee caught her ankle. She almost tripped. She righted herself and moved past him.

"Hannah? What is . . . where are you *going?*"

She shot him a look. "Stop judging me!"

As she swiveled back toward the door, her elbow knocked a lamp from the end table onto the floor. She tilted her head back and growled —at herself, at Jason, at this stupid lamp that should have never been put so close to the area where people walked. She yanked the door open and stormed down the hall toward the elevators.

Jason stared wide-eyed at the shadows created by the moon and the stars. He heard the door click shut and the faint *ding* of the elevator seconds later.

"Wow," he said. What had just happened?

With Alanna, he rarely ran into such a hailstorm of emotions. While prim and proper, she spoke directly. No confusion. She said what was on her mind, even if the words were laced with sarcasm to protect the person underneath. He cared about her. He did.

But Hannah? She *was* a wild child, in her own way.

Talk about passion.

Confused as much by his own feelings as by her actions, Jason headed downstairs to find his friend before she marched off into the night again. He hoped she knew better than that by now. To his relief, he found her in the lobby by the breakfast bar. She was situating her bedding on the plush sofa, and she froze at the sight of him.

"Go. Away."

He dropped onto the cushions beside her and sighed.

"Helloooo?" She waved her hands. "Go."

"You're not a freak, Hannah." He gave her a playful nudge. "And if you wanna know, I've never been with anyone either."

"Not even Alanna? I just thought—"

"I'm not saying it's been an easy decision. I am a guy. It's the right one, though. For both of us."

Hannah dipped her chin. She felt warm against his arm. "I didn't know."

He stretched out and pulled a cushion to his chest. She curled up on the other half of the sofa, wrapped in the hotel blanket. She looked beautiful. He closed his eyes. "Good night," he said.

But she was already asleep.

When he opened his eyes, Jason found Hannah cuddled against his chest. It was Monday morning, and they were center stage in a lobby full of hotel guests. Some served themselves breakfast at the neighboring breakfast bar, while others checked out at the front counter. Standing over Jason and Hannah, their clerk from last night wore a look of disapproval.

"Was there a problem with the room?" he said.

"No, uh . . ." Jason cleared his throat. "It was fine."

"Because there's no refund, no matter where you . . . sleep."

Hannah laughed when the man snatched the room pillow from under her arm. Jason shrugged and suggested they get out of here. Time to go back to their quest.

Chapter Thirty-Two

A Little Push

Mobile, Alabama

Monday, midmorning, and already the spring-break revelers were drawing complaints from hotels, residents, and seaside bars.

None of this surprised Sergeant Dodd. He had once been a college kid, despite what some of the younger officers believed. One particular drinking binge taught him some harsh lessons. He spent all night bowing to the toilet in a dumpy motel, and all next day trying to find his stolen wallet with his ID and credit cards.

No, he wasn't here to judge. He was here to serve and protect.

And protecting others from themselves was often a component of his job.

Hannah's hopes sunk as the Toyota rolled to a stop at Mobile General Hospital. This was her birthplace. She expected to find some answers here. Instead, she saw plywood leaned against the wall of the old entryway. The grass was patchy and yellow. Newspapers and trash blew across the lot of the abandoned property.

"Maybe we got the wrong address," Jason said from the driver's seat.

She stepped out of the car, leaned on the door, and considered her options. She was hundreds of miles from home. She wouldn't give up now.

"Could be someone inside," she said. "A janitor or security guard."

In torn jeans, her zippered hoodie, and black tennis shoes, she headed for the sliding front doors. Jason followed in his loose denim shirt over jeans. They reached the glass together, and she imagined the doors opening. As though she'd been expected.

No such luck.

A notice on the glass warned against trespassers, and another provided information about the overseeing property-management company. Hannah cupped her eyes and peered inside. She felt a tug. She had to get in there. She paced the perimeter, testing windows and doors, despite Jason's objections.

"Hannah, didn't you see the Security Alert sign at the front?"

"You really think anyone's paying to guard this old place? I doubt it."

She checked another door. When it relented a half inch, she leaned into and it screeched against the frame. She gave it a kick. Her second kick catapulted it into the wall with a *clanggg*.

"See?" she said. "Where there's a will, there's a way."

"This is a waste of time, and you're gonna get us in trouble. C'mon."

"Stay behind if you want. Stand guard or something. I'm going in."

She entered a tiled hallway, where skylights provided pale light. A wheeled laundry bin was stuffed with plastic bags and junk. A roach scurried from the daylight.

"I can't believe you just broke in here," Jason said, at her back.

"I didn't break in. The door was open."

"Not exactly. You pried it open."

"I just gave it a little . . . push."

"Well," he said, "don't ever push me like that, please."

"Pretty good kick for a girl, huh?"

"Diego would be proud. Danielle would be jealous."

Hannah worked her way through the maze of corridors. "You coming with me? Don't be such a baby."

"What could we possibly find here?"

She reached an old nurses' station. She located the switch, and the lights came on. "I used to wander around the old OR at my dad's hospital. Cool thing is, even though they upgraded the place, they still keep all the files and stuff there."

"You think you're going to find records from two decades ago? C'mon."

"I don't know. There just has to be a . . . a reason for all of this."

"Well, there's a reason that light worked. There's still electricity coming to this building, which means the alarm system's probably working. Can you just stop and think about what you're doing here, instead of playing the destiny card?"

"Don't say it like that. No, Jason. This is my life here, all right?"

"Hannah, I'm just—"

"If you want to leave, fine. Just leave."

She traced her fingers along a floor plan taped to the desk. She tapped it once, then turned and left him at the counter. Along the hallway, children's artwork still clung to the walls, reminders of all the young lives that came through here in times past.

Ahead, she saw what she was looking for.

The Records room.

Shelves of files and folders filled the small area. Boxes were stacked haphazardly, and an old photocopier cowered in the corner. Hannah didn't even know where to start, except to find information from 1991. She wished she had names to work with. Her adoptive parents' names on the birth certificate were court approved, as part of the adoption process, but those names would have been added after her actual delivery date.

She brushed dust from the first box, coughed, and thumbed through its contents.

Jason entered the room. "Where's your inhaler?" He sat across from her.

"I don't know."

"Look, I'm responsible if something happens to you."

"Don't, Jason. Please. Don't be like everyone else, telling me what I can and can't do, and how I'm so weak and incapable of doing the things I want to do. I don't need that, especially not from you."

"But I promised your dad I would look out for you."

She set aside a box marked *Sept. 1998*. She needed to go further back.

"We're done, Hannah. You're not even listening. We can't do this."

"I'm not leaving without something. I didn't come all this way just to—"

The door slammed open, startling her, and a police officer burst into the room. His firearm was aimed at them, resting over the wrist of his other arm that shone a wide flashlight beam. "Hands where I can see them," he barked. "Now!"

Hannah lifted her arms and glared at Jason. "Don't tell me. You called the cops?"

"Yeah, right, Hannah. I called the cops. More

like, you wouldn't listen when I tried to warn you, okay? Thanks a lot."

The officer shifted his bright beam between both of them. Once convinced that they were harmless, he lowered his weapon. His name tag identified him as *Sgt. Dodd*. He was a lean, middle-aged guy with a receding hairline. He looked relieved that he hadn't encountered armed thieves or a band of mentally unstable squatters.

"All right." He started with Hannah. "Tell me what's going on here."

Chapter Thirty-Three

Not Over Yet

Getting a police mug shot wasn't Jason's idea of a good time.

He went first. He stood before the white background and held up the placard with his name and number. Smile for the Mobile Police Department. The camera clicked a number of times while he offered poses of contrition, frustration, and shame. He hung his head. The trip was not supposed to unfold this way.

Hannah went next. He knew she was upset by

all this, mostly because her search had been cut short. She put her acting chops to work. She tried the poor-me look, the waah-let-me-out-of-here look, and the we-didn't-mean-to-cause-any-trouble look.

The entire process felt staged. Like something from a TV set.

Mug shots . . .

Really?

And the one phone call . . .

So it actually worked like that, huh?

A bald-headed guard led Jason to an old-school wall-mounted telephone in a hall with concrete walls. Jason hoped to bail himself out of this situation and keep his mom from worrying or ever knowing of it. He dialed Alanna.

"Babe," she said. "Where are you?"

"Hey. Yeah, I'm . . . How're you? You guys get there yet?"

"We just checked into our hotel outside New Orleans. You didn't answer my question, Jason. This number came up as Mobile City Government."

"Listen," he said. "Don't freak out, okay? Something happened, Alanna, and the long and short of it is that Hannah and I are in jail."

"Jail? Did I hear you correctly? You *better* have a good explanation."

"Well, it's not like we planned it. I . . . look, you're two hours away, and I'm just asking for a little help. Please."

"You *are* joking. No, you got yourself into this. Get yourself out."

Clickkk.

"Alanna?"

The phone was dead.

Jason hung up. Through the slat in the metal door behind the guard, he saw men marched past in handcuffs and orange prison garb. He really didn't want to go in there. He was a good guy. This was not him.

To his relief, the guard walked him past desks and ringing phones, toward a corner office with cinderblock walls and tan window blinds. He saw Hannah's long dark hair and her sad, round eyes, and he wanted to strangle her for getting them into this mess and ignoring his warnings. Almost as much as he wanted to pull her close and hug her to his chest, and assure her they would try some other way to track down her birth mother.

Hannah sat in the dimly lit office. On the desk, a placard identified Sergeant Dodd. The clock on the wall said it was 2:05 p.m. Handcuffs hung in a row along the wall, the way coats hang from a rack. Was that supposed to intimidate her? At this point, she didn't care. This entire trip was a waste. Her entire life was an enigma.

She shouldn't be alive. She wasn't wanted.

Why did she even still exist?

Sergeant Dodd came through the door behind

her and swung around to his rolling desk chair. His black uniform boasted a black tie, a polished brass badge, and yellow chevrons on the sleeve. He rested his chin in his hand on the desk and studied her.

She dropped her chin and fiddled with the sleeves of her hoodie.

"B and E. Breaking and entering. Do you understand the consequences?" Dodd's eyes were unblinking, and when she gave no reply, he said, "Look, why were you there?"

The door opened again, and a guard ushered Jason into the room. Her friend folded his arms and leaned against the wall beside her. Though she knew he wasn't thrilled with her, she drew strength from his nearness.

"Okay," she said to the sergeant. "I'll tell you."

She handed him her faded birth certificate and gave him the whole story, what she knew of it, from start to finish. He listened. His eyes were caring and attentive.

"So here I am. I came all this way," she said. "And Mobile General was the one place that gave me any hope of some answers. Well, that was a dead end. A big fat zero. If that makes me a criminal, I'm sorry. I don't know. If you're going to put me in jail, please just get it over with, because . . ." She stopped and looked at Jason.

Sergeant Dodd's gaze moved to the certificate in his hand.

"Because," she continued, "my dad, my adoptive dad, he is going to kill me. And he's going to kill you too, Jason."

Jason sighed and slumped into the chair beside her.

" 'Owens Clinic,' " the sergeant mumbled, reading from the certificate. " 'Mother transferred prior to delivery.' Hmm, that's odd." He turned to his desktop computer, typed in a few words, and hit Enter. He compared something on the screen to the document in his hand, then turned and rummaged through the shelves behind his desk. He came back up with a file in hand. "Hannah, this signature right here, the one that's marked *Informant*, that's usually a family member or maybe a guardian. Do you know whose this one is?"

"Nope. I can't even read it. All that writing looks like chicken scratch."

Sergeant Dodd wasn't listening. He was grinning.

Actually grinning.

Well, it wasn't funny, because this was her life, and her past, and now this man who controlled a part of her future was mocking all that was important to her.

"You know, this, uh . . ." He shook his head. "What're the odds?"

What was the sergeant going on about? The odds of her going to jail? Odds of her dad murdering her and Jason before going to jail himself?

"Twenty years ago," Sergeant Dodd said, "I was a new cop, brand new, and I had dealings with a local abortion clinic. There were some bomb threats, some death threats, and whatnot. I dealt with a doctor and two nurses, and the reason I recall this is because one of the nurses, well . . . she was very kind to me."

Hannah pulled her hair back from her face. "Okay?"

"Here you go." He returned the birth certificate, along with a second document. "That there is one of the nurse's statements. Go ahead. Have a look at it."

Hannah glanced between the two papers, not sure what she was expected to find. She had reached her dead end back at the vacant hospital building, and she had little hope of discovering anything new and vital here in a police station.

"These signatures . . ." She looked closer. "Huh. They're the same."

Sergeant Dodd nodded.

"Why would a nurse from the clinic sign my birth certificate?"

"I have no idea." He took back the document. "Her name is Mary, Mary Rutledge." He beckoned Hannah and Jason to come around to his side of the desk, and he typed more at his keyboard. "All right, see here, her phone number is unlisted. It's just an address, and it hasn't been verified in quite a while." He clicked his pen, wrote the info down on the back of his business card, and handed it to Hannah. "Good luck."

"Wait. What about, you know . . . all the . . . ?"

The officer lowered his voice and cast a glance through the office window slats. "Oh, I wouldn't worry about it." Pivoting in his chair, he leaned toward her. "Look, I'm very sorry for this misunderstanding, all right? I hope you won't think badly of our city and that you'll come back again."

Hannah bit her lip. "So we're free to go?"

"If you want."

She smiled at Jason. She shook her head and tried to hold back tears. She wanted to tell the man thank you but feared she would lose it if she opened her mouth.

"Jackie out there will get your stuff and check you out," the sergeant said.

She stood and moved with Jason toward the door.

"Oh, wait a minute." Sergeant Dodd rose from his chair and placed his hands on his waist. "Tell me, Hannah, what will you say? If you find your mother, what're you going to say to her? I'm just curious."

"I . . . don't know."

"Well, my wife has this thing she says: 'To be

241

human is to be beautifully flawed.' And now she's pregnant with our fourth, which we just found out, so I think I understand a little of what you're going through and how hard it must be. Life isn't always black and white. It gets messy out there. So hate the crime." He nodded. "But not the criminal."

Hannah pondered that.

Jason shook the officer's hand and dipped his head in gratitude.

"It's 2:40 p.m.," Sergeant Dodd said, "and daylight's still burning. Go on, you two. This day's not over yet."

New Orleans, Louisiana

Fat Tuesday. It was the literal translation for "Mardi Gras," the last day before the beginning of Lent—always forty-six days before Easter Sunday. It was also the name of this busy establishment in the French Quarter. Today was only Monday, but the excitement here was palpable as the city of N'awlins, as some called it, got ready for the big day.

Palpable . . . Truman liked that word. It meant you could almost feel it.

Feel it the same way that hands could *palpitate* and revive a weak heart.

"Be still, my beating heart." He drew both

hands to his chest, his eyes fixed on his blonde-headed prey across this table in Fat Tuesday's.

"Excuse me?" Alanna asked over the crowd's hubbub.

He arched one eyebrow. "You heard me."

"No, Truman, I didn't. Forget it, you freak. Just buy me another Coke, would you?"

"You know, I understand why you're so upset. You sure you don't want something a little . . . stronger?"

"No, thanks." She drained the last of her soda.

"Is it an accident that your boyfriend sits behind bars with a woman he's known all his life, while you're in this city of romance with a man you've only now begun to discover?"

"I don't know *what* you are babbling about."

"I," he said, slapping a hand to his chest, "am that man."

"Maybe I do need a drink."

"You'll be sick before the partying even starts," Truman warned her. "Believe me, I don't let alcohol woo me with her siren song. I have ears for one song only."

B-Mac, on cue, strummed his guitar at the neighboring table and sang: "That's the meaning of life. That's the meaning of love . . ."

Alanna's jungle senses were tuned finer than Hannah's. She sensed what was going on here, and she pushed back in her seat before succumbing to Truman's feral charms. "What is Jason even thinking? In jail? The whole thing makes me sick." She lurched from the table and focused on the exit.

"Where're you going? There's no need to rush off," Truman said.

"I've . . . I've got to call the doctor."

Chapter Thirty-Four

Mysterious Ways

Mobile, Alabama

Late afternoon sun drizzled like honey through clusters of oak leaves and warmed Hannah's face. She slumped in the passenger seat as Jason braked outside the brick apartment building. It was a small place, maybe six or eight units, crouched on the city's edge. A pair of men in saggy jeans were leaned against a dusty white van, but they looked up at the arrival of the shiny rental car and swaggered around the back of the apartment.

An old Chevy Celebrity was parked out front. Would Mary Rutledge be home? Would she even want to discuss an event that happened so long ago?

Jason left the engine idling. "You want me to go in with you?"

Hannah's lips parted, and she almost told him to turn the car around. She wanted the truth, but what if the truth wasn't the one wanted? If the encounter went well, she would be fine on her own. If it went badly, she would need time and space to process it.

She shook her head. She could handle this.

"I'll be right here," Jason said. "I'm not going anywhere without you."

Carrying her birth certificate, Hannah moved from the car toward the building. She turned once and saw Jason's concerned expression. She smiled at him as if to say, "I'll be fine. But whisper a quick prayer for me, just in case."

He smiled back.

She slipped into her hoodie and faced the front stairs. Time to do this.

Inside, a long hallway ran the length of the building. Although the place was in need of repairs, it was swept and clean and bore none of the graffiti she had seen a few streets back. This didn't seem like the zip code a nurse would live in. Perhaps she did in-home care for an elderly resident. Seemed like a logical explanation.

The building's main hallway had doors on both sides and a stairway to the second floor. Hannah checked names on the black metal mailboxes set into the wall.

 # 2—Rutledge.

She headed for the second door down the stone-tiled corridor.

Mary Rutledge stood at the kitchen window, scrubbed the dishes in the sink, and thought again of that woman's face. Ms. Porter. Or whatever name it was she went by nowadays. Just changing the name didn't change the person underneath.

It was certainly no accident that the two of them had been there Saturday night.

At that Publix across town.

In the very same aisle.

With her curiosity all astir, Mary had followed the woman out to the parking lot. She stayed back but took note of the license tag. She had a good memory, and the next morning she fed them numbers to her brother DeSean. Caught him on his way to work.

"Why're you doing this?" he asked her. "Mary, what's up?"

"Ain't nothing illegal 'bout checking on a car's owner, is there? You're a lawyer. You can find that sorta thing in no time. I think it belongs to the woman who almost gave birth to her baby in your car, way back when."

"You're kidding me, right?" He chuckled. "That was twenty years ago."

"Nineteen and a half. Just check for me, would ya?"

"I'll check," he said. "And, no, it's not illegal."

It was a plain fact that the good Lord worked in mysterious ways. He'd done stuff in Mary's own life, yessir. Not that she deserved it. She'd done her share of wrong, done things she wasn't proud of. And that's what made it so mysterious that He worked in her anyways, that He didn't let all that foolishness stand in the way of His greatness.

She sang of that greatness as she rinsed a ceramic casserole dish and propped it in the drain board. Her hands were still wet when the knock came at the door. She dried her hands, slipped her feet into her house shoes, and hurried through the living room.

Another knock.

Mary peeked through the hole and spotted a lovely young white girl, brown eyes and long chestnut hair. Seemed too young to be a tenant in this building, and she gazed up and down the hall like she weren't sure if she should be here.

But Mary was sure. Yes, she knew.

Must be some of that woman's intuition of hers.

"Oh, honey," she whispered. "You done come to the right place." She smoothed her skirt and opened the door.

PART THREE

Chrysalis

"Let God transform you into a new person
by changing the way you think.
Then you will know what God wants you to do."
—ROMANS 12:2 (NLT)

Chapter Thirty-Five

A Miscast Actor

After Hannah's second knock, the door opened and revealed an attractive, middle-aged black woman with alert, wide eyes over high cheekbones. She wore a long, flowing skirt and a gray knit sweater over a white blouse.

"Yes? Can I help you?"

Hannah swallowed. "Are you Ms. Rutledge? Mary Rutledge?"

"Yes."

"I hope I'm not disturbing you. I just . . . I don't know how else to, uh . . ." She lifted the wrinkled birth certificate. "Why did you sign this?"

Mary took the document, held it at arm's length to get a better look, and her eyelid twitched. "Please. Come in . . . Hannah."

The apartment's interior was modest but well kept. Plants grew in clay pots, sashes held the drapes back from the blinds, and table lamps lent warmth to the place. An old thirteen-inch TV set crouched on a cloth-draped crate. Hannah was invited to have a seat in the small dining area, where daylight still shone off the glass table near the window.

"Here ya go." Mary set down a helping of iced tea. "Hope it's not too sweet for you, but I make it with agave nectar. S'posed to be better for you than all that sugar."

She took a sip. "It's good."

Her host slipped a paper napkin under her glass and seated herself across the table with her own tea. She placed the birth certificate between them. "So how much do you know?"

"Not much."

"How'd you find me, if you don't mind me asking?"

"Probably sounds weird, but a police officer recognized your signature."

"Hmm. That musta been Sergeant Dodd."

Hannah nodded.

Mary adjusted the fruit arrangement in the bowl on the table. She wiped the condensation from her glass with a napkin. She looked up, slight dimples showing in her cheeks. "She was a pretty girl, Hannah. You do favor her."

"You remember."

" 'Course I do, honey. Somehow I always knew you'd come back."

Hannah tugged on the drawstrings of her hoodie. "Tell me about her."

"She was eighteen. Younger than you are right now, you know? Barely eighteen and the weight of the whole world on her shoulders. She came into the clinic, and I . . . well, I wasn't much older.

But I was *older*." Mary's eyes darkened. "You know, the girls that came there, they really knew what it was they wanted. They was sure of it. But your mother was different. She was . . . conflicted."

That word rattled about in Hannah's head. *Conflicted.* Was that supposed to make her feel better somehow? Was she supposed to find comfort in knowing that her mom was uncertain about ending the pregnancy?

"Hannah." Mary leaned forward and her eyes widened. "I'm the one who took your mother back and . . . and prepped her for the procedure."

"The abortion."

"That's right, honey. The abortion."

The word hung in the air, and the older woman took another sip of tea.

Despite the apartment's serene feel, Hannah's insides were churning.

"She tried to convince me she was making the right decision," Mary said. "But it was herself she was really trying to convince. Told me she didn't even know the fella. Didn't know his name. Met him at a bar, had one night together, and he was gone."

Hannah's chin quivered. So much for ever finding her birth father.

Mary turned sideways in her chair yet kept her eyes on Hannah. "I listened. Listened to her like I done with a hundred girls before her. Nodded. Told her I understood. For some of 'em girls, I was their only friend. Right to the very last minute, your mother told the doctor she wasn't sure she wanted to go through with it. But he told her it was too late. I'd already prepped her, like I said, and there was time and money to be lost otherwise. Like any business, I s'pose. Always the bottom line to think of."

"So she could've still walked out?"

Mary nodded.

"But she didn't," Hannah said.

Mary faced forward. "No, honey. She didn't."

In that case, Hannah realized, she was worse than an unplanned pregnancy. She was an undesired child. She was never meant to be here. Some part of her had hoped that her survival was due to a last-second change of heart on her birth mother's part. That hope was now dashed, and she gulped back a rush of emotion. She felt like a miscast actor on a Broadway stage, with no clue how to respond to this scene and the cast. Skin tingling and lips numb, she sat stiffly in the wooden dining chair.

"Why didn't she?" Hannah breathed. "Did she say why?"

"She wouldn't talk much about it," Mary said. "Seemed there was stuff she weren't telling me or no one else. But your mother, she had her whole life out there to be lived. She was smart. I knew that right off, just looking in her eyes. She said she had a scholarship for college and hopes for a career. 'Course, she couldn't do none of that with no baby."

"With me, you mean?"

Mary looked away. "Halfway through the procedure, something musta gone wrong. I wish I knew what. The doctor, he sent me out for fresh towels and sterilized instruments. Well, when I came back, she was just awakening. Doctor told her it was a 'failed attempt.' Said she might oughta come back the next day."

"I've read about a few cases like that. Was that normal, though?"

"For him."

"You saw it happen more than once?"

The pain in the older woman's eyes was dark and deep. She turned toward the window and took a breath. "There were things that happened there, Hannah. Terrible things. Things they had me do. When you get told something enough times, somehow you start to believe it."

Mary's black eyes widened, focused on something far away, and when she spoke again she did so in a weak voice. "It was tissue, that's what they told us. Tissue that couldn't survive. Nonviable tissue."

Hannah couldn't move. She felt her pulse beating at her temple.

Across the glass table, the older woman faced her bitter memories with wet eyes. Her lips stretched thin, and each wrinkle on her face hinted at burdens she had lived with a long time.

Hannah thought of the sergeant's words: *"Hate the crime. But not the criminal."* And her heart went out to Ms. Rutledge.

"Your mother, she . . ." Mary sat up and faced Hannah. "She came back the next day. Me, I was there in the lobby, and she told me she wanted to finish the procedure. Didn't have no man around. No family to speak of. She said this was the only way. Well, one look at her and I thought to myself, why, this girl's in labor, and she's just too young and naive to know it. I had two choices. I knew I'd lose my job, but there weren't no way I could ignore what stood right in front of my own eyes. I chose to get her to the hospital."

"Mobile General?"

"Closed down now, but that was the nearest place to go at the time. When we got there, she was ready to deliver. She begged me to stay with her. I was really the only one she had, so I did. It was your brother who came first. I'll always remember—"

"My . . . my brother?"

Mary glanced up.

Hannah's face turned warm, and her eyebrows knotted. She could hardly register what she had just heard. "I'm sorry. What're you talking about?"

"Oh, Hannah." Mary's upper lip twitched. "Your mother was carrying twins."

Twins?

No, she had never heard a thing about this. Impossible.

"Your brother came first, and I'll always remember him. He was so teeny. Less than a pound." Mary cupped her hand and stared down at it. "And he was . . . damaged. His arm, it was missing. Completely gone. Torn off in the failed attempt. And he was just . . ."

Hannah pulled the folds of her hoodie tight.

"He was shaking there," Mary said. "I saw the pain, and I . . . I didn't see no tissue. I just saw the face of a child."

A tear burned down Hannah's cheek. She shook her head.

My brother? My twin? All these years I've felt like something was missing, and the whole time I was right?

"But you . . ." Mary lifted her chin, a slight smile playing across her lips. She touched the birth certificate between them on the table. "Hannah, you were the *big* surprise. Nobody knew 'bout you, not even your mother. You came out, and you had these big eyes. Weren't barely two pounds, but there you were. Sure 'nuff. And just . . . *beautiful*."

Hannah didn't move as the woman stood and walked past her. This was all too much to comprehend. She parted her lips and drew in a slow breath, afraid she might crack and fall apart if she said a word. She was a statue. She would survive if she didn't move and didn't try to respond.

Mary shuffled back and set a small object on top of the birth certificate.

A hospital bracelet.

"I never went back to that clinic," she said. "And I never nursed again."

Hannah's eyes were fixed on the bracelet. She lifted it, so thin and yellowed with age. It not only bore the date she was born, but also identified the patient as Alyssa Porter. "Was this mine?"

"Your mother's. She gave it to me when she left the hospital."

Alyssa. That was my mom's name.

"Then," Mary said, "she just up and left. Oh, they looked for her, but she had changed her name, and she was long gone."

She left us. Wanted nothing to do with us.

"My brother. How long before he . . . you know . . . ?"

"Hannah, your parents adopted *both* of you."

"What?"

"I would come by now and again to see the both of you in the NICU. Your mom and dad, they were always there. They'd sit right by your incubators and read to you and your brother outta the Bible. They were praying people, I remember. And he fought *hard,* but your brother never did leave the hospital. He died four months after y'all were born."

Images of Grace and Jacob Lawson spun through Hannah's mind. She had seen pictures of them in their midtwenties, and she thought of them at the nursery window in the hospital now empty on the outskirts of town.

Her adoptive parents. There for her from the very start.

And there for her brother too.

Mom and Dad, I am so sorry. I had no idea. Not a clue.

Mary wiped at her eyes and sipped at her iced tea. This nurse, this abortion clinic nurse, had defied her boss and left her career all for the sake of two infants light enough to carry in a wet paper bag.

Wait a sec. Hannah frowned. Why hadn't her parents told her all of this stuff? Why had they tried to stop her from making this trip and uncovering these secrets from her past? She deserved the truth. She deserved the chance to find and meet her birth mother. They had no right to keep her from that.

Mary leaned over the table, her voice a whisper. "Hannah?"

She looked up.

"I know where your birth mother is. I saw her coupla days ago."

"Here?" Hannah gulped. "In Mobile?"

"That's right, honey."

Hannah's chin quivered.

"I knew it was her," Mary said, "the moment I laid eyes on her, but she weren't in no mood for talking. Me, I had to know. My brother's a defense attorney, real good at what he does, so I called him to help. Well, your mother did get that education and she does have that career. Really made something of herself, yessir. Her name is, uh . . . Cindy Hastings. Works at a law firm here in town. Finally come home after all that running."

Cindy? Alyssa? Whatever her name is, she's close.

"Here ya go." Mary handed over a business card.

With raised, dark green lettering on ivory stock, the card listed the website and phone number for Conwell and Hastings, Attorneys at Law. On the right, it specifically named Cindy Hastings.

"Thank you," Hannah mouthed.

"Oh, honey." Mary squeezed her hand. "Thank you. All these years, the memories I got here in my head . . . I've needed to have my say."

They stood, hands still connected, but Hannah couldn't find the courage to give a hug. She just couldn't. She would break. It was all she could do to breathe.

Instead, she thanked Mary again and made it out into the long, dark corridor. The moment Hannah heard the door shut behind her, her chest heaved. She collapsed against the wall, shredded the business card, and slid to the floor. Holding her head, she sobbed.

Chapter Thirty-Six

The Storm

Jason had never seen Hannah like this. She fed him the basics of the story—her brother, her survival, the roles of her birth mother and her adoptive parents. He didn't know what to say. He held the hospital bracelet and felt a connection to her like never before.

Per Hannah's request, he drove her to the nearest beach. She stared out her window most of the way so he couldn't read her face. When she insisted that she needed some time alone, he nodded and said he would wait here in the car. He watched her wander across the sand and slip from view behind clumps of dune grass that waved in the breeze.

Would she be okay? She was in jeans and her hoodie, but the sun was dipping low, and he didn't want her to get cold once darkness stretched over the Gulf.

He leaned back in the driver's seat and thumped the wheel with both hands.

He adjusted the cord to make sure his phone was charging.

He flipped through radio stations, where the songs sounded trite and cheery.

"God," he prayed. "What do You want me to do?"

Twenty minutes later, Hannah still hadn't returned from the gathering dusk. Jason locked the rental car and went looking for his friend. She meant so much to him. He knew how to get her riled and how to get her to laugh.

Did he know, though, how to comfort her when her heart was breaking?

As helpless as he felt, he couldn't leave her on her own.

"Hannah?"

The waves advanced in rows, their deep emerald faces winking in the final minutes of daylight, then closing their eyes and crashing cool and dark upon the shore.

"Hannah? Where'd you go?"

He spotted her at last, a familiar silhouette against the sunset. She was propped on a rock, elbows on her knees. She held something in her hand.

"Hey." He took a seat beside her in the sand. Her body felt warm beside him, and he smelled the shampoo from the hotel.

She blinked tears from her eyes. "I don't know what to do, Jason."

"You gonna go see her?"

"I don't know." She held her mother's business card. After making him stop at a corner market for a roll of tape, she had taped it back together

262

by working the pieces like a puzzle. "This is the woman who wanted nothing to do with me, remember?"

"Well, we didn't come all this way just to give up."

"What if walking away is actually the best way of facing reality? She didn't want me then. Who says she'll want to see me now?"

"Either way, don't you need to know?"

"Yeah." She nodded. "Yeah, I have to try."

That sounded more like the girl he had grown up with. "What about your parents? Are you gonna call and talk to them about your brother?"

"Ha. The second I do that, my dad would be on a plane to come get me. You know how he is. Maybe he was right, though. Maybe I shouldn't have found out about all this. I mean, deep down . . ." Hannah's voice wavered, and she stared out at the waves. "There's always been this feeling that I shouldn't be here. So now I know. I guess it's my brother who should still be alive."

"Hannah, don't even say that."

"It's true, Jason. Somehow I've . . ." She bit her lip. "Just always felt that way."

He nudged closer on the rock. "Listen, none of what happened is your fault."

She fell into him, and he enfolded her in his arms. She poured out the rest of her emotion from the day, shaking against him, and he rocked her. He told her she better not be going anywhere.

What would he do without his best friend around? He brushed her hair back from her eyes, rested his head against hers, and peered across wind-whipped waters at the setting sun.

"Here's what I'm thinking," he said. "Tonight, we find another hotel and you get some sleep—in the bed this time, not the lobby. Then tomorrow morning, I drive you over to Conwell and Hastings, and you meet your mother face-to-face. Whaddya say, Hannah? Sound like a plan?"

She nodded and snuggled closer.

After this evening's tears, Hannah had used the hotel sampler of exfoliating cream to scrub her face. Her cheeks now tingled and smelled like eucalyptus. She wore no makeup, though she wasn't one for much of that anyway. She sat cross-legged on the bed, in sweats and a tank top. Her hair was pulled up in a loose bun. Her journal was on her lap, as she tried putting into words half of the things she was feeling.

About the woman called Cindy Hastings.

About her adoptive parents.

And Jason, of course.

"Hannah?" A knock at the door alerted her to his return. "Is it safe to enter?"

"Come in."

"Hey." He stepped into the room, sunk his hands into his pockets. "You gonna be okay?"

She nodded.

"Good," he said. "I'm gonna go, uh, sleep in the ice machine. It's just better, you know, if I curl up someplace that's not . . . in here."

She chuckled. *Don't read anything into that.* Weren't guys always complaining they were too warm even while girls were bundling up?

"How're you paying for this?" she said. "I feel bad."

"Don't."

"But I'm the one getting the room and the bed."

"And you're the one who needs it. I saved up a few bucks for the trip, so it's all good. I'm gonna go sit on the balcony and make some calls. Don't worry, Hannah. I'll bill you later." He gave her a playful grin.

She looked away as he headed for the door. Was she blushing? Could her childhood friend have that effect on her? She reflected on their earlier moments along the beach, on how comfortable and safe she felt in his embrace.

"Hey, Jason?"

He turned toward her.

Staring straight ahead, she said, "You want to know the last thing I remember before I blacked out on opening night? The last thing that went through my mind?"

He braced himself against the wall.

"Falling," she said. "Falling into perfect blue water, and holding your hand." She turned toward him. "Why have you always been there for me?"

Silent, he held her gaze, and everything in Hannah told her to break it off. Forget this moment ever happened and quit with the schoolgirl dreams. Did she really think Jason would ever see her that way? Why would he, when he had the coveted girlfriend?

"You can go," she said. "It's late, and I know you need to call Alanna and stuff."

"Hannah—"

"Seriously, it's fine. I understand."

"Hannah, look. Do you see where I'm standing?" He nodded toward his feet. "I'm here for you, because that's what friends do."

"None of my other friends do."

"What does that tell you?" He pressed his lips together, shrugged, and pivoted back toward the door.

She called good night, and then the door closed behind him, leaving her with her thoughts and her journal. She closed the thing. Not another word. If she wrote down these feelings, she might ruin whatever had just passed between them.

In her dream, the storm hovered over the Gulf, swirling, growing, drawing energy from the sea. It tore at oil rigs, wobbled ships like bath toys, and shot saltwater droplets through the air. Even on the shore, she felt those drops sting her skin. She needed shelter. She ran for the pier and pushed herself far underneath, cocooned between its round, stout pylons.

With her head tucked into her arms, she prayed. *Breathe in, breathe out. Slowly. Stay calm.* And all the while, the wind roared.

Chapter Thirty-Seven

A Puzzle Piece

New Orleans, Louisiana

Truman awoke to laughter and voices on the streets below. He threw off his blanket, stretched, and kneaded the hotel pillow with his hands. Yes, the jungle cat was now alert and alive. And beware, all those farther on down the food chain.

Namely, the blonde creature named Alanna.

Alanna was on her own now, still fuming over Jason's abandonment and imprisonment. Truman was counting on her loneliness today, in the French Quarter, stuck here without her boyfriend.

Divide and conquer.

Isolate.

All had gone according to Truman's plan, and

he hoped she would be able to admit to herself how truly attractive he was.

Did Truman feel bad about this scheming? No. Well, maybe a little.

But a tiger had to appear strong.

He hopped from the bed and used the restroom, then opened the hotel-room curtains and watched the people already moving about through the city. There was one weakness in his plan. If Jason returned, Alanna would escape the tiger's claws.

Time to call Jason and make sure that didn't happen.

Still at the window, Truman dialed his cell.

"Hey," Jason answered. "Listen, we're in morning traffic and I'm driving. I'm gonna let you talk to Hannah."

"Wait. I need to—"

"Truman? Is everything all right?"

"Hannah Banana."

"Not too loud," she said. "I only let my friends call me that."

"So we're friends, is that correct? It is what your words imply?"

"Yes." She chuckled. "I mean, we've known each other since way back when. That's how you knew my favorite color, right? You could probably guess my weight as well."

"Let's see. A hundred and eighteen pounds."

"You don't actually do it, you weirdo. You

don't actually guess. Didn't your mom ever tell you that was rude?"

Truman stared at his own reflection in the room window. "Did you know that she's not my birth mother?"

"What, your dad's second marriage?"

"I was adopted, Hannah. Same as you."

"Seriously?"

"Do I look anything like B-Mac, my cousin? No. Am I the only one on either side of my adopted family with orange hair and freckles? Yes. Indeed, I am that man. You don't look adopted. You look like you fit in. Whereas I . . . well, I used to think I looked like a freak." He worked his tongue against his cheek. "My adoptive parents, they helped me understand that my importance didn't come from looking just like everyone else, but from being unique. I don't know where I'd be without them. They're the ones who gave me a chance at a good life, and, if I may say so, I think I've proven myself quite adept on social and educational fronts."

"You're definitely unique," she said. "I like that about you."

"That was not something I, uh, meant to share. I hope it encouraged you, though."

"You always make me smile," Hannah said.

"Thank you."

A man on stilts paraded past the hotel in billowing clothes and a mask, tall enough to peek into Truman's room. He seemed in a hurry. Big day ahead.

"Hannah, I understand why you came on this trip. Two years ago, I had this thing inside me, this drive, to track down my own birth mother. I love my parents, but I had to do it, you know? It felt like my life couldn't go on otherwise. Like I couldn't see the whole picture until I put that piece of the puzzle in place. Does that make sense?"

"Absolutely." She said it so quietly he barely heard.

"I found her," he said. "In Baltimore. I called to see if we could meet."

"I'm going to meet my mother right now."

"So you found her? I'm glad." Truman backed from the window and closed the curtains. "When I met my mom, it was at a McDonald's, of all places. She said it was a safe place, so I went with it. She had blonde hair, brown eyes. I thought she was beautiful, but she'd barely look at me. Turns out she felt like she'd done something wrong by letting me go to another family. I told her how hard my parents have worked to raise me and take care of me, and all I wanted to do was be face-to-face with the woman who brought me into this world."

"Exactly. I mean, most kids get that every day, right?"

"Here's the way I see it. God has a reason for

it all. I mean, who knows how my life would've turned out? If I were in Baltimore, I wouldn't have met you and Jason. I wouldn't have my friends from Oasis and wouldn't have ended up at this school. I mean, life's too short to go around second-guessing everything, right?"

"Yeah," Hannah said. "Sometimes it still hurts, though."

"Sometimes. The nice thing is that she and I still call and chat every once in a while. It's not much, but it works for me. I think it makes her happy too. Listen, you and Jason take all the time you need, okay? We'll be fine without you." He cleared his throat. "So tell me, was I close on your weight?"

"Ha. Like I'm really going to answer that, Truman. Good-bye."

Chapter Thirty-Eight

Family Portrait

Mobile, Alabama

The Conwell and Hastings building jutted into the cloudless sky. Hannah's pulse quickened. Jason parked behind an ABC bank and walked her to the sidewalk across the street from the law offices. She was in a cold sweat, despite the warm morning.

Was her mother in there? What would they say to each other?

Hannah had on her pewter necklace and regular jeans. She wore her dark hoodie over a blouse with a ruffled collar. Under different circumstances, she might have dressed nicer to make a good first impression, but she had limited clothing for the trip, and this was for the best anyway. She would either be accepted as herself or not. After all, this was about finding out who she was, right? Not about being someone she wasn't?

She stared up at the tower, twenty stories high.

"So," Jason said. "You gonna just walk in there?"

She squared her shoulders and nodded.

"I'll be right here," he said.

"Okay."

She crossed the street and wondered if she was being watched. Behind her, Jason's phone rang and he muttered something. She almost turned but kept moving forward. She had to do this. No fear. No hesitation.

She entered, checked the directory alongside the bank of elevator doors, and took the first available car up to the twentieth floor. The tippy top. The doors opened upon a lobby of buffed marble floors, polished mahogany doors, and a reception desk that stood as high as her chest.

She strolled toward it, her arms folded.

"Can I help you?" the receptionist asked. A light was blinking on the multiline phone on her desk.

"Yeah, I'm here to see Cindy Hastings."

"Oh, she's out at the moment. Would you like to wait?"

"I, uh . . . do you have a restroom I could use?"

After pointing, the receptionist lowered her eyes and picked up the receiver. "Conwell and Hastings, attorneys at law. How may I help you?"

Hannah started in the direction indicated but pivoted slowly back toward a heavy glass door that looked in on a row of private offices and an empty conference room. While the receptionist's attention was diverted, she slipped through the door and hurried along the hallway in search of her birth mother's office.

273

She found it at the end, on the corner, with a name posted beside the open door: Cindy Hastings.

Hannah filled her lungs, looked down at the carpet's edge, and stepped over the threshold. She was entering another world. Another lifetime. She was moving into unknown territory, uncertain of the response she would receive.

Although lamps glowed and an attaché case sat perched on the glistening desk, the high-back chair was empty. Tall, tinted windows offered views of lush trees and a nearby hill. A stately bookshelf bore law manuals, an American flag plaque, and knickknacks like those found at Pier 1 Imports.

Hannah inched farther in. Her hands hung at her sides, and she plucked at her sleeves. She saw a child's crayon drawing positioned on a dresser near the window. It depicted a little girl and a woman holding hands beside a house.

They were tagged "Me" and "Momy."

Framed photographs lined the window ledge behind the desk, and Hannah moved that direction for more clues about her mother. She wiped her palms on her jeans, pulled her hair back, and leaned down for a better look.

A family portrait. A man, woman, and blonde-headed girl.

"Hi," a voice said. "Can I help you?"

Hannah turned, startled. She hadn't even heard

the woman come in behind her, the footsteps muffled by dense carpet. She thought of apologizing for trespassing, but she'd already faced those charges yesterday. And after all these years, why should she be the one to apologize?

Assuming, of course, this was her mother.

She knew, though. She already knew.

Cindy Hastings had long chestnut hair pulled back behind one ear. She wore dangling earrings, and her makeup was subdued. She was dressed in a fitted charcoal-gray dress that reached her knees, very professional looking, and a pair of black heels. As Mrs. Hastings scooted by with a stack of files and paperwork, Hannah felt as though she were gazing into a mirror that offered a time-progression image of herself twenty years from now.

"I, uh, I'm sorry." Mrs. Hastings stood at her desk. "Stacey didn't tell me I had another appointment."

"I didn't make one. I guess I shouldn't have just come into your office."

"Are you one of our new interns?"

Hannah's heart fluttered, and she pulled her hands to her stomach. "I'm Hannah. Hannah Lawson."

Mrs. Hastings showed no reaction. She bent to organize the papers on her desk, and her gold bracelets shimmered beneath the muted fluorescent lights overhead. In a crystal bowl, chocolate squares were heaped in red foil wrappers.

Dark chocolate. With raspberry.

"I'd love to talk," Mrs. Hastings said, "but I have a lunch appointment."

Hannah hesitated. "I was . . . I was born October the seventh, 1991. At Mobile General Hospital."

Mrs. Hastings's eyes lifted slowly from the documents in her hand.

"I came here," Hannah clutched her pewter necklace, "hoping that might mean something to you."

Recognition sparked in her birth mother's eyes, followed by indecision and fear. She lowered her head, her hair covering her face. She leaned across the desk, tapped the intercom button on the phone. "Stacey, could you, uh . . . please cancel my lunch and hold all my calls?"

"But your husband's already—"

"Thank you, Stacey." Mrs. Hastings glanced over at Hannah again.

Hannah shrugged. Where did they go from here? Who should speak first? No one had given her a manual that described the way to handle this situation.

Mrs. Hastings pulled her hair back over the other ear and turned sideways, as though afraid to face this head-on. She looked over her shoulder and met Hannah's gaze. Her eyes were pleading. "I . . . Hannah, I don't know what you want."

"Hey, honey." A man hurried into the office, early forties, self-assured, with a kind voice. He was the man from the portrait by the window. He wore a tie over a dress shirt, with the sleeves rolled up, and a wedding ring gleamed on his finger. "You ready? We gotta go. Lily's waiting for us in the lobby."

Mrs. Hastings looked from him to Hannah.

He followed her gaze. "Oh, I'm sorry. Who's this?"

Hannah waited to hear her mother's response. Would she claim Hannah as her own and introduce them? Did this man even know Hannah existed, a child from his wife's former life? Probably not. For one brief moment, Hannah imagined the truth pouring from her mother's lips and prompting a joyous reunion.

"I, uh . . ." Mrs. Hastings looked from Hannah to her husband and back again. She peered straight into Hannah's eyes, and then her gaze hardened. "I have no idea."

The rejection pierced Hannah's chest. Her lungs seemed to collapse.

Air. Breathe. Smile. Don't drag this man into it.

"I'm Hannah," she told him.

He shook her hand. "Hey, good to meet you." His grip was firm and warm.

Her mother still hadn't touched her.

Mrs. Hastings pulled her attaché case to her chest, a buffer between them. "Hannah, I don't know where you got your information. It's not correct. I don't know what you're referring to, and I'm not able to take any more cases right now. Raymond down the hallway, perhaps he can help you with your, uh, civil dispute."

Civil dispute? Was Hannah supposed to play along with this?

"I'm sorry." Mrs. Hastings delivered the words with more sincerity than the subterfuge required. "I'm truly sorry."

Mr. Hastings threw a final glance at Hannah, then placed his arm around his wife's waist and they exited the office.

Hannah was left alone. She dragged her fingers through her hair. Could she have expected much else? Her mother had made her choice years ago, and there was no real reason for her to turn back from it now.

Stunned, Hannah took the elevator down to the ground floor. She trudged through the lobby and out the front doors. When she glanced to her left, she saw Mr. Hastings edging along the curb in a shiny black Mercedes. Mrs. Hastings reached for the back door. She held a child in her arm, an adorable little girl with blonde hair done up in a white bow.

The girl saw Hannah and waved one small hand.

That could have been me. She's living the life that might've been mine. She's my half sister, and she'll probably never even know I exist.

Hannah waved back.

Here before her was the family portrait. And she had no place among them.

While easing her daughter into the backseat, Mrs. Hastings was caught in a breeze that ruffled her fitted dress and blew her hair back over her shoulder. She noticed Hannah, held her eye for a moment, then settled into the passenger seat.

Statuelike, Hannah stared after the Mercedes as it drove away.

Cindy Hastings told herself she was doing the right thing. The Mercedes slid from the curb and left the young woman named Hannah behind.

"Does Applebee's work?" her husband asked.

Cindy nodded and kept her voice light. "Yes, they have a good kids' menu."

For a moment back in her office, Cindy had almost broken into tears at the sight of her daughter. Instead, she gathered herself. Locked things down. Told herself to think of the ramifications. She had worked all these years to shut out the past and become the person she dreamed of being, rather than the teenage girl scarred by memories.

And she couldn't bear to think of the twin son and daughter she had lost.

Simply couldn't.

She had her own family now. That's what mattered. Curt was a busy investment banker, a devoted husband of eight years and an adoring father. Together, Curt and Cindy had a good life, and their little girl was just what they had wanted before they got much older. She was named Lily, in honor of Cindy's deceased mother.

"What about you?" Cindy turned in her seat. "Do you like Applebee's?"

Five-year-old Lily's chin bobbed up and down, and she squirmed.

"Stay buckled, sweetie. Don't get out of your seat."

"I'm not, Mommy. My bottom's down."

Cindy fixed her eyes straight ahead again. Even with this good family, she feared sometimes that God had forgotten her name. Or blotted it out. Or perhaps He hadn't received the memo that she was Cindy Hastings now instead of Alyssa Cynthia Porter.

Either way, what had she done to earn back God's favor?

She'd realized long ago that she would have to build the life she wanted herself and cover the cracks in her foundation. Hard work was the penance she paid for past choices, and through her work she became a success—nearly twenty years later and twenty stories higher.

But when her nineteen-year-old daughter appeared today, everything nearly crumbled. What if her husband knew? How would her work partners view her?

Hannah . . .

So that was her name.

Before even hearing the birth date and place, Cindy knew it was her daughter, her little fighter and survivor. Yes, Hannah's voice was the same one she had heard in her head all these years.

"Hannah!"

Although she heard Jason yell and caught his movement in her peripheral vision, Hannah was transfixed by the car that faded from view.

"Hey." Jason jogged across the street and stopped in front of her, sweat on his brow, veins bulging in his neck. "I am really, really sorry."

"No, it's okay. That was her, but she . . . she didn't even say anything. She—"

"Listen, it's not that." He looked back over his shoulder as a gold sedan with a rental sticker braked across the street. "I swear, it wasn't me. I had nothing to do with this."

Her dad stepped from the car.

"No," Hannah said. "What is *he* doing here?"

Chapter Thirty-Nine

Stay Outta This

Jacob Lawson could barely control his anger. He had booked the flight last night, hopped the plane this morning, and flown from Wilmington International to Mobile. He told himself not to blame Hannah. She was on a search for meaning and roots. Yet the more he thought about her and Jason sitting in jail, and the more he imagined them shacked up the last two nights at some hotel, the more furious he became.

He slammed the door of the rental car and strode across the street.

Jason and Hannah stood together, probably corroborating their stories to avoid looking as guilty as sin. Well, he wasn't buying any of it. He knew what had happened. He'd been told everything.

Hannah took a step toward Dr. Lawson, her jaw set. "What, are you following me now? How do you even know where we are?"

"Get in the car, Hannah. I'm not gonna argue about this. I'm taking you home."

"No! I'm not going anywhere until you tell me the truth. I want to know. Everything." She jabbed her finger. "Right now."

"Jason's girlfriend called, and she told me all about—"

"Alanna? Oh, great. That figures."

"She told me where you were and also told me that you two had been arrested. Is that correct? I cannot believe you would lie to me."

Her pitch changed. "You can't believe that I . . . that *I* would lie to *you*. Wow. You're unbelievable, Dad."

"I'm not discussing this with you right here, right now. Get in the car, and we'll talk about this at home."

"No." She shifted on the sidewalk, looked away, then stared at him with nostrils flaring. "I'm staying here."

He pointed across the street, his gaze locked onto hers. "Get in the car. *Now.*"

She fidgeted, started to turn away. "Fine!" She threw her hands into the air, pushed past him, and crossed the pavement.

"Yeah. Fine." He started after her.

Lord, help him, if she gave him that defiant look again. Where had this rebellion come from? Did she even have one clue as to all he and Grace had done to love and raise her? He was halfway across the street when Jason's voice stopped him.

"Dr. Lawson, you don't even know what she just—"

"You stay outta this, Jason. Stay out."

"Listen, I know what this looks like, but—"

283

"I said, stay *outta* this."

Jason jogged after him as he headed for the car. Hannah was propped against the hood, arms crossed.

"I know how you must feel about this," Jason said. "The thing is—"

"You have *no* idea how I must feel about this. And you can't know until you have a daughter of your own." He stabbed a finger at Jason's chest. "So *stay* out of it."

Jason closed his lips.

Smart move. Very smart.

Dr. Lawson started toward the car again, still angry, yet convinced things were under his control. He was taking his daughter home. And her friend-cohort-conspirator was done flapping his gums regarding stuff he knew nothing about.

"She's *not* your daughter," Jason fired back.

Dr. Lawson stopped in the middle of the street, hands on his hips, facing away from the lippy college kid. He had known Jason over half of Jason's life, and this was the thanks he got for sharing his home and family with this punk? Some gratitude. This was ridiculous.

"I'm sorry," Jason added. "I know you've been a great dad to her. But she has every right to find out who she is."

Dr. Lawson still did not move. "Hannah, get in the car."

"Dad, can you just wait a minute?"

"Get in the car. Now."

He waited till she obeyed before turning for the confrontation. "You don't think she's my daughter, Jason? That's really what you think? I have raised her since she was in an incubator, in diapers, and in preschool. She means everything to me. Everything. I knew she wasn't ready for the truth about all this, but I gave her that chance to find out. What does she do with that privilege? She gallivants halfway across the country with you, and ends up with a ride in a police car to jail. She's broken city laws, not to mention God's laws. And as for you two, I don't even wanna know what's gone on between you."

"Nothing, Dr. Lawson. I swear."

"I'm not finished."

"You need to know that I treated her like a sister."

"Well, I certainly hope so. I've treated you like family. And this is the thanks I get from the two of you? Two brats yelling on the street because a father happens to care? I'm gonna make this very simple, Jason. From now on, you stay away from my daughter. You don't call her. You make no contact whatsoever. Do you understand?"

Jason's stare was unflinching. This kid wasn't just a kid anymore. He stood there like a man, his shoulders squared. He didn't back down.

"You lied to me, Jason. I expected much more from you."

Jason finally tore his gaze away.

"Look at me," Dr. Lawson said.

The kid seemed intimidated now, even fearful, but he locked gazes again. Well, you had to respect that about him. He was willing to face his fears for the sake of his friend.

After a long silence, Dr. Lawson believed his point had been made. He left Jason standing in the street and climbed into the rental. He shifted into Drive and headed for the airport. He had a daughter to get home and a wife who was worried sick.

"You hungry?" he said to Hannah.

She hunched against the passenger door, her face turned away from him.

"You're not gonna talk to me? Okay, I get it. I'm the bad guy right now. If you are hungry though, speak up. They don't serve much on the plane, and we won't be landing in Wilmington till later this evening."

"I'm not hungry."

That was the last thing she said en route to the airport, and he figured he could hold out as long as she could. Their flight left in ninety minutes, just enough time to check in and pass through security before boarding.

She might not be talking to him. She might not even claim him as her father. But at least he had his baby back.

Chapter Forty

Blame It on Alanna

New Orleans, Louisiana

Hammers were at work, pounding, pounding. They swung at both sides of Truman's head, battering his temples and clanging in his ears. With Mardi Gras's main activity still hours away, he had managed already to get himself in trouble.

Blame it on Alanna.

That girl had snubbed him last night at dinner, in front of B-Mac, Diego, Danielle, and the other restaurant patrons. He held the door for her, and she sneered. He offered to order for her, and she told him that she was a big girl and didn't need his help. When she stormed from their table at the mere mention of Jason's name, Truman knew he was sunk.

His plan had failed.

And, against his better judgment, he ordered a drink.

"Bad idea, dude," B-Mac cautioned.

"Just one," Truman said.

"Famous last words."

Diego folded his arms. "Drinks and depression, they don't go together. Take it from me."

Truman was determined, though. Being not quite twenty, he was glad for the loose rules here in the Big Easy. The server never carded him, and he drank from the large plastic cup. It tasted like fruit punch. He was surprised at how easily it went down.

He ordered another.

"No," B-Mac said. "You are gonna be so sorry."

Truman thought of Alanna's parting scowl, showing no fear of the tiger, and he tipped back the cup again.

Alanna the Alluring. Alanna the Alert.

And Truman the Town Fool.

Now, in the morning sun, Truman sat at a small round table on an outdoor terrace with scrolled black iron railings. He downed a Goody's tablet and some ice water, trying to wash the toxins from his system. Below, drinkers and partygoers were getting louder on Bourbon Street. Couldn't they shut up? Didn't they know about the happy, happy hammers hammering in his head?

"Dude, you look upset," B-Mac said from the neighboring table. He basked in the sunlight, thick hairy calves poking from his khaki shorts.

"Don't talk to me. Please. Nobody talk to me."

"That bad, huh? I'm sorry, man, but we tried to warn you."

"Don't. Talk."

From the third table, Danielle smirked. She wore an orange tank top—good color, at least—and threaded her fingers with Diego's. These two were hot and cold. Danielle, the firecracker. Diego, the cool cat, with his sunglasses and forearm tattoos. They joked, touched feet under the table, and fed each other bits of a beignet.

Truman thought he might throw up.

An hour earlier, Jason had texted for directions to this location, and he now joined them on the terrace in jeans and a gray T-shirt. "Hey, guys."

"Oh, look," Truman said. "The prodigal returns."

Jason took a seat. "Aren't those Alanna's sunglasses? Where is she anyway?"

"You've come back to ruin all my dreams, I see."

"Sorry. What're you talking about?"

"Forget it. She's in room 24. She said she had a lot to think about."

"Thanks." Jason started to rise.

"Well, good to see you too, buddy." Truman stared at him through the sunglasses. "You know, if you had been here, maybe I wouldn't have had the audacity to drink something called a Hand Grenade. And that would've been a good thing, because about three sips in, you don't know who you are anymore."

"Didn't the name alone give you a clue?"

"You say that now." Truman wagged a finger at

Jason. "When I tell you I have no recollection of those events, I mean I . . . don't . . . remember . . . anything. Nothing." He ticked off the list on his fingers. "Not the argument. Not the fight. And not this guy. This little shiner." He peeled the shades from his face and gestured at the black eye already circled by a deep green bruise. He squinted against the overhead sun, and that action magnified the pain of his swollen face.

Enough with the hammers. Really. Please stop.

An entire construction crew was now at work on his skull.

"Sounds awesome." Jason grinned. "Guess I missed out on all the fun."

"Oh, and look what it all comes with. A court date. For disorderly conduct." Truman tapped the triplicate form, grimaced, and smacked his forehead on the table—*ouch!* He spoke into his lap. "I have a criminal record, Jason. I just want to go home."

"Same here, actually. Where's my stuff?"

"It's all in my room."

"I need to get it."

"Now?" A glimmer of hope. If Alanna stayed while Jason left, Truman might still have a last shot at working his magic. "But we're not taking off till tomorrow."

"Now, Truman."

He held up the key card. "There you go. You drive safely."

●●●

Jason stared at his clothes and toiletries. Should he really do this? He still had the rental car, but if he left now, he would not only forfeit the gas money he'd chipped in, but also leave Alanna alone in the van for the long drive home. She would never forgive him.

So be it.

Behind him, someone knocked on the open hotel-room door. He turned and saw his girlfriend. She wore a loose blouse over a green tank top. Hoop earrings shone through layers of glistening hair. Her eyeliner was thick, and her eyes a little bloodshot.

Had she been crying?

"I heard you were back," she ventured. "Good to see you."

He stuffed his belongings in . . . She stepped closer. "I went too far. It wasn't my place to get Hannah's father involved, but I was worried, babe. What was I supposed to do? I figured Dr. Lawson might be able to help, at least. I mean, you called me from a jail." When he didn't say anything, she kneaded her hands. "I'm sorry."

"Little late for that, dontcha think?" Jason continued packing. He was confused and angry. He felt betrayed.

"Where're you going?"

"Home."

"We're going back tomorrow. That's what Truman told me."

"Good. You and he can keep each other company."

"Please don't do this. I don't want to make the whole trip back without you."

"I don't think we have a lot left to say right now. Anyway, Truman's good at making people laugh. He'll make the trip go quicker."

"He's . . . you know, I think he likes me."

"I've known Truman for years. He's a good guy."

Alanna moved a step closer. "What else do you want me to say? Are you going to just stand there, Jason? Aren't you going to hug me or kiss me or tell me you're glad to see me? Babe, I've been so worried."

"Yeah, you said that already." He snapped his gaze toward her. "I'm headed home, Alanna. I'm leaving right now."

"So that's it?" Her voice faltered. "Just . . . just like that?"

"We can talk more back in Wilmington, all right?" He slung the bag across his back and moved toward the door. "I need some time to think."

Chapter Forty-One

Hurting Child

Wilmington, North Carolina

Hannah didn't say a word to her father during the boarding process in Mobile, the northeasterly flight, or the descent into Wilmington. From her window seat, she viewed the whitecaps on the Atlantic, the bridge over the Cape Fear River, and the skyline of her hometown.

There was nowhere else she could call home, was there?

This was it.

Jacob and Grace were it.

She leaned her head against the window's hard plastic and watched the images blur. She sniffled once but covered the emotion by sucking on her inhaler. Her fingertips rubbed the worn butterfly stickers. The passion butterfly was her favorite, with its velvety burnt-orange wings and mottled markings. Even though faded after all these years, the stickers reminded her of Jason's thoughtfulness and friendship.

She was the butterfly, wasn't she?

Growing from that unlikely egg, never even meant to survive.

Crawling along as a caterpillar, full of doubts that she would ever fly.

Tucking away into the protective chrysalis, cocooned from the elements until that moment of final metamorphosis.

And now I'm not even given room to stretch my wings.

Her birth mother refused to acknowledge their relationship, and her adoptive parents didn't trust her to take flight.

Hannah followed her dad from the plane into the terminal. They stood in baggage claim and waited for her bag to appear on the carousel. When he asked if she would talk to him about all that had gone on, she moved one step away and avoided his eyes.

"Listen," he said, "until we get this whole thing straightened out, I don't think you should go back to school. I see no reason in the world that I should continue funding this kinda behavior."

That's how this would go down? He would use his money as a means of controlling her? Well, that was just fantastic.

"What happened down there anyway?" he pressed.

She grabbed her rolling luggage as it passed by. "Why do you care?"

"Why do I care?" He followed her through the

baggage area, past passengers, pilots, and flight attendants. "I care because I'm your father. I love you."

"If you loved me, you would've told me."

"Told you what?"

"The truth."

She rushed through the exit. He caught up with her at the curb of the loading zone, where taxis and vans impeded her progress.

"You wanna know the truth? Okay, I'll tell you the truth. It was three months—"

She saw a break in the traffic and tromped through the pedestrian crossing toward the parking lots.

He caught up again and kept stride. "It was three months after we adopted you, Hannah, when we found out that the . . . that the medical bills weren't gonna be covered by the insurance. We lost everything. The car and the house. All of it. Gone. We had to file for bankruptcy. I was one year—one *year*—away from finishing med school. So tell me, how does that make me the bad guy?"

"Well, I'm sorry." She reached the parking lot. "Sorry I was such a burden."

"C'mon. That is not what I said."

"It's what you meant."

"Stop. Please, just stop."

She put more distance between them. "What was his name?"

"What was whose name?"

"My brother." She spun toward her father and

his eyes widened. "Yes, I found my mom. I know all about it."

"Sweetheart, I always meant to . . . meant to tell you about that."

"Right. Just like everything else."

He winced. His earlier rage seemed to dissipate, and all that was left were faint wrinkles, lips gone pale, and moisture pooling on his eyelids. "Jonathan. Your brother's name was Jonathan."

Hannah froze.

Jonathan.

Until this moment, her baby brother, her twin, had been a faceless image in her head. With the name came instant identity. She could see him. She could feel him. He was here, a part of her, and she believed he would stay with her till the day she died and they were reunited beyond this life.

Her father trudged toward her. He eased the luggage from her grip and carried it the rest of the way.

Grace Lawson set the plates on the kitchen island, one at each of the two stools. Her husband and daughter would be famished after their flight, and she hoped this might serve as a peace offering of a sort.

Hannah's favorite: deli turkey topped with provolone, lettuce, and sliced tomato. Sourdough bread. Light mayonnaise and mustard. A glass of iced tea. And three individually wrapped dark chocolates with real raspberry filling.

The raspberry Grace could do without, but her daughter loved it.

The automatic garage door opened and her husband's truck rumbled inside. They were home. Grace hurried to the living room couch and took a seat with a magazine on her lap. She didn't want to pressure either of them into a response.

"Hey." Jacob led the way into the house. He caught her eye, gave a slight shake of the head, and continued toward the bathroom. He left the luggage on the step into the living room.

Hannah appeared from the hallway, lifted the bag, and started toward the stairs.

"There're sandwiches in the kitchen," Grace said.

"Just . . . just give me a minute, Mom. I'll be back down."

Mom? That was all Grace needed to hear.

"Sure. You take your time, honey."

She gauged her daughter's mood by the footsteps. They weren't the hard, hurried strides of an angry teen, but the softer steps of a hurting child. She closed her eyes and whispered another prayer.

Since it was still spring break, Hannah decided there was no rush to get up in the morning. She wrote in her journal. She turned off her lamp at midnight. The last few days had wrung every emotion and teardrop from her, and she fell asleep in seconds.

When she woke, her bedside clock told her it was nearly noon the next day.

Almost twelve hours of rest.

Well, no more need for her to do the early-bird-gets-the-worm routine now that her dad was pulling her out of school. What would she do? She couldn't talk with Jason. She couldn't be involved with the theater group. She was closed off from everything she cared about.

That evening, her mom drove her into town to New Hanover Regional Medical Center, where Hannah sat through an appointment with Dr. Stewart. She had nothing against the man. He was a good doctor, a longtime family friend, and she knew everyone meant well. They were doing what they could to help.

Wearing a blue-and-cream sweater, Hannah sat across from the doctor and listened to his assessment and advice. If she was going to have any chance of stretching and strengthening her wings, she needed him to reassure her parents that she was okay.

"So you think I'm doing better?" she said.

"Better? Perhaps, yes. Yes, I'd say your condition has stabilized and shows signs of improving." Dr. Stewart scratched a note on his pad. "I am prescribing a smaller dose of medication, and I want your feedback on how that goes. Be sure to take it twice daily."

She nodded.

After supper that evening, Hannah requested permission to take a walk down to Smith Creek Lake. No, she was not sneaking over to Jason's place. No, she hadn't had any contact with Jason. Her father let her go, and she strolled through the tall grass toward the dock. Distant house lights reflected off the water. Though the sun was down, it left an indigo afterglow and an apricot-colored strip along the horizon.

She leaned against a post and watched the stars flicker overhead. In this great big universe, she was only one person. Did any of it matter?

Yes, for her brother's sake, it mattered.

She was here. She was alive. She couldn't let that go to waste.

Chapter Forty-Two

The Power of Choice

Jason had arrived back at UNC-Wilmington around noon. He spent the rest of the day in his dorm room in Graham Hall, unpacking, snoozing, thinking. He read from his Bible, the first time in a while that he had taken it from the shelf on his headboard. It spoke of young men learning from older men, and it was no accident that he opened to this passage.

As the sun was setting, he propped himself on the mattress with his pillow.

Time to make a call.

Sighing, he dialed his cell. It went to voice mail and he left a message: "Dr. Lawson, this is Jason. Jason Bradley. But, yeah, I'm sure you know that. Look, you need to know that I . . . I treated your daughter with respect. That's the truth. But I also wanted to tell you that you were right, and I was wrong. I, uh . . ." He cleared his throat. "I won't be seeing Hannah anymore. I'm sorry for everything."

He pressed End.

The End . . . How fitting.

And just when something was beginning to change in his heart.

If this was the night for dealing with stuff, he may as well get it all out of the way. Why stop with one call? He still had another to make.

Atlanta, Georgia

Truman tried to sleep, though that was a difficult task in this rattletrap van. They still had hours to go, despite the shorter route inland that cut through Atlanta. B-Mac was hunched over the steering wheel, his fro-locks swaying. A Neanderthal would have looked just as comfortable in the driver's seat.

At least this caveman could sing.

"That's the meaning of life," he mumbled. "That's the meaning of love . . ."

Truman dropped his passenger-side visor. Through the small inset mirror, he saw Diego and Danielle leaned into each other, fast asleep, with a blanket over their legs. On the middle bench seat, Alanna was alone. No Jason to keep her warm. She had answered a call from him earlier, and when it ended she sounded more resigned than dejected.

"That's all you need to know . . . about everything . . ."

Truman was admiring her through the mirror when she looked up and caught him in the act. Before he could lower his gaze, he realized she wore a half grin. He grinned back. They were both grinning at each other. Yes, an actual, unforced, real-life grin.

"You're awake," he said. "You okay back there?"

"It's getting chilly."

"Well, milady, allow me to crank up ye old heater and . . ."

What're you doing, you jungle cat? Pull yourself together.

This here was his opportunity, if not an outright hint from Alanna. Clearly, he had won her over.

Everything he read in those store-rack magazines said humor was one of the sexiest things to a woman, and he was bringing sexy back. Yes, indeed.

"Hmm," he said. "I don't know that it'll reach back that far. Let me, uh . . . I'll just come and sit by you. That is, if you find that suitable."

"Suitable? Sure."

Tiger on the prowl. Watch out.

He stepped over the plastic drink holder, the Igloo ice chest, and a half-dozen empty soda bottles on the floor. The VW hit a rut in the road, and his head slammed into the metal roof. His glasses popped onto the floor. He stumbled, tried to right himself, and landed sideways in Alanna's lap the way a baby might cuddle in its mother's arms.

He expected her to snap at him.

Instead, she laughed.

"You know," he said, "my mother also has blonde hair. Maybe that explains my attraction to you, some Freudian thing."

"If you're going to talk Freud, get off my lap, Truman. No, thanks."

"And if I don't, can I stay?" He gazed up and batted his eyelashes.

"No." She laughed again. "But you can sit by me. I'd like that, actually."

Truman positioned himself on the bench seat beside her, slid his arm around the back, and ignored his cousin's rolled eyes in the rearview mirror.

Wilmington, North Carolina.

Over the next two days Hannah cleaned her room, caught up on laundry, and organized. Her mom joked that she must be feeling ill. Hannah knew something was different, though. She was well aware of the nesting instinct that came over expectant mothers and felt driven by something similar. Something instinctual. Almost over-powering. Of course, being pregnant was an impossibility, considering her no-longer-secret virginal status.

She thought instead of a butterfly, everything tidy and compact in its cocoon until it was ready to fight loose and take wing.

Yeah, that pretty much described it. She craved tidiness.

As for her schooling situation, she had printed forms from the UNCW website and fanned them out on her bedspread. She sat among them now, trying to make sense of all the facts and figures and instructions.

A knock sounded at the door. It was her mom, wrapped in a buttoned sweater over a blouse. She was always modest, with the poise of the silver screen's most elegant actresses. In her own acting, Hannah tried to combine modern sensibilities with some of that old-school charm. Had she picked up some of these mannerisms from her adoptive mom?

"Hey," Mom said. "Can I come in?"

"I guess."

"What's all this?"

"Financial-aid stuff. It's all due by the end of the week, and even if I get it in on time, it's nowhere close to enough to cover tuition. So basically, yeah . . ."

"Honey, your father's not going to take you out of school."

"He said he was, and he sure sounded like he meant it to me."

"Oh, he's just upset." Mom slipped around and joined Hannah on the bedspread. She straightened Hannah's collar and rested her arm around her shoulders. "He loves you so much, honey. He's just terrified he'll lose you. We both are."

"And you don't think I'm scared too?"

"Yeah, I think you're scared. I think you're upset. And you have every right to be." Her mother tugged a folded photograph from the pocket of her sweater. She flattened it on her knee and showed it to Hannah. "I'd like to try to explain, if you'll let me."

"Is this you?" Hannah took hold of the photo. "You look so pretty in this picture. And you . . . you look pregnant."

"I was. I was twenty weeks when that was taken. I was carrying twins."

"Twins?" Hannah snapped around.

Her mother nodded, her face aglow in nostalgia.

"Mom, what happened?"

Her lips turned downward. She drew in a breath, brushed her hair back, and her upper lip trembled. "Oh, bother. I didn't want you to see me like this." She had a difficult time meeting Hannah's eye. "We, uh . . . we lost them. I was only a few months along, and we were so excited, and then it was all snatched away. That's how it felt at the time. I'm not blaming anyone. In the weeks that followed, I could barely get out of bed. Hannah, I was so despondent. I lost twenty pounds because I practically stopped eating. One day, I . . ."

"You what?" Hannah ventured a glance.

"I was reading the Bible, and it talked about caring for the orphans and widows. I felt like God said in that specific moment that I needed to stop thinking of my own pain and reach out to others. I would only find healing by tending to others' wounds."

Hannah chewed on her lips and listened.

"So I started volunteering," her mother explained. "At this pregnancy crisis center downtown. It was amazing being able to help others. It was healing, that's true. But it also hurt. Hurt deeply. Some days I had to take a break. Well, there was this beautiful cathedral around the corner, and I would go there at lunch to pray. I'd talk to God, begging for answers. For hope."

Mom teared up. "I will never forget October seventeenth. I walked back to the crisis center after my prayer time, and I saw a bulletin. It said, 'Twins. Abandoned. Only twenty-four weeks.' It was posted by the priest from the cathedral."

Her voice caught as he looked in her daughter's eyes.

"Honey, don't you see? The twins I lost would've been the same age as you and your brother, and that was all I needed to know. That sealed it. Hannah, *you* are our miracle. And that's why it's so hard to let you go." She pulled Hannah close and touched her forehead to Hannah's. "You mean so much to us."

"I know," she mouthed. She gazed at the picture. "Which cathedral was it?"

"Oh," Mom said. "It was beautiful."

Sodium streetlights lined the street that led to the cathedral. In the dark, the city was alive and sparkling beneath the moon and the stars.

Hannah meandered down the sidewalk, tracing the same path her mom used to follow between the crisis center and the church. Her mother had found solace and guidance at this place, and Hannah needed the same. She had said very little to anyone about the encounter with Cindy Hastings, and the emotions were still raw.

Where was that sense of closure she had hoped to find?

Or, on the other hand, the door to new possibilities?

Neither had presented themselves, and she was left with a hollow spot in her heart. If she ever needed some direction, now was the time.

Hannah clutched a Bible to her chest, climbed the wide stairs to the cathedral, and slipped inside. She moved through the entryway to smaller doors with beveled glass. Beyond them, a marble baptismal font stood at the back of a sanctuary with soaring pillars and a vaulted dome. Stained-glass windows ran along the sides, each depicting biblical stories, and statues represented apostles and saints in acts of service and humility.

While a far cry from her upbringing, there was a true sense of reverence here. She found a pew a few rows in, and the wood creaked as she took a seat.

Lord, I'm listening. Or trying to anyway.

A priest appeared only moments after she arrived. He wore black, with the traditional white collar. As he approached down the center aisle, she saw the coat draped over his arm.

"Excuse me?" he said. "I'm sorry, but we need to close for the evening."

"Oh, I didn't know. I've . . . never been here before. I'm Hannah."

"Hello. We have services daily, if you'd like to come back."

"Actually I'm . . . I'm Baptist." She shrugged. "I guess you should know that.

He chuckled, and his gray eyes sparkled

beneath a balding head ringed with snowy white hair. The deep wrinkles on his face reminded her of her grandfather, cantankerous Papa, but the priest seemed more relaxed.

"You guys sure know how to build churches," she said.

He sat a few feet from her, an arm rested along the back of the pew. "Why did you come, if you don't mind me asking?"

"I don't know. I guess I'm trying to figure out how to let go of . . . things."

"Things?"

She moistened her lips. She had nothing to lose by talking to this man, and she wanted to talk. She needed to. "I don't know how to . . . to let go of the fact that I feel hatred for myself and others. There. I said it."

When she fell silent, he gave her an understanding nod. "What is it you want to say, Hannah? Just say what you feel."

She nodded. "Well, three weeks ago I found out that my entire life is a lie. So I went on a trip to Mobile, Alabama. That's where I was born. I thought if I went, I would get all these answers, and that somehow when I got back, I would feel different." She pursed her lips. "But I don't."

The priest remained quiet, his gaze steady.

"My parents aren't really my parents. And my birth mother, she tried to abort me. And I have a brother. Well, I had a brother. We were born only minutes apart, October seventh, 1991, but he died only months after the . . ." She ducked her head to hide her face. "I'm angry at my parents for not telling me sooner, for making me think I was just like everybody else. I'm angry at my birth mother for not . . . for not *wanting* me. I mean, why didn't she want me? What's so wrong with *me?*" She tossed a look at the priest, her eyes wet. "I found her. And she still doesn't want me."

His empathetic eyes encouraged her to go on.

"And I feel guilty. Part of me feels like . . . like my brother should be alive, and I shouldn't. I wonder if he would've been a better person than me." She tried to smile. "I wonder what he would've been like. I just hate myself for feeling this way."

The priest nodded. "I see."

They sat in the pew, side by side, beneath the dome and the golden lighting and the large crucifix above the central altar.

"This cathedral," he said, gazing around, "was built in 1893, named for Saint Paul the Apostle. Magnificent, isn't it? He wrote a letter to the church at Colossae and said, because we have been forgiven by God, we should forgive each other." The priest leaned closer, fixing her in his gaze. "In Christ, you are forgiven. And because you are forgiven, you have the power to forgive. To choose to forgive. Let it go. Hatred is a burden you no longer need to carry."

"How'd you get to be so smart?"

"A lot of mistakes, Hannah. I have done things I'm not proud of, and I need forgiveness as well. Don't we all? Only in forgiveness can you be free, Hannah. A forgiveness that is well beyond your grasp or mine. One that can't be found on a trip or even in this cathedral." He sat back again, his eyes moving upward. " 'If the Son sets you free, you will be free indeed.' "

She pondered those words, and the crucifix served as a reminder of the price paid for that freedom. Smiling, she set both hands on her legs. "Well. I guess you'd better close up, huh? I won't keep you any longer."

He led her to the front doors. "What was your brother's name?"

"His name was Jonathan."

"Well, Jonathan wants you to live your life, Hannah. Live it to the full."

As he headed back toward the altar, she turned toward the doors and exited into the warm night air. She descended the stairs outside the cathedral and noticed the form to her left. It was a young blonde woman, the last person she expected to find in these evening shadows.

"Alanna? What're you doing here?"

PART FOUR

Completion

"He who began a good work in you will carry it
on to completion until the day of Christ Jesus."
—PHILIPPIANS 1:6 (NIV)

Chapter Forty-Three

Into the River

Alanna realized long ago that she had very little control of her surroundings. It was one of the hard lessons of growing up with an alcoholic father. As a means of survival, she learned to manipulate. She showed a tough exterior. She used her looks and sharp tongue to take control and to keep others on their heels.

Then Jason left her. No longer under her control.

Though she was saddened, it came as no surprise. They had been friends since her arrival at the university two years earlier, and they'd walked with each other through some tough times. He didn't deserve the cutting words she used against him. The more their relationship grew, the guiltier she felt for trying to control him through such tactics.

Jason deserved better.

And so did Hannah, as much as Alanna hated to admit it.

"Alanna? What're you doing here?" Hannah emerged from the cathedral. "You're the last person I expected to see."

"I was looking for you." Alanna was seated on

the stone steps. "Don't think I'm a stalker or anything."

"How'd you find me here?"

"I tried calling you first, and when that didn't work, I called your mom. She told me your cell was broken and you were here. Can we talk for a minute?"

Hannah hesitated.

"Please? All I'm asking for is a few minutes."

"Okay." Hannah sat a few feet away, her face pale in the moonlight.

"I looked inside, and it's beautiful. I can see why you came."

"Did you hear any of, uh, what I said in there?"

"No, I came back out here to wait. I didn't want to disturb you." Alanna pulled one knee up. "I need to tell you why I treated you the way I did."

"Hey, you had every right to be jealous. I should've never let Jason take—"

"We're not together anymore. It'd been coming for a while, and it's not your fault. That's not the reason."

"I didn't know. I'm sorry."

"He and I, I guess we're just better as friends." Alanna shrugged. "He says that he's not even allowed to talk to you. I . . . I should've never ratted you out, Hannah. That wasn't my place, and I didn't even know all the details."

"It caused me a lot of trouble."

"Yeah, I'm sure I'm not your favorite person right now."

"What's done is done," Hannah said.

"I need to explain. Will you let me do that?"

Hannah gave a slight nod.

Alanna stared off, her thoughts swimming. "His name was Adam. He was nineteen. My parents had just sent me off to boarding school in California, a good three thousand miles away. That tells you something, doesn't it? And I was only sixteen. To be honest, I was glad. I was suffocating in my home. It was tough, though. I didn't know anybody on the West Coast, didn't know how to act. And Adam, he . . . he made me feel alive, you know? And safe." She flashed a painful smile. "I hadn't felt safe in a long time."

Hannah's brown eyes looked up.

"Before I left," Alanna continued, "my dad said, 'If you come home pregnant, then you can't come home at all.' He said it like a joke, but I knew it wasn't. Even when he was drunk, that wasn't something he would joke about. Well, six months later, Adam handed me four hundred dollars and told me if I didn't get an abortion that he would leave me."

"How old were you?"

"I dressed and acted like I was older, but I was just seventeen."

"Wow. I can't even . . . I can't imagine."

"It was tough, Hannah. I was afraid of my dad.

Afraid of losing Adam. So I . . . I did what Adam wanted. And then he left anyway."

"I had no idea." Hannah's voice was low. "That must've been awful."

"Before the spring-break trip, Jason told me why you were going." Alanna glanced over, surprised to find such kindness in Hannah's eyes. "The way I acted, you need to know that it had nothing to do with you, and I apologize. Thing is, when I look at you, I . . . I hate myself." She swallowed hard and looked away. "There's nothing wrong with you. I treated you the way I did because there's something wrong with *me*."

A city bus passed by, shaking the ground. The streetlights created hazy cones of yellow up and down the avenue.

Hannah nudged closer. "You know, my mom used to come here and pray before I was born. It's the first time I've ever been inside, but I couldn't stop looking at the crucifix in the front. It reminded me of what she used to tell me when I was little. She said that Jesus' arms were spread out so wide on the cross because of how much He loved me. His hands were open, offering forgiveness, no matter what I had done."

As much as Alanna wanted to be in control, she couldn't stop the tears that pricked the corners of her eyes. Hot droplets. Salty and bitter.

"I don't want this to sound trivial or cliché," Hannah told her. "And it, well, it might sound trivial and cliché. But even if you've heard it a thousand times, it can change you if you accept it and let it sink in. Truth is, I'm still working on it myself. I know that His arms are big enough for you."

Alanna's hair fell over her face. Tears dripped from her chin.

"If you want, I know some people you could talk to, Alanna. My pastor, he's pretty awesome. And my shrink? Well, he's a little strange, but he means well."

That brought a faint smile to Alanna's lips.

In her Al-Anon meetings, she had been told the importance of self-disclosure and forgiveness. She resisted those steps, yet knew how vital they were. She had come searching for Hannah as a step in the right direction. While Alanna appreciated all the support from others who had gone through similar struggles, there was something different in tonight's encounter. Here was Hannah, someone she had wronged, reaching out with a care and concern Alanna didn't deserve.

"His hands are open . . . no matter what I had done."

She thought of Adam. Of the thing he had asked her to do.

She thought of her father. Of his tirades and violence. And of how, in middle school, she never knew which man he would be when she got home from volleyball practice.

She even thought of Truman. Of his earnest desire, his confidence, and his ability to make her laugh.

"What do you say?" Hannah asked. "I could take you sometime, if you want."

Alanna looked over. "I'd like that."

Mobile, Alabama

Mary Rutledge stared out her window into the darkness. She cupped a mug of hot tea in her hands—African red bush, s'posed to do a body good—and went round and round on the events of the last week or so.

First, there was Ms. Porter. Who was now Mrs. Hastings.

Second, there was Hannah. Whose last name was now Lawson.

So much confusion in this great wide world, so much heartache and grief. On Tuesday, though, Mary had offered answers to Hannah. She hoped that mother and daughter had reunited, but there were no guarantees, were there? Sometimes you followed the truth till that road ran out. When it did, you carved out a new trail and moved on.

She mumbled to herself over her tea, "Time you move yourself along, Mary. Or time gonna pass you by."

The Good Book had its share of nurses. Why,

back in the days of the Hebrew slaves, nurse midwives were saving Hebrew babies. Pharaoh told 'em to throw the boy babies into the Nile. He didn't want no army rising up against him. But those midwives were brave and smart. When it came to baby Moses, he was tossed into the river all right. Tossed in all bundled up in a basket. And nowadays, everybody knew 'bout him. That li'l baby led God's people to the Promised Land.

Mary nodded to herself. Whichever way she came at it, she didn't see no other choice. Oh, sure, she had choices. Women had choices. The men, they had choices too—and often left the womenfolk with the hardest ones, after the fact.

But when it all boiled down?

Well, she knew just what she had to do. It was the visit from young Hannah what settled that for her. Mary was a nurse at heart, and even though some of 'em years had been wasted on foolishness, she had plenty of good years left. She was forty-three now. Still half her life ahead of her, the good Lord willing. There wasn't any reason she couldn't update her credentials and get current. Hospitals were always saying how they needed more nurses.

She'd had her say, at last. And, Lord, how she needed that.

Time now to move along. Yessir.

"In the morning," she told herself, "you go on down and find out whatcha gotta do."

Chapter Forty-Four

Ready to Fly

Wilmington, North Carolina

Hannah was curled on her side under the covers, her journal open next to her. She had so many thoughts still tumbling through her head.

Today was Friday, the last official day of spring break, and they were halfway through the month of March. Would she be back in school on Monday? No word yet from her father.

After only three days apart from Jason, she realized more than ever how much he was a part of her life. She couldn't let that slip away. All these years. All their talks. The races to the lake, the birthday parties, and his teasing about her chick flicks and her love of *Anne of Green Gables*—which was all the more intense now that Hannah knew both she and Anne were adopted.

The most pressing thought pertained to her relationship with her birth mother. She didn't want to hate the woman for rejecting her. It was hard, though, to accept what had happened on that twentieth floor.

"Who's this?"

"I have no idea."

Stabs through the heart.

Hannah heard a soft knock on her bedroom door. She gathered the crumpled papers on her bed, her failed efforts at drafting a letter to Cindy Hastings.

Even last night Hannah had curled up in her desk chair, listened to music on her old CD player, and tried to put her thoughts into words. She would probably never get back to Mobile. Why put herself through that pain again? But she still might send a letter to the Conwell and Hastings building.

Another knock.

"Yeah, come in."

"Hi." Her dad wore a pale blue sweater over a dress shirt. His hair was its normal curly wildness.

"What's up?"

"I, uh . . ." Her dad sighed. "I've been giving this a lot of thought, Hannah. And I wanted to tell you that I am sorry. I'm sorry I overreacted. So you're still enrolled in school, and I took the liberty of calling your drama professor. I reminded him that your mother and I are both alumni, and we are still very, very, *very* good friends with the dean of students." He tilted his head. "I think he got the message."

Hannah smiled.

"So you have a pretty good shot at staying in the theater group, if you want it."

"Thanks, Dad."

"And I think you should probably pack."

"What for?" She stifled a yawn.

He dropped an envelope beside her on the bed.

She gave him a quizzical look, then opened it and found an airline ticket. It bore her name and showed the destination as Mobile, Alabama. Leaving this evening.

"I know you need to finish this, Hannah. With your permission, I'd like to be there when you do."

She nodded. This was unbelievable.

"Plane leaves in a few hours." He turned, ready to go, then looked back. "But there is this one place I would like to take you on the way. If that's okay with you."

Jacob held his daughter's hand and led her across the fresh-mowed cemetery lawns, between rows of tombstones and memorial markers. The sky was clear and blue. Jacob was still in his pale blue sweater and tan pants. Hannah was in black sandals and a summer dress covered with a thin wraparound. Their bags waited in the car. Their flight left in three hours.

Jacob aimed for a familiar spot. A large oak tree. Its sprawling branches and dark green leaves provided shade to the gravestone underneath.

A vase of roses and baby's breath stood at the stone's base.

"My brother," Hannah whispered.

Jacob reached for her hand, and his voice turned husky. "We hoped beyond all hope. We truly believed God would heal him. The doctors said there wasn't much brain activity, but I . . . I saw him smile. We prayed and prayed, but sometimes it's so very hard to understand."

Hannah squeezed his hand a little tighter.

"We were just so young," he said. "We didn't know what to tell ourselves, so naturally we never told you, Hannah. Months became years, and years became decades, and you still didn't know."

She looked away, her eyes round and wet.

"After he died," Jacob said, "I just remember holding you. I would hold you for hours. I would not let you outta my sight. Because I was afraid that if I lost you too, I would . . ."

He took a moment to collect himself. He needed to say this for his daughter's sake. "So I would just hold you, because I couldn't let go. And, sweetie, I still haven't. I'm sorry, Hannah. I'm sorry for the journal. For keeping so much from you. For how controlling I've been. It's not that I don't trust you. It's that I'm . . . I'm

323

trying honestly to learn how to trust God again. So please don't . . . don't . . ."

"Dad."

"Yeah, baby?"

She turned, her gaze meeting his. "I . . . love you." She leaned into him, and he engulfed her in his arms. "And it's okay."

"Yeah?" He swallowed. "I love you too. I love you so very much."

They held each other, with Jonathan's memory only feet away. Jacob cupped the back of Hannah's head and kept her close, the way he used to do when she crawled onto his lap as a little girl.

"Thank you for bringing me here," Hannah said. "Thank you."

She was no longer that little girl. She was a young woman. She was ready to make her choices and live her life. She was ready to fly.

Speaking of which . . .

"We better go," he said at last. "We have a flight to catch."

Chapter Forty-Five

One Shot

Mobile, Alabama

Hannah and her dad arrived at the airport and checked into a nearby Drury Inn with two queen-sized beds. The law offices at Conwell and Hastings were closed for the evening, and Hannah would wait till tomorrow to complete this last part of the story with her birth mother.

"You know, why didn't Mom come?" she asked from the desk beside the TV. "She totally should have been here. We could've played a fierce game of Yahtzee."

"Would've been fun." Her dad was stretched out on his bed, arms folded under his head. His curly gray-blond hair fell across the stacked pillows. "Thing is, sweetheart, this part's tough for her. She's raised you and loved you. You're her daughter, our daughter. And even so, she's afraid she could never compete with the woman who shares your blood. She knows how important this is for you, but what if, you know, she doesn't measure up?"

"I'll always love her. No matter what."

"She's worried that she'll lose you," Dad explained. "I mean, not physically. She's afraid she'll stop being that first woman in your life. The voice you listen to. The shoulder you cry on."

Hannah looked over at him. "Is that what you think too?"

"Sweetie, it's not about what I think. You need to settle this."

"But you're worried too. That's why you flew here with me."

"I think you're a grown woman who deserves the truth. You're the one deciding how to respond to that, and whenever my girl's facing tough situations, I wanna be there as much as I can. That's all, Hannah. That won't change, no matter how old you get."

"Even when I'm your age?"

"What? You'll never be my age," he kidded. "You'll always be my baby girl."

"Parents." Hannah shook her head.

"Kids." Her dad echoed her action.

They both laughed, and she returned her attention to her journal. She wanted to get these words just right. She would only have one shot at this.

Hannah walked in her summer dress toward the offices of Conwell and Hastings. She and Jason had traveled this same route from the parking area on Tuesday. This time she held her father's hand and came with a different set of expectations.

"You sure this is how you wanna do it?" her dad asked.

She pulled her lower lip through her teeth, studied the imposing structure, and gave him a nod. "Yeah," she mouthed.

"All right then."

She slipped her hand from his, waited for a gap in traffic, and crossed the street. She and Dad had shared a continental breakfast at the hotel, and it was now lunchtime. She wondered if Cindy Hastings would be away from her desk as she had been last time.

Hannah checked her pocket and took a deep breath.

She was ready.

Cindy Hastings came up in the elevator alone, her attaché case dangling from her right shoulder. She wore a jacket over a purple silk top, fitted black slacks, and black pumps. She had her hair pulled back into a ponytail, ready for many more hours of work.

She texted Curt on her BlackBerry. She was finishing the discovery process on a case for the county, and that meant she would be home later than planned this Saturday afternoon. Lily needed to be taken to her ballet class at four o'clock. Not Curt's favorite errand, but he knew where the tutu was in the closet, and she could count on him to take care of this.

Work, work, work. It never ended.

Not that Cindy minded, since it kept her thoughts occupied.

Before the elevator car reached the top floor, she heard a voice. Not any voice. *The* voice. The one she had heard throughout the years and finally matched with a face, four days ago in this very building.

"Mom, can you hear me?"

It wasn't audible or real. Of course, it wasn't.

Cindy strode down the hallway to her corner office, where she set down her case on the desk. By nature, she was not an organizer, yet her career and her job as a mommy had honed her skills. Rarely did she lose anything these days, and she kept her desk immaculate. Everything in its place.

The single, slightly crumpled sheet of paper caught her eye.

And that wasn't all.

Cindy glanced toward the open door. Although she heard discussion from the conference room, there was nobody in her view.

She picked up the paper, which bore only three handwritten words.

And touched the yellowed hospital bracelet as well.

"Mom, can you hear me?"

The rush of memories was overwhelming. Her lip started trembling. Her knees nearly buckled.

She pressed the intercom button on her desktop phone, knowing she could not see anyone in this current frame of mind. She couldn't even breathe.

"Yes, Mrs. Hastings?" It was the receptionist.

"Stacey, could you . . . ?"

She couldn't finish the sentence. She released the button and smoothed the paper in her hands. That bracelet was her own, worn on her wrist during that one horrible day at Mobile General Hospital. She had birthed a son, maimed by her own choices, and a daughter, who was tiny, whole, and beautiful. On Tuesday, she had spurned that relationship, despite every broken part of her heart that wanted things to be put together again. She couldn't put Curt through that. Or Lily.

Nobody in her world knew.

The secrets of Alyssa Cynthia Porter were safe.

And after the way she responded to Hannah, Cindy knew she would never see or hear from the poor girl again. That was for the best, wasn't it? Best for all.

These three little words undid her:

I forgive you.

She waved her hand over the paper, as though to wipe away the past. There was no wiping it away, though. She had lost her own parents, and she'd inflicted that same anguish on her nineteen-year-old daughter. She lifted her face toward the ceiling and sniffed.

Forgiveness?

Who was she to deserve such a thing?

She pulled her office door shut and read the words again.

The sob started deep in her stomach, deep down where all this had started and where the wounds still hid. Cindy thought of Hannah at the curb outside, watching as the Mercedes drove off. She thought of Lily waving, with no clue that it was her half sister a mere ten yards away. Cindy wiped a tear from her cheek and held her mouth, trying to keep it together. But the message on the paper was impossible to ignore.

Tears ran down her face, and sobs shook her chest and her shoulders. She leaned her back against the solid wood door and cried. Two decades' worth of shame and regret churned to the surface, all those wounds she had buried.

Her knees gave way, and she slid down to the carpet. She gasped for air. Her throat tightened, and she could hardly make a sound. She clutched the paper to her chest and pressed those words into her skin.

"Can you hear me? I forgive you."

Was it even possible?

Healing sobs shook her. The weight that lifted from Cindy's back was more than she realized she had been carrying, and despite the heated flush at her neck and the burning in her eyes, she felt lighter than she had in years.

● ● ●

Hannah looked up at the sky, at the clouds that swirled and floated over Conwell and Hastings. Her gaze lowered to the corner windows where her birth mother worked.

Had she found the note?

This morning, Hannah had decided there was no need to leave an address. They both had their lives to live, and freedom to do so was what mattered most. The past was behind them, and the future stretched ahead.

"Beautiful day, huh?" her dad said.

She pressed her lips together and nodded. He took her hand, kissed it, and guided her back toward the rental car. They had a flight back this afternoon. Back home.

When they reached the car, Hannah spotted a butterfly clinging to the passenger-side windshield wiper. It lifted and headed toward a nearby tree, fighting gusts of wind, getting nowhere. And then the wind shifted, an updraft caught its outstretched wings, and it floated upward on the current toward the freedom of the highest branches.

Chapter Forty-Six

Short and Sweet

Wilmington, North Carolina

Truman sat in the back of the Dharma-blue VW van and watched the student apartment building loom large through the front window. There was no hiding the van's arrival. The entire UNCW campus probably knew she was here. Although her smiley-face logo had fallen off during the spring-break trip and specks of sand still appeared on the plastic seats and black rubber flooring, she would have to do for this evening's plans.

"Take a right here, trusty chauffeur."

B-Mac shot him a look through the mirror. "Don't push it, man."

"Well, you could've let me drive her myself."

"Drive Evelyn? Dude. That is *not* an option."

"I meant Alanna. I do have a license. I am a licensed man. It wasn't my idea to bring you along on my date."

"You are in serious luck, cuz. I'm not only your driver, but also your free and live musical entertainment. That's right. My guitar's still in the back."

Truman groaned. He reached under his glasses and rubbed his eyes.

"There she is," B-Mac said.

And there she was. Alanna the Alluring. Seated like a model on the dorm steps, she had one leg bent, the other tucked beneath her, and long hair gathered over one shoulder.

"You do the talking," Truman instructed B-Mac. "You're our chauffeur. Be smooth."

B-Mac raised an eyebrow, tossed back his locks of curly hair, and adjusted his thick glasses on his nose. He edged to the curb and killed the engine. He called through the open passenger window. "So, uh, I was wondering if you're ready to go to dinner with my cuz."

"Where?" she played along.

"There's this place on the coast called Lighthouse. I think it's, like, literally a lighthouse."

"I've heard that's almost five hours away and—"

"Two, tops. You've seen how fast Evelyn can go. She's magic."

"I have class tomorrow."

"Tomorrow's Sunday. C'mon, you know you want to do this."

Alanna caught Truman's eye through the sliding door's window. She gave him a grin. They were grinning. Grinning at each other. Grins all around. She turned back to B-Mac and acted coy. "I'm not so sure about this. I've heard your cousin's a real tiger." She clawed the air with her fingers.

"Forget the tiger. They've got she-crab soup at Lighthouse that will . . . will literally change your life. It's that good." He beckoned. "C'mon. Get in the van."

Alanna stared off, her high cheekbones and profile statuesque in the sunlight.

"I'll show you my M. C. Hammer dance," B-Mac told Alanna. "I even . . . I have a set of parachute pants in the back. I will *nail* it."

She giggled at that.

B-Mac wiggled his eyebrows in the mirror at Truman.

"Enough," Truman hissed through clenched teeth. "Just get her in here."

"For parachute pants, you've almost talked me into it." On the steps, Alanna rose and brushed off her backside. She moved to the passenger window. "Here's the thing, B-Mac. I need to know your real name before I'm willing to let you drive me just anywhere."

"Are you serious? I just drove you to New Orleans and back."

She folded her arms. "I can stand here all night."

"Hannaford," B-Mac whispered.

"That's not so bad."

"Hannaford Tobias Soloskowitz the Third."

"Oh. Well, I'm sorry. I, uh . . . B-Mac's good. It's short and sweet."

Truman's patience reached its limit. He

yanked on the side door's handle and slid it wide open. "Enter," he said, with a sweeping gesture. He reached for her hand.

"Thank you," Alanna said. "You look nice, Truman."

"I hope you're hungry, milady. I have arranged for a premium table at the Lighthouse. I trust that will meet your high culinary standards."

Her airy laugh was all the answer he needed.

"You heard the lady," he snapped at B-Mac. "To the castle, and quickly."

The van rattled back to life and circled away from the dorm.

Chapter Forty-Seven

Man of Mystery

Jason sat in his dorm room, barefooted, with one leg up on an open drawer of his desk. He had an old hardback of *Anne of Green Gables* open on his lap. His English Lit instructor wanted a full report on a book's theme and setting, and Montgomery's classic was on the list students could choose from.

Of course, no one knew of his choice. Sure, he lived in the 2000s and embraced his artistic, sensitive side. But that didn't mean he was ready to give up his man card.

Not that easily.

Had to admit, though, it was an entertaining book. Anne Shirley was one funny girl, and she reminded him at times of another girl who could make him smile.

Jason was still reeling from the encounter with Dr. Lawson. He hated the way things had gone down in Mobile, and he still didn't know the full story of what happened in the Conwell and Hastings building. He did know that the look in Hannah's eyes was nothing short of heart-breaking, and he wished more than anything that he could call and hear the details. Even better, they could walk down to Smith Creek Lake and chat into the night.

Not gonna happen. Not till her dad changes his mind.

Jason thought of defying the man's orders, of backing off from his own apology. None of that would be right, though, so he prayed that God's will would be done. Sometimes that was the only prayer that seemed to fit.

The cell phone rang on his desk. Some of the guys were going out to the Gazebo area to shoot hoops, and he figured this might be the call to join them. He could use some fresh air, as well as a brief escape from the land of Green Gables.

"Hello?"

"Jason. This is Dr. Lawson."

He tossed his book onto the desk, sat up in the cheap desk chair, and wondered if something was wrong. Was Hannah hurt? Was she in the hospital again?

"Yeah, listen." Dr. Lawson cleared his throat. "I wanted to say that I . . . assumed the worst about you. That was unfair. Hannah talked to me, and she told me how you treated her with respect. How much you cared. And I . . ."

A long pause followed. Had the call been dropped?

"And I think that you should call her."

"I, uh . . ." Jason was dumbfounded.

"Listen, I'm not saying that you *have* to call her. I'm just saying that you *should*. I mean, I'm not trying to pry here. Guess I've done enough of that already, huh?"

That was a loaded question, and one best left unanswered.

"I just wanna know, Jason, what your intentions are concerning my daughter."

There it was. That was the real question, wasn't it? It was all Jason could think about, ever since he watched Hannah storm off from the Windy Shores Motor Resort in the middle of the night.

He knew the answer. He had known it all along.

Time to put it into words.

"I love her," he said.

"Then you need to call her."

"Yeah." Jason chuckled. "Yeah, I . . . Wow. Okay, I definitely will."

"Thanks."

"Thank you."

Jason disconnected and stared at his dorm-room wall. That hadn't just happened. Hannah's dad hadn't just told him to call his daughter. Where was the fiery-eyed father who seemed ready to pummel Jason on the streets of distant Mobile?

Just go with it. Don't even hesitate.

Hannah's number was still on speed dial, and he placed the call.

With her dad's approval, Hannah drove the gold Acura to the Randall Library on campus. She would be back in school on Monday, and she wanted to be prepared.

Before heading home, she stopped by Professor Watson's office. He wore an electric-blue vest over a black dress shirt. He peered up through his glasses, smiled, and came around the desk to shake her hand. He welcomed her back into the theater group, expressing how much they needed her passion and talent. He trusted she was feeling better. Yes, he had been informed that Dr. Stewart and Hannah's psychologist agreed she was fit once more for the pressures of school and stage.

"And we'll be the richer for it," the professor said.

"You're sure this isn't because my dad pulled some strings with the dean?"

"Your father is a persuasive man, I'll give him that. But no, Hannah, I believe in your gift. That's why you got the part in the first place. We'll be auditioning soon for a new production, and I expect you to be there. Can you promise me that much?"

"What's the role? One of your originals?"

"Let's just say that you would fit the part well."

That was a half hour ago.

Hannah eased into the driveway at her home back in Murraysville. She tugged her wheeled bag of books into the house, her ponytail flopping against her chest. The bag caught on the carpet runner that divided the dining room from the tiled kitchen.

"Hi, baby," her dad said from the sink.

"Hi."

"You need help there?"

She smiled. "I'm good." She noticed the phone in his hand, as well as his strange expression that suggested he was hiding something. "Things good here?"

"Very good."

She didn't know how to take that. She headed up the stairs, her heavy bag thudding against each step. Halfway up her cell phone rang in her jeans pocket. She sighed, stopped, and flipped it open.

Before putting it to her ear, she caught the name on the display:

Jason B.

Should she even answer this? Her dad was just down the stairs, and his restrictions hadn't been lifted as far as she was aware. Still, this was Jason. He hadn't called her in days, honoring her father's wishes, so this sudden breach of protocol must mean he was in some trouble.

It rang again.

"Hello?"

"Hannah, this is Jason. Don't worry. From what I can tell, I've got permission to call you again. Yeah, so . . . Listen, we have a lotta catching up to do, right? I'm wondering if I could, uh . . . you know . . . take you out to dinner."

"What?"

"Yeah. I mean, take you on a date."

"A date?" Hannah's bag slipped from her hand and tumbled down the stairway. She thought she heard her father snicker, but of course he had no clue why she had dropped her stuff. If he only knew. "Like, just you and me?"

"That's usually how it works."

She pressed her back against the wall and said softly, "What about my dad?"

"He's the one who told me to call you. If you don't wanna, then—"

"Yeah. I mean, I do. I will." She was making a fool of herself. She clapped her hand to her forehead and closed her eyes. "You're not just asking me out just to make him happy, are you? Because the last thing I need is some sympathy date."

"Hannah, I *wanna* take you out. I want to do this. Me."

"Okay. When're you thinking?"

"Tonight."

"What? Nope, that's too—"

"Soon," he said. "I knew you'd say that."

She laughed.

"Hey, if knowing you over half my life means this is too soon, then I won't be taking you out till I qualify for the senior discount. Tonight, Hannah. I'll pick you up at seven, if that works for you. Not too formal or anything, but I'm gonna be wearing a tie and dark slacks."

"Where are you thinking?"

"Sorry. That part's a surprise."

"Hmm." She pursed her lips. "Sounds mysterious."

"Jason Bradley, Man of Mystery. See ya in two and a half hours."

She did a quick dance, a smile splitting her face from ear to ear, and dashed up the stairs to her room. She didn't know what had gone on between her father and Jason, but somewhere between the pier and the hotel and here, Jason had come back into her dad's favor. And back into her life.

If she had any say in this, she would never let him go.

Chapter Forty-Eight

Going Off-Script

Jason believed in facing your fears. He believed that pressing through those fears brought freedom and peace. He also believed the Bible when it said "perfect love casts out all fear."

Which was why he brought Hannah here.

Thalian Hall.

"This is stupid," she said, her eyes squeezed shut.

"You're stupid. No peeking." He guided her by the hand down the hall's center aisle. Usher lights marked the rows of empty seats and the exits. The stage was softly lit. He had talked to Professor Watson, made a few connections, and arranged the whole thing at the last minute. "No cheating, Hannah. Do you wanna ruin the surprise?"

"Yes, I do. I dressed for dinner here. Five times actually."

"Five times?"

"I'm not proud of it, okay? It's just I don't go on a lot of dates."

"I don't know why. You look amazing."

Even in a dress shirt, belt, and tie, Jason felt inadequate next to her. Hannah wore a short, strapless evening gown, light pink, with a woven bodice. A beaded choker graced her neck. A sheer wrap was threaded around her lower back and draped over her arms, giving her an angelic look. She was a butterfly ready to open her wings and soar. When had his childhood friend transformed into such a beauty?

"Thanks," she said. "I wondered if you would ever notice."

"I'm that slow, huh?"

"Well, let's see. How old are we now? I mean, the first time I—"

"Wow." He caught her arm as she stumbled on her heels. "Okay, I've got ya. One foot in front of the other."

"You know, I would go out more, but my dad is scary."

"Yes, I know that." Jason swung around in front of her and eased her to a halt. "Here we go. Three, two, one . . . Open up."

Hannah opened her eyes and discovered that she and her lifelong friend were by themselves in the vastness of Thalian Hall. It was beautiful, the way the lights glimmered along the balconies, the way the empty seats shimmered in velvety crimson. Only steps from the stage, she felt the way she had at her first middle-school production, ready for the curtain to rise and the spotlight to come on. She imagined herself a princess, a star.

Jason waved his arms. "Tada." He hopped onto the stage.

She tilted her head and smiled at him.

"I thought you should finish," he said.

"Finish what?"

He scooped two scripts from the floor, both with *Annabella* printed across the top. "This time, let's forget about Lance Prescott. Nothing against the guy, but he is sorta . . ."

"Be nice."

"I just think I'd do better in the role. Whaddya think?"

"I think we need actors." She strolled up the steps at the side of the stage.

"Unfortunately, we're gonna have to make do. But don't worry, I was in a play once. Kindergarten. I was Sheep #5. Don't laugh."

She laughed.

"How 'bout a little respect?" He helped her up the steps and handed her a script. "I mean, I was this close to landing Shepherd #2."

Hannah took her spot, the same spot where she had stood weeks earlier on opening night. The *Annabella* production was still running, with Julia Armen as the lead, and some of the props were visible now at the back of the stage. Hannah pushed back her fearful recollections, refusing to let anything ruin this moment. She took a deep breath and exhaled slowly.

"You good over there?" she asked.

Jason reached his mark and nodded. "Hello, Annabella."

"Hello, Desmond." She turned her chin his direction. "You can dispense with the pleasantries. A bit trifle, don't you think?"

"I think, uh . . ."

She rolled her hand. " 'They have . . .' "

"They have high expectations for—"

"Standards."

"High standards for me." He dropped his script at his side. "I'm pretty terrible, aren't I?"

"Yes."

"Well, look, when I was Sheep #5, I didn't have lines."

Grinning, Hannah moved toward him. "Ah, so that's how you got the part."

"Yep. All I did was stand there in a sweaty wool suit and . . . I did not just say that, did I? That was ridiculous."

"Even the great actors have to start somewhere, right?"

She was at his side now. She caught a hint of his cologne. He looked pretty suave in his dark pants, belt, tucked-in shirt, and tie. It wasn't his preferred attire, and that made it all the more special that he had gone the extra mile for her.

Hannah ran through the lines of the script, using a faux-Victorian cadence and diction. Jason stepped closer, attentive. She turned the page and continued, reading past the point at which she had collapsed on this very stage. The talent scouts, the worried whispers, the campus rumors —that was all behind her now. There was no reason she couldn't dream and believe again.

"You're really good," Jason said.

"It's a lot easier without a whole audience."

"I'm your audience."

She stared at the script and watched the lines blur. Her heart thumped, and the heat of the stage lights warmed her bare shoulders. Jason's hand brushed her cheek and pushed her hair back over her left ear. His touch was light, his fingertips feathering over her skin. Her eyes turned upward and peered into his. She loved the solid lines of his face, his wavy sandy-brown hair, and his slightly parted lips.

Their hands met. Their fingers intertwined.

Hannah pulled in her bottom lip, and her thoughts swirled.

They were kids again, racing across the dock, holding hands, diving into the liquid blue of the lake. They were teens in youth group, singing songs of praise, raising hands in worship. They were friends, riding in the VW van and exchanging glances. They were best friends, with his arms around her on the beach as she clutched her mother's taped business card and cried.

And they were so much more.

"Hannah," he whispered.

She couldn't hold back her smile. She rested a

hand on his chest, looked at his mouth, and a laugh burst from her lungs.

"What? Why're you laughing at me?"

"I'm not," she said. "It's just . . . it feels strange, doesn't it? Maybe even ridiculous, but that's not the right word."

He waited for more, his eyes serious and unblinking.

"We've been friends all this time, and now, I don't know, it's like we're turning into adults, and the whole thing is awkward, and it's like they always say about that transition between being just friends and more than friends, and—"

"Hannah."

"I'm doing it again, aren't I? Rambling when I get nervous."

"*Are* you nervous?"

She faced him, only inches apart. She tilted her chin up. Her pulse was steady and strong, thrumming through her entire body, and she wasn't having any trouble breathing. She felt light as a feather, light as the sheer wrap threaded through her arms. "Not at all. I always feel safe with you."

Jason cupped her cheek with his hand. "I hope so."

She bit her lip, flashed a playful smile, and spun away.

With his other hand, he squeezed and spun her back. She pivoted on her heels, her dress flared about her legs, and she found herself pressed lightly against him.

He cupped her face with both hands this time and lifted her chin. "I love you, Hannah. I'm sorry it took me so long to figure it out. Guess I was just scared."

"And you're not scared now?"

"I'm more scared than I've ever been." He reached down and kissed her, his lips parted, his breath warm and sweet.

She lifted on her toes, pressing her mouth against his. He slipped one arm around her lower back, pulled her close, and kissed her forehead, her cheek, and earlobe. Then their lips met once more, even softer this time.

Chapter Forty-Nine

Special Delivery

Mobile, Alabama ~ August 2011

Sergeant Dodd couldn't have planned his daughter's birth any better, despite the fact that the timing went all wrong.

In March, his wife had gotten confirmation that she was at last having a girl and then she had insisted she would deliver Cesarean. "At my age,

I don't know about y'all, but I'm done. Boy, am I ever. Nineteen hours in labor, like I did with Tommy? No, thank you. I'm gonna set my own date and do this with as little fuss as possible."

Dodd didn't argue. He had learned a thing or two over the years.

"And this way, darlin', you can be there when she's born," Kelly added. "You've been on duty every other time, showin' up after the fact and still in your sweaty uniform."

She made a good point.

So they set their schedules and charted things out.

And then, little Kristina Dodd arrived six days early.

Sergeant Dodd rushed his wife to the hospital and held her hand in the delivery room. Despite the change of plans, it was his day off, and he wore a buttoned denim shirt over black Dockers. He was there when the cut was made. And he was there to make his own cut, severing the umbilical cord and taking his newborn daughter into his arms.

Never had he experienced such pride and joy.

"You did great, Kelly. She's perfect."

"Is she healthy? Have the doctors said anything?"

"They took her for some tests, but it's all standard procedure. She's fine, just fine."

The sergeant smoothed his wife's matted dark hair and gave her bold assurances, even as he squelched his own concerns. A child born this early was a candidate for complications and postnatal care. At least she was whole and alive. She had squeezed his finger with her tiny hand.

Movement in the hallway nabbed the sergeant's attention. He turned toward the open door, then stepped back from what he saw.

Nurse Rutledge's eyes widened as she read the newborn's file. Could it be a mistake? What were the odds? Forgetting all about her sore feet in white nurse's shoes, Mary wrapped the baby girl in a hospital blanket and adjusted the pale pink cap on her head.

She checked the names again, just to be sure.

Sure 'nuff. Plain as the nose on her face. Baby Kristina belonged to Kelly and Richard Dodd.

"Is she good to go on back to her momma?" Mary asked the doctor. "She's done been screened for phenylketonuria, and her Apgar tests came out good."

He signed off on the chart and gave her a nod.

Mary cradled the sleeping girl in her arms and carried her through hospital corridors that were all shiny and bright. The profession had changed over the last twenty years, but she was glad to be helping people. If she weren't here, then she would be home and thinking 'bout herself. And she'd done her share of that already.

"Hello," she said, entering Mrs. Dodd's room.

The sergeant turned her direction, and his jaw dropped. He didn't look much different, just older, that's all. Few wrinkles 'round his eyes, less hair sitting up top, but still the same kind-eyed officer she remembered.

"Nurse Rutledge? Did I get that right?"

"Yessir, that's right."

"How is Kristina? Is she okay?" Mrs. Dodd sat up in the bed. "Can I hold her?"

"Hold her all you like. She done missed her momma, and it ain't right to keep the two apart. Go on now." Mary handed over the warm bundle. "She's good as can be."

Sergeant Dodd took a knee on the other side of the bed, he and his wife both putting their faces close to Kristina's.

Mary picked up the clipboard on the counter, marked things off, and made a note. She glanced over and saw the Dodds sharing teary-eyed smiles.

She turned to go. Weren't no reason to stay and be a nuisance.

"Mary?"

"Yessir?"

The Dodds looked up at her, their eyes glistening, their faces a-glowing.

"I'm glad it was you," the sergeant said. "Thank you for being here."

Cindy Hastings strode past the reception desk and reached for the glass door. Despite the workload ahead of her, her thoughts were on the past. For months, the forgiveness in Hannah's simple note had seeped down into her being. Those three little words were sunlight, oxygen, and water, and her soul opened again in ways she never expected.

With the healing came the freedom to let go of her secrets, and Curt deserved to know. He was a devoted husband, and she trusted that he would love her just the same.

As for Lily?

Cindy would need Curt's help for that decision. Hannah was gone, having left no clues to her whereabouts, and the questions might be too much for their softhearted girl.

In the manner she had mastered as an attorney, Cindy compartmentalized these concerns and shelved them until later. She did not want to jeopardize the tasks at hand. This was a big case, with a large potential payout in court fees and rulings, and she wasn't one to bill her clients for time she spent on herself.

She hurried down the hall to her office and soldiered through the rest of the afternoon. At six o'clock sharp, she closed up her attaché case, turned off the lights, and rode the elevator down to the underground parking. She drove home, realizing she was out of excuses. She couldn't hold on to these secrets any longer. It was time to sit down and tell Curt everything.

"How was your day?" he said, greeting her from the living-room sofa.

"Where's Lily?"

"Out like a light in her bed. I think she's in another growth spurt, and first grade's got to be tiring, with all the new challenges it presents. Teacher says she's doing well."

Cindy nodded. She sat on the plush cushion beside her husband, set her case on the floor, and fished out the crinkled note. Curt stiffened, aware that something was up. She asked him to listen without interruption, and she would answer any questions when she was finished.

"But you're not sick, are you?" he asked.

"It's nothing like that. Please, just let me speak."

Seeming satisfied, he turned toward her and took hold of her hand. "I'm listening."

Cindy explained about the unwanted pregnancy, her fateful visit to the clinic, and Hannah's appearance all these years later. She reminded him of the nineteen-year-old girl in her office back in March, and he nodded. When Cindy showed him Hannah's handwritten note, her emotions rushed back to the surface. She searched Curt's eyes through her tears, and he pulled her close.

"I love you," he said. "It's all right."

"I should've told you earlier."

"You told me now, Cindy. I love you all the more for being honest with me."

Chapter Fifty

The Leap

Wilmington, North Carolina

Jacob and Grace stood at the end of a walkway stretching across the lawn to the dorms. He lifted the final box from the bed of his Chevy truck. The morning sun cast long shadows from the lamp-posts and oak trees. Students milled about.

"You ever miss it, Grace?" He straightened his corduroy sports jacket over his jeans.

"Our college days? Not so much. Though I will admit, you were quite the handsome young man."

"And now?"

"Quite the handsome gentleman." She took his hand. "I'm proud of you."

"I dunno, sweetheart. Not so quick. I haven't let go of her yet."

He touched the items in an open box—old photos, books, and a trophy that poked from the other stuff like a miniature angel. This was the beginning of Hannah's sophomore year, and she was moving on campus. It would be her first time living away, and he wasn't sure how he would handle the void in their home.

Jason and Hannah reappeared from the dorm, their arms emptied of the last load.

"Oh, honey." Grace leaned closer. "Look at them. Aren't they cute together?"

Jacob shrugged.

"Don't be jealous."

"I'm not jealous. C'mon, Grace, whaddya think? No, I . . . I'm happy for them."

She raised an eyebrow.

"I am. I'm, uh . . . I'm happily adjusting, all right? Gimme time."

"We'll have plenty of it, just the two of us." She placed a kiss on his cheek. "And who says we can't relive our college years?"

"What if she comes running home by next week?"

"Don't get your hopes up, Dr. Lawson. I think she's well on her way."

"Hey, Mom and Dad. So what do you think? Isn't it nice? I mean, you've been here before, but it's different knowing it'll be my home."

"And mine." Jason pointed at the neighboring dorm.

"Okay, here ya go." Jacob handed him the box. "That's the last of it."

Hannah beamed. She wore a loose top over a peasant blouse and jeans. Her hair was combed out, catching the rays of sun. He caught a hint of melancholy in her eyes, and then her excitement swept it away. She bounced on her toes. She was ready to go find out the name of her assigned roommate.

"Don't forget why you're here." Grace held her daughter's hand.

"I won't."

"Will you be able to handle the shooting schedule and your class load? I don't want you falling behind."

"Professor Watson says he'll talk to the faculty and make sure I get my assignments with plenty of advance warning. Plus, I'll be stuck in a trailer half the time, waiting for lighting and makeup and all that. I will do my classwork. I promise."

While Jacob did worry about his daughter around a movie set, he couldn't deny the talent that landed her a role in the upcoming Nicholas Sparks film. Wilmywood was in business, and shooting started in early September. Hannah had a part as the lead's best friend.

"School's first priority, okay?" He dropped his hands to his sides. "You call us, let us know who your roommate is. Don't let them give you anyone too weird."

"I'll be fine, Dad. I promise."

"I'm holding you liable," he said to Jason.

"I'm on it, Dr. Lawson."

They shook hands.

"We've gotta go." Hannah hugged her mother. "I love you."

"Love you too, honey."

● ● ●

Hannah heard her mom echo back the words, and she smiled. This was really happening. She could barely contain herself. She was thrilled to have a room on the bottom floor, where she wouldn't have to lug her books up and down the stairs. It was just like her dad to think she would get the weird roommate. So far, she and most of her classmates got along just fine, but she knew it was different when you shared living quarters with a stranger.

Hannah saw her mother now trying to hold it together, lips pressed tight, eyes crinkled at the corners. She didn't want this to turn into a cry-fest. This was her big day.

She adjusted her braided necklace and turned to Dad.

"Hey," he said.

Make it quick, Hannah. A quick hug. Quick pat on the shoulder.

She wrapped her arms around him, squeezed once, and backed away. Jason had the box under his arm, and she knew he was as anxious as she was for this next step. Hands brushing, they turned and started toward the dorms.

A bittersweet feeling welled in Hannah's chest. She thought of all her parents had gone through to get her to this point in her life. This was what they had raised her for, right? They had trained her up in the way she should go, and she was ready for that leap into adulthood—the good, the bad, the dreams dashed and brought back to life. And speaking of dreams, she hadn't had a nightmare in months.

Yes, Mom and Dad had walked her this far. How could she simply flit away?

She stopped, her shoes settling into the lush grass. Jason waited, his eyes questioning. She pulled her hand up through the back of her hair, and her brow knotted.

Oh, who cares what anyone thinks?

Hannah turned toward her parents once more.

Mom wore a brave smile, regal as always, and Dad took a step forward. Hannah ran to him, a little girl all over again, her heart full and beating and alive. She threw herself into his arms and clung to him.

When they pulled apart at last, she gazed up into his eyes. "Thank you."

"For what?"

"For wanting me."

He pressed his lips together. His eyes clouded, and he looked away.

"Okay." She patted his chest.

"You gotta go," he said.

She returned to Jason's side and they strolled, hands linked, toward the rising sun. She looked back one last time, hair cascading over her shoulder, and heard her father's parting words.

"I love you, baby."

Armed with those words, she could take on the world.

Acknowledgments

Thanks from Eric:

To Linda Wilson (now with the Lord) and to Mary Ann Daniels—For bringing me and my wife into this world, even while pressured to do otherwise.

To Carolyn Rose, Cassie, and Jackie, my wife and daughters—For helping me know, day in and day out, what women of all ages deal with. I am blessed with three beautiful, spirited ladies.

To Jonathan Clements, my literary agent—For being both personal and professional. I couldn't find a better fit.

To Theresa Preston, Jon Erwin, and Andrew Erwin—For trusting me with your baby and letting me dress the story in various outfits.

To Julie Gwinn, Julee Schwarzburg, and the B&H staff—For allowing me to partner with you in this creative process, even under time pressure. And for catching my mistakes in the manuscript.

To Cecil Stokes—You've tossed other ideas my way, but this one actually stuck. Who knew?

To Chris Sligh, musician and actor—For adding heart and humor to the film, and providing some great tunes for my writing times.

To the 77s—Nearly three decades later, our nation's laws remain unchanged, but many lives have been saved due to lyrics such as those in "Your Pretty Baby."

Thanks from Theresa:

To my Heavenly Father who has always known the plans He has for me . . . resting in that knowledge makes anything possible.

To Stephen—my amazing husband, my true love, and my best friend—Thank you for letting the stories in my mind unfold into your patient ears. Even when my ideas are crazy, or I blurt them out at weird times . . . like in the middle of watching TV. Your willingness to walk hand in hand with me into my made-up universe means so much to me. Your support gives me wings.

To my family—Thank you for reminding me that I've always been a writer in my heart, and for encouraging me and supporting me as God's plan for my life continues to unfold.

To Jon and Andrew Erwin—I will be forever grateful to you for taking a chance on me. Thank you for your friendship, your mentorship, and for always encouraging me to trust my instincts, be myself, and write from my heart.

To Eric Wilson—Thank you for your partnership, your honesty, your flexibility and your heart for this story. Getting to work with you on *October Baby* has been a true honor.

To Bill Reeves—Thank you for your work behind the scenes to makes it all happen. You are the oil to the engine, and we know it.

To Julie Gwinn and B&H—Thanks for putting up with the rookie. You are a lightning fast bunch, and it was a pleasure trying to keep up with you.

To Julee Schwarzburg—Thanks for your fast work, guidance in the process and love for the story.

To Gianna Jessen and Shari Rigby—Your courage, honesty, and authenticity is an inspiration to me and to many others.

To my church family—You have loved and supported my family throughout the *October Baby* journey and so much more, and we are so grateful that God has given us a body of believers to truly "do life" with.

To my beautiful daughter, Sarah—You have taught me so much since you came into this world. Being your mommy is my favorite and most important job. You inspire me. Your life is truly beautiful.

A Glimpse into the Making of the Film:

OCTOBER**BABY**

by Theresa Preston

"The Beginning"

Fall 2009

I blinked a couple of times wondering if I had heard him right. I was pretty certain that Jon Erwin, standing in the middle of my living room, had just said that he wanted to write a movie about an abortion survivor.

A what?

Big, "out of the box" ideas were not a surprise coming from Jon and Andrew Erwin. Their creativity and ingenuity were what inspired my husband, Stephen, and I to pack up and move from Boston, Massachusetts, four years prior so that Stephen could work as the audio designer in their start-up film company.

I had become very comfortable with the idea of storytelling, having seen and been a part of numerous projects and music videos over the time my husband had worked with Jon and Andy. Jon and I had even written one screenplay together already, and we knew that we wrote well as a team. I loved the idea of writing again. It was a passion God was starting to awaken in me, and a talent I didn't even know I had until my mid-thirties. God had been ordering the steps of my life one by one in the direction He intended for me. Writing. Who knew? Yes. I wanted to write. But this story? I wasn't so sure.

It's too controversial.

That was my first thought. *Nobody talks about this.*

I told him the idea was interesting, but I was secretly relieved when I didn't hear more about it for a while. What I didn't know was that in that time, God was moving and stirring Jon's heart. The whole idea was born when he saw a video of Gianna Jessen telling her story. Gianna is a vibrant, beautiful, strong and inspiring woman who survived an abortion and speaks around the world proclaiming the glory of God in her life. He was shocked that the words *abortion* and *survivor* could go together, and as he researched it more, he was all the more determined that this was the right story, and this was the right time.

He approached me again a little while later

asking if I would be willing to come on board in the writing process to help with the female voice of the film. This time he had come up with the bones of the story. It went something like this: The main character is a college-aged girl who is wrestling with her heart and emotions that she doesn't quite understand. She's quirky and lovable and there's a boy she likes, but everything is turned upside down when she finds out she's been adopted because her birth mother had a failed abortion. She goes on a trip across the country with her friends in search of her birth mother, but ultimately she finds herself.

It wasn't dark and heavy. It was a coming of age story of a girl who needed to find who she was. I understood that . . .

And so *October Baby* began.

"The Middle"

2010

I still wasn't entirely sure about how we were going to tell this story, and I felt like I was tiptoeing around the topic, still trying to convince myself that this was a good idea. We began to brainstorm, and once the scenes were roughly drafted, they traveled around on a long white poster board stuck and re-stuck, mapping out a journey for our young character.

A journey to find herself. To find answers. To find God.

I was struck with how familiar this journey is to all of us. Perhaps not in a beat up old VW bus with a bunch of quirky school buddies, but maybe with a beat up old Bible on our laps thumbing through the pages for answers to questions that are hard to even ask out loud. Or maybe we search for answers somewhere else, finding nothing but a sea of more questions.

The journey is familiar somehow to every one of us.

As we began writing, there was much research to be done. Who would this character be? How would she think? What questions would she have at her very core? And what about the others she would meet along the way? Her birth mother? The nurse she would encounter who worked in an abortion clinic, but chose to save her life? Her adoptive parents who raised her, loved her, and risked everything for her?

The responsibility of telling it "right" was palpable. I was still concerned. We were embarking on something that would surely stir things up. Was I ready for that? Wasn't it easier to just stick with the simpler stories? Not put ourselves out there so far?

And then I started reading about abortion survivors and my heart was overwhelmed. And not just survivors, but many others who had the courage to speak out for the sanctity of life, even at risk to themselves and their reputations. People who had been pro-life their whole lives, and those who had come to the stance later in life after wrestling with themselves, their life experiences, and their faith. They had the courage to tell their stories—to glorify God in the hardest of circumstances. God was challenging me: "Theresa, do you trust me?" What if this was my journey?

As I read their stories, God was tugging on me, putting pieces together. He was making a connection in my heart. My husband and I had been blessed with the most beautiful little girl in 2008. Sarah Grace Preston. Born at 39 weeks gestation, but only after three months of bed rest, six hospitalizations and a lot of anxious prayers. The doctor discovered I was in preterm labor when she was just 23 weeks gestation, a dangerous time. By medical standards, she was barely viable. They wanted to prepare us for the worst should she come so early. When they began telling Stephen and I all that would have to happen to give baby Sarah her best chances, I remember thinking "I would do anything to save her. *Anything*." Her life was already beautiful. Her body was still forming, but there was no doubt in my mind that she was worth every ounce of my being to protect. *I would have done anything to save her . . .* is that how God sees me?

Did I believe that every life was beautiful? And if I did, what was I doing about it?

Jon Erwin was in a similar frame of mind. While working as a cameraman for Alex and Stephen Kendrick on the film *Courageous*, they talked with Jon a lot about the challenges of being a Christian and a filmmaker. They asked him, "What is your purpose?" Convicted and stretched, Jon talked about it with his brother, Andrew, and God continued working in their hearts, emboldening them to take their own journey . . . stepping out into the great unknown to make their first feature film. They were told it was risky. Maybe they should start with something lighter, but they trusted God to go before them and prepare the way.

The screenplay was written. The story was complete, or so we thought. Standing on our little piece of the puzzle, we could have never begun to see or understand God's big picture. The Erwin Brothers began sending the screenplay to actors they envisioned playing the parts, one of whom was Shari Rigby, an actress Jon and Andy had worked with before on a music video. We soon discovered how far this story could reach into peoples hearts and lives. Shari called Jon and told him how moved she was. She herself was a post-abortive woman, and some of the details we had written in the life of Hannah's birth mother, the part we were asking her to play, were amazingly similar to her own life. Playing the part in the film would prove to be immensely healing for Shari, meeting God and finding forgiveness herself in the very scene in which her character is forgiven. It started her on a journey across the country, boldly telling her story and letting God use and stretch her to point people to the amazing healing power of the grace of Christ.

"A New Beginning"

2011

Shari's story was just the beginning. It seemed that as God continued to grow and spread the story of *October Baby* into different places and forms, the people He brought on board had their own stories to tell of how *October Baby* had touched their lives. The circumstances of each person's story are different and unique, but the truth of God's grace and love are at the heart of every one.

When it came time to expand the screenplay into a full-length novel, it was, honestly, a little nerve-wracking. Would someone else understand these people we created? Would they catch the vision? Could they see and hear our hearts for these characters we had labored with and loved? And then Eric Wilson came on board, and as the story began to expand and unfold in the pages, it was clear that God had gone before us yet again, and prepared his heart to tell this story with us, with passion and honesty and excellence.

Organizations from all over the country also came on board, helping us to spread the word, knowing that there was something special about *October Baby*. The story could reach people with the message of God's forgiveness, and that could make so much difference.

2012

As the film has been seen by audiences throughout the country, we have been completely humbled by the way God has been using it. Abortion survivors have a voice and are telling their stories. Postabortive women share that *October Baby* has helped lead them toward the journey of finding healing. Adoptive families find joy in the celebration of Hannah's relationship with her parents who loved her so completely. The door was opened to talk about what no one was talking about, and suddenly, as though people had been waiting for someone to just utter the first word, the conversation began and it continues, growing and challenging and stretching each one of us.

Today. In your life. Right now.

We may have written this story, but it was never ours in the first place. It was always God's. His story is the ultimate one of sacrifice, healing and forgiveness. It is in His story that you will find He loves you so faithfully that He patiently pursues you as you take whatever journey you must to find Him. His love is so complete that He sent His Son to die on a cross for your sin, and in so doing He has paid the price for anything and everything in your past, present, and future that you think could keep you from His loving embrace. His forgiveness and grace are free gifts. If you just open your heart to Him and run into His waiting arms, your loving Father will wrap them around you and tell you that you are wanted. You have always been wanted. His eyes are perfect and they truly see you. All of you. And what He sees is beautiful.

Your life is beautiful.

Discussion Questions

1. What was your reaction to Nurse Mary Rutledge? Did you have difficulty empathizing with her and her position at the clinic? What did you think of her final choice?

2. Do you know personally an adoptee or adoptive parents? Under what circumstances would you consider adopting a child?

3. Hannah, like many abortion survivors, suffered from nightmares. Did you notice any symbolism in her dreams?

4. When Hannah was in the doctor's office, she discovered a betrayal from someone close to her. Did you have a hard time forgiving the person responsible? Or did you understand the motives behind it?

5. In what ways did Hannah grow in her relationship with her parents? In what ways did they grow through her experiences?

6. Hannah's life was turned upside down after her collapse on the stage, yet this led her on a

life-changing journey. In what ways has God used difficult circumstances to bring about good in your own life?

7. Did you know, before reading this book, that there were abortion survivors? Does that awareness change or solidify your own views regarding abortion?

8. Did Alanna's backstory, revealed toward the end of the book, help you understand her tough exterior and demeanor toward Hannah? Why or why not?

9. How did you feel toward Hannah's birth mother? Did you relate to her in any way?

10. What did you think about Jason and Hannah's relationship? In what ways did it frustrate you? In what ways did you see honor and respect between them?

11. Were there any scenes that brought tears to your eyes? Were you moved by the sad scenes, the happy ones, or both?

12. When the priest talked with Hannah, what did he challenge her to do? How did she go about responding to that challenge?

Center Point Large Print
600 Brooks Road / PO Box 1
Thorndike ME 04986-0001 USA

(207) 568-3717

US & Canada:
1 800 929-9108
www.centerpointlargeprint.com